BURY OUR SECRETS

CRAIG BEZANT

'BURY OUR SECRETS'

International print edition - Australian English

Copyright © Craig Bezant 2023

www.craigbezant.com

ISBN Print edition   978-0-6456895-0-1

ISBN eBook edition 978-0-6456895-1-8

Cover image by Graham Earnshaw/Shutterstock.com

Cover design by Craig Bezant

Typeset in Palatino and League Gothic

Many of the locations within this novel are real.
The story itself is fictional, which means creative flair has been given
to locations and characters – descriptions and actions are purely for
plot and entertainment and are not intended as critiques
of existing entities, people, or places.

The Margaret River region in Western Australia is
a wonderful place, as are its people.
If you haven't visited, do so when you can.
If you have, it's time to go back.
After (or while) reading this novel, of course.

To the family that gets me through each day,
And the ones I've loved and lost along the way.

CHAPTER ONE
CURIOSITY IS A STRANGE ADDICTION

A letter arrived in the mail today, from Uncle Graham. It's Wednesday. He died on Monday. It's not a message from beyond the grave; rather, a shining example of our crippled postal service—no more overnight deliveries. He could have emailed or texted, but it wasn't his style. He was far more traditional —handwritten notes, printed books, CDs and records. Physical things you could hold. Proof of your existence. Still, the letter is a strange sight, because we'd just spoken on Sunday, over the phone. Fifteen years, I hadn't seen him. Then out of the blue, he calls to say he's dying.

'Henry,' he'd rasped, 'I'm not long for this world. Doctor's given me another five to ten days.'

He hadn't lasted the night.

I'd known he was sick a week earlier. Aunty Janice, Graham's sister, had rung, told me my uncle had fallen off a ladder, hit his head. The resulting scan had revealed more than a bruise. You can only ignore the symptoms of a tumour for so long. I'd promised her I'd get down to Margaret River to see him. I let my days fill with excuses, thinking I had more time.

Over the phone, Uncle Graham had asked if I would give his eulogy, speak well about him. I'd tried to tell him I couldn't. He'd helped my mother look after me when I was a teenager, a replacement father-figure for a few years, but that was a long time ago. He'd chosen to live closer to his remaining siblings down south, in Margaret River. Mum and I were city folk, though. I was born in Subiaco, raised in Perth's northern suburbs. We had no interest in country living. So, we'd stayed, survived. Time flew by as we lived separate lives.

I invited him to my wedding, of course. He turned up, gave a speech, laced it with his weird humour. Got a little too drunk and told me to keep a short leash on my wife, Lucy, lest she go wandering. He'd argued with my wife's relatives, leaving in a fit of embarrassment. I should have asked if he was okay, but I was angry. We lost contact. For fifteen years. I have no idea what he's been up to. What could I say in a eulogy to fill the gaps of a life I've largely missed?

But you can't refuse a dying man's request.

Still, why the letter? Had Uncle Graham posted it hours before he'd died, or had he sent it last week? Had he called on Sunday because I hadn't replied? The letter starts by doubling-down on his wish for me to give his eulogy, but it includes additional requests he never talked about. On a yellow slip of paper, there's a list of things to find for his ceremony and wake. Some esoteric items, music, photo albums. It seems he's also made me his unofficial funeral planner.

Which would be okay, I guess, except I don't understand the last entry:

Find Lillian

I have no idea who Lillian is. In my forty-one years on this earth, I've never heard that name uttered from the lips of anyone in my family. Not in any meaningful way. Was I meant to trace and call this person, bring her to the funeral? Was she a special guest? If she knew Uncle Graham romantically, she'd know about his death, so what was her connection?

Two words. No further details—no address, phone number, description. Two words and Uncle Graham thought I'd make sense of them.

I've sat on this for a while, part of the phone conversation lingering at the back of my mind.

'How's the force treating you?' Uncle Graham had asked. His memories must have been playing tricks on reality since I was only a police officer for two years before shifting professions. 'I remember you'd solved some cases the big boys had no clue about.'

'I helped tie things together, Uncle Graham. That's all.'

Ruffled feathers, more like. Overstepped my place, my duties, until it almost got me killed.

'You kept digging. That's what it was, Henry. I need you to keep digging for me now. Can you do that?'

'Sure. I'll keep digging,' I'd said. I didn't mind agreeing to something he wouldn't remember.

With the letter in front of me, I can't help but make the connection to Lillian. I know I must find the other items on the list, too, but they seem straightforward—things I'll collect throughout his house. Lillian is elsewhere. There's every chance she could be

3

an ex-partner, an old colleague, a childhood neighbour. But if Uncle Graham thought I was still an officer, there's also a chance she's someone who requires the skill set of an officer to find. Skills that will require me to dig for information.

Problem is, I don't dig for information anymore. I've moved on, buried that part of my nature.

Haven't I?

Digging feels so unnecessary, anyway. Why hadn't Uncle Graham just told me who Lillian was? Or where and why I needed to find her? Why leave a cryptic list that death has robbed of explanation? Why involve me at all? If Lillian is missing, or worse, why not call or write to an actual police officer in his local area?

I try to calm down, try to tell myself I'm reading too much into this. Uncle Graham's death is hitting me harder than I'd like to admit. It's just a request to find someone, invite them to his funeral. It's only one item on a long list of things to seek. Achievable, over the upcoming weekend, before his ceremony on Tuesday. I'll ask around. I haven't heard of Lillian, but other relatives may know her. They may have seen her in the last fifteen years.

Which is why I can't shake the feeling…

Uncle Graham has two surviving brothers, a sister, their partners, and countless cousins, nieces, and nephews. Most of them have seen him more than me; are more qualified to talk about him, to sort through the items on his list and find the person he wanted at his funeral.

And yet, he'd chosen me.

Writing it all in a letter, for my eyes only. No digital trace.

I need to know why.

Curiosity is a strange addiction. It's calling once more.

CHAPTER TWO
HIDING SOMETHING

Uncle Graham was my father's younger brother, eight years separating them. I'd known him longer than my father, though—William Herbert died twenty-six years ago, when I was fifteen. My father was a gardener, or landscape artist, depending on how much my mother romanticises it. He'd booked a job in Mandurah, an hour's drive from the city. The job was supposed to last a few weeks. Some big, new house alongside an estuary development, nothing but sand around it. A landscaper's blank canvas. And a big payday. And, if he did the job right, more money from other residents surrounded by sand. Mum said my father was so excited to work there, he'd leave the second sunlight crept over the hills. But he worked one long shift too many. Exhausted himself. On his way back to Perth one evening, he ended up wrapping his car around a tree.

Uncle Graham came to stay with us after the accident. Mum had lost part of herself. She would never be the same. She withdrew when I needed her, fracturing our bond. So, Uncle

Graham took over. Helped with the chores, kept me in line. When I think back, it's easy to see how I could have let misery and teenage angst plunge me into darker places. It did, at times, but Uncle Graham made sure I kept going to school, challenged myself, became independent, did my father proud even though grief distorted my memories of the man.

The phone rings, tearing through my thoughts. It's the landline. There are only three types of people who call my landline: telemarketers, my mother, and people who've got my number off my mother. I wait, let it ring longer. Nobody else is going to answer the call. My wife is at work. We have no children. I wander over to the phone, pick it up. A one in three chance.

It's my mother.

She wants to know how I'm doing. Aunty Janice has called her, relaying details about the funeral. I tell her I know; Aunty Janice called me, too. This morning. Mum's called me about this already. This morning. My mother forgets these things. Her brain is all over the place. Ever since my father passed away, she's fluttered in and out of conversations and consciousness.

'Henry? Are you listening?' she's saying. 'They've scheduled his funeral for Tuesday.'

'I know, mum.'

I've tried having her see different doctors, but each one says she's fine. No strokes or disorders. They even clear her for a driving license each year, ignoring the fact that she's one of the world's worst drivers. Maybe she has a tumour like Uncle Graham. Maybe—

'It's down in Margaret River. Can you believe that? It should be back here, where he used to live.'

'He's lived in Margs for twenty-odd years, mum. It's his home.'

'But still, when are you heading down?'

I think of the letter. 'As soon as possible. Just need to make a few calls.'

'I don't think I'll come down till Monday.'

'You've told me that. I've arranged things so you don't have to…' I reel myself back, soften my voice. 'Aunty Janice is sending Trent to pick you up.'

'Who?'

'Trent, her son.'

'Can you pay him for petrol?'

'Sure.' The conversation's going nowhere, so I try to change its direction. 'Can I ask you something?'

'Go ahead.'

'Lillian. Have you heard that name before?'

'There's a lady named Lillian at our library. She loves her Mills and Boon.'

'No. I mean, in our family. Connected to Uncle Graham.'

There's a pause.

'No,' she squeaks.

I want to push for answers, but I say we'll talk later and end the call. That *No* gives me enough for now. The long pause, the way my mother's voice changed pitch, it's enough to suggest she's hiding something from me.

I need to get down to Margaret River as soon as possible, rummage through my uncle's belongings and dig up as much as I can on this mystery person. My mother's not the most reliable source, but if she *is* lying, I can assume that Lillian exists. She was involved in my uncle's life in some capacity.

At least that's a start.

CHAPTER THREE
IT'S NOT A SHACK

The drive down south from Perth to Margaret River is a test of endurance. It's under three hours if attempted without resting. If you stick to the speed limit, varying between eighty and one hundred and ten kilometres per hour. If you have no problem navigating nefarious stretches of forest-lined highway, dodging nature, slower cars, and road trains.

Usually, I wouldn't test my endurance. I'd stop in Mandurah for a coffee, then Busselton to stretch my legs. But I've missed most of the Thursday morning peak hour traffic and the road trains seem non-existent today. The weather is yet to reach its almost-Summer warmth, too, so it would be foolish to disrespect good fate.

Uncle Graham's property is a fifteen-minute drive from Margaret River's main strip. I've passed houses that wouldn't look out of place in Perth's fringe suburbs, but the scenery switches fast. Now I'm heading along gravel-lined roads that take me past interchanging patches of forest and farmland. I've always imagined my uncle having a small, weather-ravaged house in the middle of nowhere. As I pass fields full of cows, most seeking shade beneath trees, I get the feeling I'm going to wind up at an even more dilapidated shack.

My phone announces I've arrived at my destination. I pull into a bitumen-lined driveway, stop before a rusty gate. I squint at the mobile's screen. The signal's been shifting between 3G, 4G and No Service, but I'm confident it's taken me to the right spot. I exit the car, unlatch the gate, swing it wide open. There's no point in closing it. As far as I know, Uncle Graham has no livestock on his property, and I'll go out for lunch later. I return to the car, accelerate along the driveway. It turns into a red-earth track surrounded by shrubland, taller trees visible in the distance. The track bumps me along until the shrubland halts, giving way to a cleared area. Ahead, the ground is made of rock so dark, it looks like fire has scorched its surface. It's a dam-slash-bridge, water on either side. I hold my breath and push on the accelerator, trying not to imagine my tires catching a slick of truant water, swerving me into unknown depths. I cross to the other side in seconds, though, and can't help but laugh out loud. A bird swoops past the windscreen as if to silence me, drawing my attention to the house up ahead.

It's not a shack.

It's an ordinary house. Single storey; brick and tile. Old but freshly painted. Bigger than mine. I park by its closed garage door, step out and gaze around. The water I crossed widens in the distance. Some kind of irrigation reservoir? Huge berry bushes are along its banks. How long will this take to falter without anybody maintaining it?

There's a large tin shed near the end of the reservoir. Beyond it, more towering trees. Above the shed, a pair of fairy-wrens chase each other in a dance for love or territory, two dots swirling through the air.

I check my phone. Lucy hasn't called me. We had a slight disagreement last night, another reason I wanted to get to Margaret River as quickly as possible. I message her, let her know I've arrived safely. There's an older message from Aunty Janice, a reminder she's left keys in a planter by the front door. I find them in a drip tray, an assortment of unlabelled colours. When I finally unlock the front door, instinct makes me call out *hello*.

Nobody responds.

It's cold, the air thick with a stale waft of cigarettes and something I can't place. The lounge room has floor-to-ceiling windows looking out at the water. They're covered by thin white curtains. I flick a light on, relieved the electricity is still working, then ease my way inside, taking in every detail, cautious of shifting shadows. The interior throws me more than the lack of a shack. I expected this to be a bachelor pad—clothes strewn over couches, movie cases stacked up against a TV cabinet, a pizza box open on a coffee table. It's not like that at all, though. I know Uncle Graham wasn't a young lad, but I never expected his place to be this spotless. Maybe Aunty Janice and her team of relatives have already worked their magic?

I never asked where Uncle Graham died. Was it right there on the couch? Or was it his bed? I find the main bedroom, see a stripped mattress, no signs of life. The bedside table and robe are bare, no signs of a second person sharing the space. No sign of Lillian.

My phone pings. Another message from Aunty Janice. She's having a dinner tonight, for family. Her son, Trent, will be picking me up. Refusal doesn't sound like an option. I type a response, agreeing to her terms, but the service drops to SOS Only. I head back to the lounge room, walk its length into an open kitchen. I find what I'm looking for on the counter, an old landline phone. It has no dial tone, though. The electricity's still running; I doubt someone cut the service. Maybe it's just a fault on the line?

Fate's guiding me again. Time to look for some of the easier items on Uncle Graham's list, or clues pointing towards Lillian's location. I take the yellow slip of paper out of my pocket, unfold it, and decide. Uncle Graham wants me to find a set of four photo albums. That would be an excellent place to start since photo albums are distinctive. Now, where to look first?

I head back through the lounge room, round its long wall, enter a passageway. Beyond the main bedroom, the first doorway leads to a bathroom that reeks of bleach. The next doorway is closed. I open it, find a light switch, flick it. Gasp. This room is so cramped, it's a struggle to get inside. There are plastic tubs stacked in piles at least six feet high, filled with random chaos. Clothes are strewn over a cardboard box near the door, and there's a framed picture leaning against a stack, depicting a forest scene.

It's the complete opposite to the front of the house.

I back away, try the next room. It's just as bad. More tubs, more clothes. A James Bond movie poster, framed. There are at least twenty plastic tubs between the two rooms. It's impossible to calculate the hours it will take to rummage through them. *And* there's one more doorway.

I retreat to the last room at the end of the passageway, hoping someone's marked a tub: *Everything on my list, for Henry.* But the room is empty; void of tubs, furniture, life. Had my uncle suddenly stopped hoarding things? Or was this the next room to be filled, the collection cut short by his death?

I spot something. I walk a few steps into the room and crouch, run my hand along the carpet. An indent is worn into the pile, a long line turning at right angles. I scan the rest of the carpet. More indents. This room was once full of tubs, too.

So why is it empty now?

CHAPTER FOUR
BOXED IT ALL UP

I take a break, walk along the bank of the reservoir. Its water is so murky I can't see beyond the surface. It seems symbolic. I've just stared at rooms full of boxes, a room absent of boxes, and can't fathom why. When Uncle Graham lived at our house, he had the spare bedroom and nothing more: a bed, a small bedside table, and a cupboard. He didn't have many possessions, content to share what we already had around the house. A suitcase, a backpack. Nothing more. Which made it easy for him to leave when he did. Is that the reason for the hoarding now? Maybe he's kept *everything* since leaving our house, sentiment imprinted on each item.

I should have visited him. Should have known.

My phone rings. Maybe Lucy's on a break?

'Where are you, man?'

It's work. Gavin, second in charge. He sounds like he's stoned. There's a high chance he is.

'You know where. Margaret River. My uncle's funeral?'

'You said that's Tuesday.'

'Seriously, Gavin? We had this chat yesterday.'

'Who's taking your shift today?'

'Not my problem.'

'Boss says it is.'

'I've got your text message saying I can have till next Friday off.'

'I said that? Shit. Was I high?'

'Are you high now?'

Gavin chuckles. 'Okay, Hen-dog, I'll cover for you.'

'Good. You're supposed to.'

I pick up a loose stone by the water's edge, hurl it across the gap, into the trees. I'm too old to put up with shit from a twenty-something-year-old whose daddy owns the store. That's what I get for selling consumer electronics now, though. At my age, if I'm not gunning for manager, I'm stuck telling customers that name-brand equipment is far superior to cheaper overseas counterparts.

I head back to the house.

Working there was my choice. I've dropped two stable, long-term careers and need to be okay with that decision. Even if my wife didn't sound like she was last night.

My phone pings. It's my boss.

Gav just saw me. He's an idiot. Have now till next Friday off, but ur needed for the following weekend rush. We've got a Wacky Weekend sale. Sony TVs cheap if you want one

I start typing a reply, but the phone drops its service again. Never mind. I enter the house, go to the first room full of tubs. After a quick breather, it doesn't seem so daunting. If all of Uncle Graham's possessions have been bundled inside these tubs, that means most items will be here. I'll waste a day or too looking for them, but I can afford that, can't I? Then I'll focus everything on Lillian.

With renewed determination, I grab a tub, open it, look inside. Winter clothes. I carry the tub into the passageway, go to the next one. Gardening equipment—rusted handles and soil-crusted prongs. I carry that one out, try a red tub. It's full of nails and other fasteners in plastic bags, tubes of sealant and other fix-it gear I should use more in my home. Another tub is full of assorted cables. And so on. No photo albums, just assorted junk that should have been in the large shed outside, or the rubbish tip.

I remind myself I'm not just looking for photo albums. I focus on finding a couple of other list items: an Akubra hat, a compass, a shark tooth necklace. I expect them to stand out, but they don't. The passageway starts getting too crowded, so I use the empty room; repeat the process of open a tub, rummage around, find nothing, carry it to the empty room. This consumes me enough to stop any thoughts of lunch, and it's not until there's a knock at the door that I finally allow myself a break.

'Cousin Henry! It's Trent, Janice's boy.'

A poster boy for farmhands stands before me. He's wearing a red plaid shirt, blue jeans, and red Converse sneakers. There's no cowboy-style hat; just black hair streaked with shiny pomade. He flashes a smile practised a thousand times in the mirror and offers a hand to shake.

'Trent?' I shake his hand, then check my phone. It's five. In the evening. The day has disappeared, a big a waste as the contents of my uncle's tubs. I try to disguise my shock, say, 'I remember you when you were half your height and twice as cute.'

Trent chuckles, peers inside the house. 'You, um, looking for something?'

I turn, catch his field of vision. A trail of assorted junk has spilled out of the passageway. 'I've, ah, got a list of things to find. For the funeral.'

'Oh yeah, the list.'

The words are like a slap to the face. 'You know about the list?'

'Uncle Graham sent one to mum. In case you didn't have time, I guess.'

'She's got a list?'

'Better than that. She's found most of the stuff on it. Boxed it all up. Got it at her house for you.'

'She's found most of the stuff?' I ask through gritted teeth.

'Oh yeah. She's busy getting us to do a lot of things. I seem to be everyone's designated driver. You're the third rellie I've picked up today.'

'Boxed up?' It takes all my strength to withhold a string of cursing. I take a deep breath, exhale. 'Well, I don't want to hold you up. Let's get going for dinner.'

I try to look at the bright side. Sure, I've wasted hours looking through tubs of random crap, but if Aunty Janice has found almost everything, I'll have more time to search for Lillian. Maybe I'll even find her tomorrow, after speaking to family tonight. Then I can have a relaxing Margaret River weekend, before the final funeral preparations.

My phone pings as I get into Trent's car. At last, it's Lucy. Replying to my message about arriving safely.

Good to hear. X

I call her, but it goes straight to voicemail.

I try to look at the bright side. At least she replied.

I hold on to that positivity as we head off to face my father's family.

CHAPTER FIVE
BEAUTIFUL COUNTRY

It's hard to enjoy a twenty-minute car ride when the conversation is one-sided. I hear all about Trent's desire to leave Margaret River, his dreams of city life, the wonders of the Diploma of Hospitality Management he's about to finish, and his goals of running a café. He tries to make it sound like he'll be saving the fucking world by adding to an already overcrowded market. I can't get a word in to caution him, though, and thank the heavens when he slows to pull into a property.

'Well, here we are in boring Boranup,' Trent says as we enter a homestead that looks anything but boring.

I have vague memories of this place from when I was a teen. It looked big then, but it hasn't lost its sense of scale. It's a vast property, with a sprawling house surrounded by a Karri forest. I remember Uncle Graham saying the land has wild kangaroos, an intermittent stream and even a tiny cave. My house has a tiny yard and they've got a freaking cave? Trent doesn't realise how lucky he's had it. His parents bought the property decades ago for next to nothing. Now it's worth a million, at least.

We pull up behind a train of cars. I was expecting to dine with the inhabitants of the house only, maybe one or two extra relatives; it seems Aunty Janice has summoned a welcoming party. Nothing like a death to bring everyone together.

'Is this why your mum arranged a lift?'

On cue, Aunty Janice opens the oak doors to her house, wine bottle in hand. She lifts it up, beaming. I can't tell if she's delighted to have me or the alcohol in her presence.

'Henry!' she shouts in her unmistakable nasal twang. 'I've got a McHenry Zinfandel. See, it's got your name in it!'

I guess it's both.

Like Uncle Graham, I haven't seen her since my wedding, although we've talked sporadically on the phone. Her face hasn't aged since the day I said, *I do*. I'd love to know her secret. Her hair seems to be the one thing that has changed, cut from a long-flowing black braid to a red-tinged bob. She hugs me with more warmth than I was expecting, then filters me through the house. The alcohol has made her merry, but I still remember her shifting temper, the way she used to yell at my mother when the two of them were too stubborn to admit they were wrong. Maybe the years in Margaret River have changed her temperament? There's an abundance of wine here. That would be a big help.

I have seconds to admire the décor within. There's an abundance of family photos hanging along rust-coloured, rammed earth walls. Someone has taken up the guitar—three models lean against the wall where the hallway expands to a lounge room, two acoustic and one electric. I tried the guitar once, couldn't strum two chords together.

'Henry!' Two of my uncles turn and announce my arrival. I recognise them straight away—Uncle Daniel and Uncle David. They're the odd fits of the bunch. While most of us clear six feet, they're at least half a foot shorter. David's twice as wide, though, suited to the rugby field. Daniel's got his wiry, leathery skin and faded tattoos to make him look older than the others, even though he's the youngest. They approach as Aunty Janice leaves to fetch me a wine glass. I'm expecting handshakes, but they take turns pulling me in for a hug.

'Great to see you,' Uncle David says, stepping back to take me in. 'Age has been kind to you, son.'

'Not so to Graham,' another man says as he stumbles into the room, beer in hand. I don't recognise him at all. He has a shock of white hair, his polo shirt struggling to contain a distended beer belly.

'This is Kevin,' Uncle Daniel says. 'He worked with Graham.'

'Partners, we were,' Kevin says, trying to shake my hand but missing. He's had a few beers already. 'Though I might have ta dis-dissolve the business now.'

'Fancy a smoke outside, Kev?' Uncle Daniel says, leading the man to honey-coloured bifold doors, winking back at us.

As they leave the room, there's a brief pause in the conversation. All I'm thinking is, *I didn't know Uncle Graham had a business.*

Uncle David points to an archway. 'Shall we go back to the party?'

'Party?'

Trent slaps me on the shoulder. 'These oldies don't want to call it what it is, cause then they'd be admitting they're getting closer to their own send-off.'

Uncle David clips him on the back of his head. 'I'm one of those oldies, idiot. Now fetch me some of the good stuff your dad's got hiding.'

We laugh, and I've got to admit, it's nice to be amongst this type of family dynamic. My mother and I are so isolated from my father's family, I've only held on to disjointed memories of what they're like. Half a dozen people occupy the adjoining room, their chatter drowning out some Nu Jazz. Aunty Janice reappears with two glasses filled to the brim with red wine. She hands one over, then announces me to the other occupants one-by-one. Most are relatives I don't remember. None are named Lillian. They're all eager to share quick tales of me as a child. I give them my time, listening to my life as if it were someone else's, unable to connect with anything they're saying. The level in my wine glass lowers, but before I can blink, it's topped up. Trent and Uncle David have disappeared to find the harder stuff. I try to turn the conversation, ask my relatives for stories about Uncle Graham. All I get is snippets.

'He cared so much about you and your mum, when your father passed...'

'He was a bit of a loner, always trying to do things himself...'

'I told him he should get a smaller property, come live near us...'

'You should move down here; it's beautiful country.'

'Beautiful country.'

I ask everyone if we have a Lillian in the family. From the puzzled faces, it seems they don't know. Whether that's the truth is another story. Aware Aunty Janice is no longer in the room, I finish my red wine and excuse myself, faking a need for the bathroom. I find a staircase, ascend it, end up in a long, attic-like room with a sloping roof. I run my hand along a dark timber overhead beam, then plonk myself on a beanbag. This night has differed from my expectations, but there's only so much extended-family dynamic I can take.

I look around, enjoying the silence. There's a television in the corner. Part of me wants to turn it on and watch whatever crap is running, escape for the rest of the night.

'You travel all this way, and you're hiding?' Uncle Roland, Janice's husband, is standing at the staircase. Flashing his bright-white veneers. He and his wife are both tall and thin, with such similar body shapes, it's as if they eat and exercise in unison. But Uncle Roland's the dapper Englishman to Aunty Janice's capricious Aussie. Decades earlier, Uncle Roland would even dress as Timothy Dalton's James Bond for Halloween, putting on the deep voice. Except he's far from a secret agent. He works with numbers—accounting or investing or property management, I'm not too sure. It changes all the time. He walks past me to a wooden cabinet, picks a bottle off the top and shows me the label. 'Don't suppose I could persuade you down with a drop of this?' As I rise from the beanbag, he swoops in for a hug. 'It's been too long.'

'I don't know why I'm here.'

'Of course, you do. Graham loved you; he deserves a eulogy from the best.'

'I mean—'

'I know what you meant. It's this strange concept called being hospitable. Now, you aren't a kid anymore, and you can't hide when you don't feel like talking. Have some of this stuff. It'll make it easier. I presume you're allowed alcohol now.' He gives me the Dalton smile. 'Don't know what you're worried about, anyway.

Janice has taken care of most of the eulogy stuff. She's got everything from the list in a box for you.'

'So I've heard. Has she been packing all of Uncle Graham's belongings in tubs, too?'

'Graham was packing away his life, or so he put it. But yes, Janice was helping him, before he passed.'

'Did she bring some tubs back here?'

'She's been bringing all sorts of things in for this funeral. Honestly, she's done so much, there's little to worry about now.'

'What about finding Lillian?'

Uncle Roland forces a blank expression before saying, 'Who?'

'Never mind.' I try to mask my excitement. He lying. Just like my mother.

CHAPTER SIX
I'M FIXIN' SOPHIA TONIGHT

A bell rings as we head down the staircase.

'We're being summoned,' Uncle Roland says. 'I'll get that box for you later, put it by the front door.'

He leads me outside, down some limestone steps and along a paved path to a gazebo. Everyone else has already gathered here—at least twenty guests. Two large tables stretch into the distance, covered with candles and enough food to fill us twice over. Aunty Janice is at the far end. She raises her wine glass and addresses the crowd, welcoming travellers. She recites a poem about death. I ignore the words, scanning the crowd, imploring memories to resurface. Aunty Janice urges us to continue catching up over the weekend. To both honour Uncle Graham and become closer as a family.

I fight the urge to laugh. Aside from Uncle Graham, my father's family moved away the second he was buried. Maybe losing two siblings has changed her sentimentality? That, and the wine.

As she winds up her speech, I learn that Uncle Graham was an agnostic who liked to talk about eternity with the local priest, something he never discussed with me. His service will be at a church, the wake at a brewery. That seems more like Uncle Graham; a compromise between two worlds. Aunty Janice says something about Uncle Graham being welcomed in whatever afterlife he imagined. She appears sincere.

'Henry? Henry?' I'm shaken from my thoughts by Uncle David. My wine glass slips from my fingers, smashing against the paving.

'Henry Herbert, everyone,' Aunty Janice calls out. 'He'll be giving Graham's eulogy, so if you have stories to share, use this opportunity while he can still remember them.'

A few people laugh, then we're instructed to grab a plate, help ourselves to the buffet, the drinks, and leave when we've had enough of both.

'You might wanna ease up, there,' Uncle David says, handing me a glass of water.

'I'll try.' I put the glass on the table, heading for Aunty Janice.

Three relatives cut me off. I try to excuse myself. There are things I need to ask Aunty Janice, but they have other plans. They recount a quick tale about Uncle Graham, then the interrogation begins.

'You look fit, Henry. Are you working out a lot?'

'I go to the gym when I can. Helps my back.'

'You look as tall as your father, too. How tall are you now?'

'Six-two. Still an inch shorter than him and his sister.'

'I remember you being waist high.'

'I don't. I've kind of blanked out most of my earlier years.'

'And you're a teacher, right? How's that going? At least ten years now, isn't it?'

'Almost. But I earned my long service, and I didn't go back.'

'Oh.'

My blunt answers aren't going to move them away. 'It's not simply teaching any more. It's being a bureaucrat, a psychologist, and a witness to shitty parenting, where everything's your fault when it's not going right.'

'Oh. You've definitely quit teaching, then?'

'I'm keeping up my registration, in case I need to go back, but I'd rather work anywhere else.'

'But your wife's a teacher, isn't she?'

'Yes, she's still teaching. She's far more committed to the job than I ever was. She should be running her school.'

'Weren't you with the police for a while, too?'

I could go on a ten-minute tangent, talk about the times my work left me hospitalised. Best to keep it brief, though. 'I left for similar reasons.'

'And what does your wife think of your decisions?'

I pull my mobile phone from my pocket, check the screen. No new messages or missed calls. 'Lucy encouraged it to start with, but I don't think she approves of my latest choice. Says it has no direction.'

'And what choice is that?'

'Something less stressful. I sell televisions and other electronic stuff to people who think they've got money to burn.'

'Oh. We bought a TV last year. Hisense. Nice for the price.'

It's back and forth for a few more minutes before I can ask if there's someone at the party named Lillian. The three gossip-fuelled relatives should know. They're adamant there's nobody here by that name, and I finally I excuse myself. Aunty Janice is no longer at the end of the table. The forest beyond is an inky void, a world of shadows I don't wish to enter. Maybe I should eat? No, food holds zero appeal. I retreat towards the house, drawing in some much-needed fresh air.

Kevin is sitting outside the house, a glass of water pressed against his lips. I can't peg the man's age. The white hair doesn't help. Sixty? Seventy? He has bags under his eyes, something I'd started getting from years of primary school teaching.

He jumps when I get close. 'Scared me, son. It's Harry, right?'

'Henry.'

'Your uncle was a good man.' He sighs. 'Didn't mean to mention our business before. The poor bastard's just died; it sounded shellfish. *Sell-fish.*' He holds up the glass. 'Sticking to this from now on.'

'I didn't even know he owned a business.' I sit down on the paving beside Kevin.

'He was a bit of an odd-jobs man for years. We met at a market, where I was selling my notebooks.' Kevin places his glass on the ground with so much care it's clear he's still part-alcohol. 'I cut the leather covers, do the binding myself. Pays some bills, but not many. I just love doing it, you know. Then your uncle, he says an old lady gave him a typewriter for fixing her retic. A typewriter! But he's spent a bit of time doing it up, so it looks almost brand new. Works and everything, like it did seventy years ago. He says he has an idea. He wants to sell it at my table, pair it with my paper. So, next market he brings it in. It's a pearler. I charge him ten per cent. A table fee. You know, for the bills. It looks great but I don't expect a typewriter to sell. Everyone's on iPads now, right? Same reason my notebooks aren't selling. But within ten minutes, some young guy comes up and wants it. Nine hundred dollars! He paid it without hesitating. I can't believe what's happened. I ask your uncle if he's fixing any more typewriters, and a partnership is born.'

'Typewriters.' I can't help but shake my head. 'I can't imagine Uncle Graham fixing one.'

'He was good for fixing lots of things.'

'So, you made a lot of money?' I ask, unsure whether to query what else my uncle fixed.

'Enough to pad my savings account. We'd go around to markets, use our connections with the locals, get typewriters for fifty dollars and make ten to twenty times on resale. Course, lots of work went into them. Difficult to fix typewriters. Not something I've learned. I was more the sales guy. Plus, I used the paper from my notebooks and made packs to go with them. Gotta have fancy paper with a fancy typewriter.'

'Where did he fix them?' I ask, thinking I might already know the answer.

'Back at his house, in a big shed. You know the place?'

'I'm staying at his house. Finding things for his funeral. I know the shed, haven't been inside.'

Kevin chuckles. 'You know, he gave every one of them a name, after someone he knew—like a local. "I'm fixin' Sophia tonight," he'd say, as if he had some romantic deli, um, dalliance. He said a piece of Margaret River was going out into the world. I wonder if that's what all the wineries think when everyone's getting drunk off their grapes.'

I force a chuckle, but my mind's racing. 'So, Uncle Graham named his typewriters after people he knew?'

Kevin nods.

'Did he ever call one Lillian?'

The man's eyes widen. He leans closer, as if we're part of a conspiracy. 'How did you know?'

My whole body shudders. 'This is important,' I manage, my heart racing faster than my mind. 'Did you sell the one called Lillian?'

Kevin leans back, slaps his leg as if it were a joke. 'Lillian? He's yet to fix her. Truth be told, I think he just wanted to keep it for himself. He showed me plenty of times. Can't blame him, it's a beaut. A Smith-Corona. All black, a marvel of the '40s.'

'Do you think it's still in his shed?'

'I don't see why not.'

I'm already standing. The world lurches around me.

Kevin gets up to provide balance. 'Easy there. It's not going anywhere.'

But I need to be going. I need to take the box of items from Aunty Janice, get into that shed and find Lillian. I shake Kevin's hand, remind him to catch up with me at the funeral, then look around for my ride.

CHAPTER SEVEN
A DIFFERENT STAGE OF MISUSE

My ride consumed far too many drinks, so I'd waited for one of the few taxis available. Uncle Roland had been true to his word, leaving the box of items by the door. I couldn't get a moment alone with Aunty Janice, but she did tape a note to the top of box letting me know the items were going to be put on a table near Uncle Graham's coffin. It answered some questions—now Kevin's revelation has left me with more.

The second the taxi drops me off, I put the box by the front door and hurry to the shed. I'd assumed it was just full of the tools and vehicles someone needed to maintain a property like this; now I know my uncle was using it as a workspace for an interest I was clueless about.

I swipe on my phone's flashlight function, slice a beam of light through the darkness. Something glints on the shed door. I race forward, see that it's a padlock. I check the house keys. None of them fit the lock. I'm kept out of the one place I need to go. I kick the door, screaming. The metal ripples, sending a thunderous boom into the night.

I have no choice but to go inside the house. For now.

I sit on the couch, leave the box on the coffee table. Stare at it for a while. I should open it right away, shouldn't I? But I don't know how I'll react if the box has the wrong stuff inside, or if it ends up being useless junk that I can't attach to Uncle Graham. So, I pull my legs up and stretch out along the couch, staring at the cardboard until my eyelids close.

A weird scratching noise wakes me. Sunlight is filtering through the curtains. The scratching turns into a series of thumps—something running across the roofing, passing straight overhead. A rat? Heavier. Maybe a possum or bandicoot. Do they get those here?

Now something's buzzing. My phone, vibrating against the coffee table. I don't remember putting it there or setting it to silent mode. I scoop it up, see the caller. My heart skips a beat.

'Morning.' I cringe as my voice falters.

'Morning. How are you?'

Just hearing my wife's voice is enough, for now, a lingering sense of unease dissipating. 'Recovering. I went to Aunty Janice's house for dinner. Lots of family there, lots of alcohol.'

'Nothing like a dead person to get people drunk.'

'Yeah. Listen…' I ease upright on the couch '…I've tried calling.'

'I've tried calling, too. It's just going straight to voicemail.'

I look at my phone. No missed calls registered. 'I don't see any—'

'Are you in a blackout area? The connection now is pretty choppy.'

I think of the numerous times my phone has jumped between connection strengths and No Service. I slap my forehead. 'It's the area. I think they want you to stay off your phone down here, appreciate nature and stuff.'

I get a little laugh. It sounds like heaven. I want to blurt out my apologies, tell her how much I need her with me right now, but something stops me.

'I've got Monday to Wednesday off, okay,' she says, maybe feeling the same way. 'Bereavement leave or family care or something like that. Catherine's filing it for me. They were close to saying I had to stay or take leave without pay, till I kicked up a fuss.'

'You can't come down tomorrow?' Fuck it. I know I sound needy, but I have to ask. It's my wife, after all. I *do* need her here.

'I'd already agreed to help Sarah this weekend, remember? Katie's got basketball and netball games. Thomas has swimming lessons. Then there's food shopping and cleaning to do. All the fun chores.'

I reach out to the box on the table, pull at the cardboard flaps.

'How is Sarah?' My sister-in-law's family is doing it tough since her husband broke his arm and leg at work, one of those freak industrial accidents.

'Desmond's still in a wheelchair. Arm's good, leg not so much. So, he's not helping her, well, at all.'

'That's crap.'

'Mum keeps calling. She wants to come down to help.'

Lucy's parents live in Singapore. They met at a conference in Melbourne, a shared Malaysian heritage creating a connection.

'What about your dad?'

'He'll do whatever she does.'

I chuckle. Aqil Morias is the most laid-back man I've ever met, an expert at going with the flow. They'd moved to Perth when Lucy was five, Sarah born soon after, so they know the area. They'd moved back to Singapore to be with Aqil's sick mother, the kids old enough to stay here.

'It'll be a big help,' I offer.

'It would make Sarah feel important.'

Even though Lucy's parents are in another country, they're always available. I'd love to know what that's like.

'Send my love,' I say, because it seems the safest option. 'You still love me, right?'

I can hear a muffled groan. 'Is this because of our fight?'

'Yeah.'

'You're overthinking how bad it is. And it's not the first time. We'll talk about it on Monday, okay?'

'I can't call you over the weekend?'

'You can, but message me first. I might be busy. You've got to write that eulogy, too, don't forget. Concentrate on that.'

'I'm almost ready to start it. Got a few stories last night.'

'You can remember them?'

'Hah, hah.'

'Er, I've got a parent standing at my door. They're thirty minutes early for our interview. Sure, no problem, I'll change everything for you.'

We end the call. I stare at the screen for a while, willing Lucy's voice to continue. Fifteen years, and I can't seem to function without her. We still make each other laugh, but we also know how to make each other cry. I know she said I'm overthinking things, but she'd laced her words with anger the night before I left. And she'd just called it a fight. I need to prioritise some solutions once I finish this list and the eulogy.

I flip open the cardboard flaps of the box and look inside. There are more sheets of paper on top. One is another note from Aunty Janice. It's got a few dot points about Uncle Graham. Date and place of birth, where he grew up, first job and other accomplishments. What she assumes I'll work into the eulogy. There's yellow paper below it, a note in Uncle Graham's handwriting. It's addressed to Aunty Janice. There's a quick message saying he's sent a similar request to me, but he's afraid I might not show up to his funeral. Should I be offended? He asks Aunty Janice to give the eulogy if the family doesn't hear from me. Is Aunty Janice furious that Uncle Graham hadn't chosen her first? Maybe that's why she's thrown everything into a box, why she's cleaned his house so quickly, boxing possessions away as if eager to be done with it all.

The letter also includes a list. I get mine out to compare. They're not quite the same. Aunty Janice's list is missing three items: a CD made for the wake, a fourth photo album, and the instruction to find Lillian. So, Aunty Janice has no idea that I've been asked to find someone. I put this observation aside for now, begin taking everything else out of the box. The items cover the coffee table. I use my original list to cross off what I can see:

> ~~Photo album #1~~
> ~~Photo album #2~~
> ~~Photo album #3~~
>   * use these for images of my life
> Photo album #4
> ~~Akubra Hat~~
> ~~CD - labelled 'music for funeral'~~
> CD - labelled 'music for wake'
> ~~Book - The Secrets She Keeps - Robotham~~
> ~~Book - Australian Ghosts~~
> ~~Flask of Limeburners (Roland has plenty)~~
> Indiana Jones Lego Minifigure
> Typebar with Letter C
> ~~Movie Poster - Back to the Future~~
> ~~DVD - The Castle~~
> Framed $100 Bill
> ~~Shark tooth necklace~~
> ~~Compass from Pop~~
> Find Lillian

There's a Lego mini-figure in the box, but it's not Indiana Jones. It's the warden character from Jurassic Park. The one who tells a raptor she's a clever girl. They've got similar hats, and Aunty Janice isn't enough of a movie buff to notice the difference. So, an honest mistake. Uncle Graham bought me heaps of Lego sets when I was younger, his go-to gift. Maybe he's included the mini-figure as our connection, to prompt something for the eulogy?

I feel like I need to find the right one, pray there's a solitary tub holding all the Lego.

I get up, walk towards the tub-filled rooms, stop myself. First thing's first. Waking in an unusual place, coupled with Lucy's call and the contents of the box, distracted me from my focus. The shed. The typewriter.

I hurry out the house. Reach the oversized tin building, try all the keys again. It wasn't the darkness or my consumption of alcohol—none of the keys make the padlock budge. While there's mobile reception, I browse the internet for ideas. I watch a quick video demonstration, then hurry indoors, rummage through a tub of fix-it gear, return with a hammer. I copy the video, tapping the side of the lock. Having little faith until the padlock drops to the ground.

I pull on the doors, slide them open. There must be clear panels in the ceiling—there's plenty of sunlight streaming inside. There's a small tractor to the right, a quad bike in front of it, some larger gardening equipment like pitchforks and shovels hanging off the adjacent wall. A wooden bench runs down the left-hand side, continuing along the far wall. On top of which looks like the bulk of my uncle's repair business.

There are at least ten typewriters. A few are in pieces atop grey, cloth mats. I know nothing about their history but there's something calming about rubbing a hand along their exterior. I read the labels that aren't damaged: Remington, Olivetti, Royal, Olympia, Sterling, Imperial, Empire. Each typewriter is in a different stage of misuse; some have keys missing, some have the typebars stuck together, others have their paintwork damaged, rust set in. I tap a key on a decent-looking green Olivetti and smile as it clacks. With keyboards evolving into panels on a digital screen, kids these days might not experience pressing on a tactile, three-dimensional keycap letter. No wonder my uncle's business was thriving, with parents spending big to preserve a piece of history and a life experience.

There are smaller tubs stacked between the typewriters, containing assorted mechanical pieces, rags, paint, and cleaning solutions. Between a Remington and a Royal, I find a giant ledger. I flick through it. Uncle Graham listed every job he's attempted, including what make the typewriter was, where he found it, and when he sold it. Cost and sale price are there, plus the name he gave each typewriter. But there's no record of who he sold each one to or the full name and address of who he'd named the typewriter after. Maybe he kept a separate document? I scan the last few pages. No listing for *Lillian*. The typewriter must exist. His partner knew all about it, but my uncle hasn't listed it.

No need to panic. I work my way around the corner, to the bench along the back wall. A few machines down, there's a typewriter covered by a thin cloth. An assortment of magnifying glasses and precision screwdrivers lay scattered around it. I know it's the right typewriter before I even pull back the fabric. One quick tug and I can't help but smile. It's a sleek machine, the surface matte black metal with three shiny stripes on either side above the keys. Written on the surface, in a yellowish-white, are the words *Smith-Corona* and *Silent*.

'Hello, Lillian.' I place a hand on its surface. A cold tingle rushes through me. 'I'm so happy to see you.'

There's a small card tucked under the typewriter. I pull it out. It reads:

Lillian. For my nephew, Henry. Not for sale.

I could stop now. Could assume this is the Lillian my uncle wanted me to find, an object he treasured, something to display at his funeral. I could assume I only have to find five more items on his list, then write a eulogy, and use my remaining time to enjoy a brief escape from the city. I could look up popular tourist destinations, visit as many as I can, sample offerings from wineries and food factories and pretend I don't have responsibilities back at home. But Kevin had said that Uncle Graham named the typewriters after people he knew. Often locals.

The typewriter's existence confirms a real person is out there.

CHAPTER EIGHT
EXPOSING THE INNER WORKINGS

I stare at Lillian. A few of the typebars are stuck halfway out, as if awaiting their chance to imprint onto paper. I remember another item on my uncle's list: *typebar with letter* C. That letter is one of the stuck ones. Maybe I can snap it off? I wiggle it a bit, but it's hanging on. I know my uncle treasured this typewriter, but it's not as if he's going to use it anymore. Maybe I can open the metal casing, use a screwdriver to prise it apart?

I pull at the top casing. It flips open, exposing the inner workings. I reach in, pause. Why pull out a typebar when it already comes with the whole typewriter? If it turns out there's no human-version of Lillian, I can cross two items off my list for the price of one. If not, I can take a typebar from another machine on the bench. It's not like they'll be fixed by anyone now.

Idiot.

Something catches my eye. There's a small object taped to the underside of the casing. It's black, too, but the sticky tape is reflective enough to be noticeable. I pull at the tape, take the black object. It's thin card. I unfold it. A small piece of photo paper drops out and onto the bench. I pick it up. It's part of an old square print, the word *Kodak* repeated across one side. I flip it over. One edge is jagged, the paper ripped or cut. I'm missing half the picture, but I've got enough.

The photograph is of a woman, seated at a round dining table. There's red and green décor in the background; I notice a candle in a vase, on a brick shelf. An Italian restaurant? There's part of an arm draped over the woman's shoulder, a white hand visible, but I can't see who it's connected to, that half of the image missing. It's like one of those cliché lover-scorned mementos, the relationship ripped away. Was this an ex-girlfriend of Uncle Graham's? No, he wouldn't have kept this half of the image, would he? I'll have to find the owner of that arm, but for now it's more important to focus on the woman. She looks to be in her mid-twenties, though I'm hopeless at pegging ages. She has bronzed skin, a broad face with an uncomfortable smile, and curly black hair. I can't tell her ethnicity. Given the restaurant, she could be European, but she could also be from South America, South Africa, or closer to home, of Aboriginal descent. Anywhere in the world—I'm also hopeless at pegging people's origins, even with a Eurasian wife.

Regardless, I've never seen the woman in the photo before now. It might be presumptuous, but I can't shake the feeling I'm staring at Lillian.

I have a thought, begin checking every other typewriter. I pull back casings, turn over machines. Inspect every area Uncle Graham could have hidden photographs. No more, though. None of the others have a name card, either; just the one Uncle Graham wanted me to find. I hang on to that thought, look at the picture again. Use my mobile's camera to photograph the photograph.

Backup, just in case. Then I grab Lillian the typewriter and bring her to the house.

I sit on the couch, staring at the image some more. The photo paper is old, yellow spots in corners, the image itself screaming of an era long past. The woman's gravity-defying curly hair looks late-eighties. She's wearing a black-and-white striped Benetton jumper. I remember a short craze in Australia in the '90s. So, the photograph is thirty to forty years old?

What am I supposed to do with it? Drive around and show everyone in my family in a vain attempt to see who recognises her? Stand in the middle of town and ask every local the same question? Or go through my uncle's photo albums, see if she appears in any other images? Maybe she'll be in the fourth album, the one I need to find.

I flip the photograph around my fingers, as if it will spin to life. Maybe I can show my family the image while looking for that missing album? I pull out my phone, bring up the photograph of the photograph, and send it to everyone whose details I exchanged last night. I include the message:

> Hi family, do you know who this is? Uncle
> Graham wanted me to find her for his funeral.
> If you know, MSG me ASAP. Henry.

I leave Lillian the typewriter on the coffee table for now, wander to the second room of tubs, and start my search. I'm only into the third tub when my phone rings. It's Aunty Janice.

'I thought I'd invited everyone to the funeral,' she says, 'do you need me to handle that?'

'I don't know who the woman is, so I can't even call her.'

'Ah. I can take over then. You've got the eulogy to do.'

'You know who she is?' My hand grasps a cloth-bound book deep in the tub. I drag it out. A few photographs trickle out, onto the carpet.

'Someone's bound to know. But the photograph looks pretty old. The fashion she has, I'm thinking eighties, early nineties.'

'I thought that, too.'

'Do you have any more photographs?'

'No.'

'Why didn't Graham ask me to find her in the first place?'

'I don't know.'

'I wouldn't expect much, but I'll ask around.'

'Okay. Thanks.'

Aunty Janice talks about last night's wine for a little longer, then bids farewell. I've flipped through the book while listening to her, filled some empty slots with the photographs that'd fallen out. There's a yellow sticky-note on the first page, with #4 written on it. Scratch one more item off the list. I'm getting good at this. Although, it's not as if I've had to search around town.

I wonder why Aunty Janice didn't find and box this album, then remember her list included photo albums one to three. She wouldn't have looked for more. I restart my perusal and scan the images with greater care. Even after replacing the fallen photos, there are still at least ten blank spots throughout the album. With no annotations, I don't know what's missing. Did Uncle Graham always have bare spots, or did he take the photos out and leave them somewhere else? I hope this is the case, but my gut's telling me someone has taken the photos; that there were at least ten images with Lillian in them, and someone removed them.

Another thought occurs to me. I head back to the couch, photograph the typewriter, make a call.

'Harry?' Kevin sounds like he's forgone the water, returning to the alcohol.

'It's Henry. I found the typewriter. Are you busy?'

'I'm at Brauhaus. It's right in town. Near a teensy little bridge.'

I need to see Kevin in person. Need to read his face when he sees the images. 'You going to stay there a while?'

'If you're buying me a pint, I'll wait around.'

'Done.' Time to see if he calls both the typewriter and the woman Lillian.

CHAPTER NINE
CAN'T HELP BUT FEEL INTIMIDATED

'That's her. Ain't she a beaut?' Kevin hands my phone back, then takes a long sip of his new pint.

I swipe away the photograph of the typewriter, show him the woman. 'What about her? Is that Lillian? Is that who he named the typewriter after?'

Kevin downs another mouthful of beer, wipes his lips. 'Geez, I don't know.' He studies it for a long time.

I look around, taking in the scenery, hoping he's going to say *Yes*. We're sitting outside on wooden bench seats. A gentle breeze tries its best to remove a yeasty smell from the air. Brauhaus is at the northern tip of town, a short walk to the rest of the shops. Since I'm out, I should visit one of them to get something to eat. Or have something here. It's almost noon, and there are already lots of people stuck into a drink. If all goes well, I might join them.

'I've stayed in town a relatively short time,' Kevin says. 'My sister lives here, but I'm a Busselton lad.' My phone pings. Kevin frowns. 'Looks like you're not having much luck.'

He hands it back to me. There's a message from Uncle David:

Sorry Henry, don't recognise her.
Will ask around.

'Well, I'm just going with what you said about how Uncle Graham named his typewriters.' I send a brief reply to Uncle David. 'If this typewriter was so special, surely people know the woman it's named after?'

'And you're sure your uncle wanted her at his funeral?'

'He wrote a list of items, and it said to find her.'

'For the funeral?'

'I'm just assuming, again.'

'You know what they say about assuming and your arse.'

'It's all I've got.'

Kevin swipes my phone out of my hand. 'Just gonna borrow that for a second.' He leaves his empty pint glass on the table, walks inside to the bar.

There are lots of people on a grassed area nearby, their chatter echoing around me. I'd love to be so carefree, but Uncle Graham's left me all kinds of frustrated. If the photograph isn't of Lillian, why leave it taped inside a typewriter of the same name? Was I supposed to find the photograph at all? Maybe it's just the typewriter I should focus on. Maybe the image was just a memento that Uncle Graham or the previous owner hid inside the machine.

And maybe pigs really can fly.

'Henry?' Several pints in and Kevin gets my name right. A man's standing beside him, dressed in a black shirt and chequered boardies. His grey curly hair catches the sunlight, carving the rest of his face with shadows. 'This is Jock. He's part-owner here.'

'Jacque?'

'Jock. Like the undies.' The man reaches out, shakes my hand with a firm grip. 'I do the hard stuff here, make the beer.'

'Tell him what you were explaining,' Kevin says.

'That photograph…' Jock strokes his chin, a sandpaper scratch audible over the chatter '…where did you get it?'

'My uncle. Graham Herbert.'

'Ah, Graham.' Jock smiles. 'He loved my stout.'

'Do you know who the woman is?' I snap, needing to cut to the chase.

'I went to school with her. Name's Charlotte Harris. Good sort, though we weren't with the same crowd.'

My heart skips a beat. 'Charlotte. Not Lillian?'

'Definitely Charlotte.'

'She couldn't have changed her name?'

'See, here's the thing. Charlotte passed away a long time ago.'

Everything inside me sinks. 'When?'

'We were all pretty young, few years out of high school. She can't have been much older than that photo. It was a car crash. I'd lost touch with her group a bit, so I didn't hear all the details. I'd check with the local cops, they'd have the info.'

'What about her parents?'

'Moved the hell away. Wanted nothing to do with the place.' Jock pats me on the shoulder. 'Sorry I can't be any more help.'

'That's a huge help, thanks.'

'We'll be seeing you soon. Your aunt's arranging for us to hold Graham's wake. I'll make sure you have one of his stouts.'

'Sounds like a plan.'

Jock walks off, does the rounds amongst the crowd. Kevin hands back my phone. 'Listen, I've gotta be going. Work calls. A future to sort out.'

'Okay.' I wonder how well he'll be working after a few drinks.

'Cheers for the pint,' he adds, as if reading my mind.

'Thanks for getting the info.'

'I'll keep asking around, see if I can dig up more.'

We shake hands, then Kevin disappears. I look back at the bar. I could order several drinks, make another day of it. I got some information worth celebrating, didn't I? A start to my search, even if it's the wrong woman?

My phone pings again. It's a message from Uncle Daniel. Are the brothers talking?

We need 2 talk about that pic. Where
are u, ur not at tha farm

Why's Uncle Daniel made his way to Uncle Graham's property? I reply, tell him I'm in town. He suggests I wait outside IGA, a supermarket down on the main strip. No point taking the car, the walk will do me good. Within five minutes, I reach the entrance. Uncle Daniel's nowhere to be seen. I enter the supermarket, use some cash to buy a snack bar—one of those protein ones that are just sugar in disguise—and a cold brew coffee. It takes a few quick gulps to down the coffee. The caffeine buzz is instantaneous.

A car horn beeps on the street beside me; makes me jump. It's a black four-wheel-drive, a monstrous vehicle; so shiny it seems an unnatural part of the country scene. The window winds down.

Uncle Daniel leans over the empty passenger seat, his leather-tanned arm waving at me.

'Get in, young Henry.' He keeps leaning over the seat as I edge my way inside, then slinks back and thumps my arm. 'Good to see ya again. Mind if we go for a drive?'

I glance back to see a huge Māori bloke occupying the bulk of the rear seats.

'This here's Lynden.'

I offer a greeting and receive a grunt. Uncle Daniel cuts into traffic and appears to be heading for the brewery, then turns left onto Carters Road.

'Where are we going?'

'Just wait.'

It's a long, silent drive through winding roads and towering trees, onto Caves then Wallcliffe roads, until the scenery disappears and there's nothing but scrub, white sand and a floor of ocean.

My uncle eases into a carpark, pulls up beside a burgundy Kombi van. Nobody's inside the van. It's a go-to vehicle for surfers; they're probably out on the waves.

'Get out,' Uncle Daniel says, yanking his seatbelt off and all but jumping from the car.

Lynden takes a little longer to ease out. The second he does, the suspension rocks on the vehicle. I turn to see him crossing his arms, a gaze of daggers thrown my way. Is he wanting me to react, to start a fight? I'm pretty tall and I've maintained a decent level of fitness, but I haven't had to fight in well over a decade. If you don't count stepping in to break up a playground brawl or stopping students from throwing furniture. Lynden is half a foot taller than me, and an extra person wider, and looks like he pummels people for a living. I can't help but feel intimidated.

How does my uncle know this guy?

'Are we going for a surf?' I joke. Lynden gives me nothing. Sometimes a guy that size smiles and turns into a huggable teddy bear. He isn't one of those guys.

'Walk with me, Henry.' Daniel's already on his way down a long concrete staircase, rubbing a hand along timber railing.

I follow him to the beach, Lynden trailing. I've gone along with this, but I can't keep ignoring that something's off. Uncle Daniel's whisked me to a remote location. Some hired muscle is watching my every move. I reach into my pocket, feel for my phone. Maybe I pretend it's ringing, step away, call the police or simply run for the car park?

No. It's my uncle. He's family. Maybe he just likes the ocean, eager to talk to me at his favourite spot?

How fucking naïve can I let myself be?

We reach the sand and ceremoniously slip our shoes off. Ice-cold particles trickle between my toes.

'You know, Henry,' he shouts against a creeping wind, 'so many people come to Margaret River and hit the wineries and caves and have no idea they're on the doorstep to the most magnificent coastline in the world.' He closes in, wraps an arm around my shoulder and starts guiding me to the water. 'They're having a problem with sharks again, did you know that? Might have to cancel the big surf tournament. Lynden's brother's in that. Isn't that right, Lynden?'

The Māori bloke grunts again, right behind me. I hadn't realised he was so close.

Uncle Daniel points to a small group of surfers on a distant break. Probably the Kombi owners. 'They live for the waves, but know their place. Respect the balance of the ocean. They know sharks aren't just dumb, hungry beasts. They're hungry, all right, cause their supply's all messed up. But sharks are smart. They know lots of people will surf here this time of year, for the tournament. They've started turning up, feeding. They've realised we're predictable. They're forced to attack to survive. You know what that's like, Henry? To be forced to attack?'

I'm sinking into the sand, my legs losing their strength.

'You shouldn't have sent that photo, Henry. Half the family got it.' He leads me to the water's edge, water frothing at my feet. 'Did you send it as a joke?'

'I'm just trying to find the woman.'

'She's dead. You need to leave it at that.'

'I thought she…'

'You thought *what*?'

I should stop, keep my mouth shut. But part of me wants to try something, wants to see how Uncle Daniel will react. 'The woman might know someone I'm after. For the funeral. Her name's Lillian.'

Uncle Daniel's eyes widen. 'Who?'

'Lillian.'

Uncle Daniel pulls away from me, takes one step into the water. He stares at the horizon for a moment, then faces me, hands on hips. 'What are you trying to do? You think you can come into our life again, stir shit up? Do you even know who Lillian is?'

I shake my head, brace myself. Will my uncle attack me, or is that the reason for the colossal mate?

'Nah, you don't,' Uncle Daniel says.

'But she exists?'

His face sours. 'Look, give a quick eulogy about my brother. Talk about the good times you remember when you were little. No need to worry about the rest of his life. No need to worry about finding Lillian, or showing the photo around. Give the eulogy, then fuck off back to the city. Stay away for another fifteen years. Longer would be great.'

My uncle side-steps away as a weight presses against my back. It's over before I feel it, a lightning-fast shove that buckles my legs and sends me down into the water. A wave rolls in against me. I'm on all fours, coughing out a lungful of seawater. I try to turn, brace for the second blow, but my uncle and his friend are already heading up the beach.

Another wave crashes over me, water ebbing against my shirt.

When I can stand, I hear a car screech in the distance.

I'm alone. Left to wonder what the hell just happened. Already knowing the crux of it is, I've uncovered someone who's likely dead, linked to someone I'm trying to find. Striking a nerve with my father's family.

I kick the water and laugh. My uncle thinks his threat will make me walk away; yet we know so little about each other. He's left me with two options. He gave me one: do the eulogy. He tempted me with another: prove Lillian exists.

CHAPTER TEN
SHOVE BACK

My mother, Uncle Roland and Uncle Daniel have all reacted to the name Lillian. Two of them lying, another getting angry, threatening. Did Uncle Graham know the last request on his list would affect my family this way? Is that why he entrusted me with it?

Uncle Daniel was right. In a way. I can do what I need to and, if things fall apart, never see most of them again. It'd be a shame, though. We may have lost touch, but family is still family. There's comfort in knowing you *can* see them when you need to, even if you don't.

I've had time to consider this, waiting for the owners of the Kombi to appear from the surf. When they emerge, I bribe them for a lift. For twenty dollars, I endure a bumpy ride back to Brauhaus. Still better than walking, which would have taken all day. I wave goodbye to my two chaperones, bronzed gods with straw hair, and return to my car. I *could* go inside the brewery for a drink and something to eat. My rumbling stomach thinks that's a great idea. But one sip of alcohol would start a downward spiral, so I drive halfway up the main town strip and pull off into a car park behind a row of buildings. A Coles supermarket adjoins the car park, which I'll return to for stockpiling future sustenance. There's a café across the main road I've wanted to try, one I looked up before my trip. I walk around traffic and find it, far enough from the main strip to afford a slight reduction of noise. It's a wasabi-green coloured building. An old house converted to feed the masses.

I open the door and noise returns. The building is full: of furnishings, food and customers. I'm asked to wait outside on a stainless-steel chair, assured me a couple is just finishing up. I order a long macchiato, sit down and stare towards the main road, at an endless stream of cars. There's a bizarre piece of street art spray-painted on a grey wall to the right, a cow getting milk from a milkmaid's breast. I try to laugh at the sight, try to sit back, relax and enjoy things.

I start crying.

It's a shoulder-heaving, guttural sob. I do everything I can to shut it off, but my body won't let me. Before I know it, I'm using my shirt as a tissue, wiping tears from my eyes. An employee comes out to hand me my coffee and freezes, unsure whether to back away or offer some solace. I explain that my uncle just passed away, that's why I'm down in Margaret River. She flickers a smile, placing my long macchiato on the closest table. She says my seat inside will be ready soon, hoping that'll make me feel better.

I should tell her to forget about it. I can't have a breakdown outside their café then devour a meal like nothing happened. Uncle Graham used to tell me you should only cry when someone's died, or you've been really, really hurt, as if weeping is an emotional flaw. I know that sounds fucked up, but at least he would have approved of this outburst—he's dead *and* I'm hurt, though he'd tell me it was just a little shove. He'd say I should pick myself up and either get over it or shove back.

I need to shove back; by finding Lillian.

I open the web browser on my phone, sip my coffee from its takeaway cup. If I'm going to ignore Uncle Daniel's warning, then Uncle Graham's farm is no longer an option for my accommodation. I need to reduce the times my family could 'pop in'. After searching a few sites, I find a property on Carters Road that has self-contained studios: a bed, television, kitchen, fridge. All that I need, plus a spa bath. It's limited to four studios on the property, well-spaced. Roughly three hundred dollars a night, but worth it for peace of mind. I could sell it to my wife as a romantic getaway, despite the occasion. Plus, there's one available, and accommodation in town seems scarce. I book through the property's website, and by the time I've finished my coffee I've already received a call saying the room will be ready at two.

I enter the café, throw my drained coffee cup in a bin and pick a few bakery items from a refrigerated display. The person who'd served my coffee walks past, asks if I still want my table. I decline as politely as possible, pay for the drink and takeaway then leave, hoping nobody noticed that guy who cried outside the café.

An almond croissant gives me sustenance on my way to the supermarket. Inside, I grab whatever food appeals to my stomach, plus some bottled water, toiletries, and a notepad and pen. My stomach reminds me I haven't eaten anything substantial since reaching my uncle's farm, just snacks. I can't even recall having anything at Aunty Janice's. It's like I'm back teaching, where classes and duties and a thousand distractions meant you were lucky to get ten minutes a day to eat, if at all.

I notice a flyer near the supermarket register for a Farmer's Market, held tomorrow morning. I doubt Uncle Daniel would think I'd turn up at a Farmer's Market. He might think I'm already retreating to Perth.

Shove back. I shove everything into a cooler bag and put it in my boot, then go for one last walk. While waiting in line at the supermarket, I'd checked the local police station's location. It's on the same road as the wasabi café. In a matter of minutes, I'm passing the café and heading up a sloping hill. If Uncle Daniel appears, I can sprint the rest of the way.

A large building comes into view on my left. It has a white sloping canopy of a roof and a low rock wall, a modern structure compared to most buildings on the main strip. It should be the police station—a building celebrating the good the police do for their community. But it's another supermarket.

I check the directions on my phone. The Maps app places a marker across the road from the aesthetically pleasing building. I turn to find a real-world match. There's a dark-blue and white Police sign hoisted in the air like a frozen flag, a single-storey building to the right of this labelled *Court House*. It's a product of the '70s: tan-coloured brick walls stained black in high-traffic areas, white-framed case windows high on the front wall, leftover from the '60s, and a red-and-black tiled roof that's seen better days. To the left of the sign, on a corner lot, is the police building, continuing the same tan-coloured brick design but with modern windows. I cross the road and round the corner to see a checkerboard design of white and blue running door-height across the width of the wall. There's a tiny white canopy added out front, as if to blend with the new building across the road.

The buildings look like houses once belonging to Margaret River residents, as if the police came upon a crime scene one day, cleaned it up and claimed the area for themselves. They deserve a structure matching the size and modernity of the supermarket, but I'm sure budgeting sways to support the policing itself. I haven't seen the statistics for a while, but they'd put up with an endless stream of drunk tourists and the resulting car incidents, theft and assaults—aside from the usual struggles plaguing the locals—all for the same pay as the people working in air-conditioned luxury across the road.

I know it's ironic that I'm about to make an officer's work even harder, but I'll need their help to shove back.

I enter the building. The lobby smells like peppermint. I spy a diffuser hiding in the corner on a desk displaying pamphlets. Ahead, there's a counter with Perspex panes providing a barrier from the public. There's a wall behind it, blocking the rest of the building's operations. It has a large WA Police emblem mounted to it, kangaroos standing either side of a black swan. There's a closed door to the left of the desk. I'm alone in the lobby. There's a bell to ding. A lady appears through another doorway, walks up to her side of the desk, sits down on a padded chair. She has long black hair and a friendly smile, but her eyes are already sizing me up.

'Help you?'

'I'm not sure if you can help. I'm looking for someone.'

'Okay.' Her eyes flicker to the doorway; she's wondering who to call over.

I pull out the photograph and hold it to the transparent pane. 'Well, details on someone. Her name's Charlotte Harris. Deceased. But I'm also looking for a Lillian. I believe they lived in this area. Lillian might still be around here.'

'And how are you related to them, sir?'

'I'm not. It's just, my uncle—'

'We can't provide personal details to the public.'

I'm pretty sure she rolls her eyes at me.

'But my uncle has passed away, and he wanted Lillian to be at his funeral. He left a note.'

'A note?' The woman's still smiling, but she turns in her chair and raps her knuckles on the desk.

In a flash, a man appears beside her. If I knew for certain we didn't have bears in Australian forests, I would have sworn one was standing before me. He's not like Uncle Daniel's Māori friend, though. He's tall and wide but more sculpted, his trunk-like arms the product of years in the gym. His exposed arms and chest are extremely hairy, a thick forest of brown curls, but he has a bald, glowing head.

'What's the go, Carla?' he says, his gravel-laced voice adding to my bear comparison.

'We've got a male looking for a couple of females.'

'Is that right?' The bear looks me over like I'm a suspected pervert.

I sigh. 'It's not like that. My family's asked me to find one of them for my uncle's funeral. I'm honouring his wishes.'

'And your family won't help?'

I can still feel the sting on my back. 'They don't know the person, that's why I'm here. The police are supposed to help, right?'

'Not if you're snarky, mate.'

I can't figure out why these officers are hostile. Is it because it's obvious I'm from out of town, or because they assume I'm trying to find women for nefarious reasons? If it's the latter, why would I go to the police?

'Let's start again.' I hold up the photograph. 'Jock down at Brauhaus told me this is Charlotte Harris. Do you know her?'

The bear and woman exchange a glance. 'Can't say we do,' the bear says. 'You sure she's a local?'

The bear's voice faltered. He lied, showing his human side. Unless bears can lie, too. Either way, I'm getting good at picking out liars.

'I'm sure she was. She'll be in your case files. Car accident. I need to find her connection to Lillian.'

'Woah there, Sherlock Holmes. What was your name again?'

I realise I haven't given it yet, and I'm tempted to make one up and walk away. If I can't think of a better way to get their attention, I'm not getting much help.

'Look, I'm concerned for Lillian's safety,' I try, hoping it doesn't sound like I'm the one who's the threat. 'My uncle, Graham Herbert, passed away, and she should know about it. She should have contacted me, and she hasn't. His funeral's on Tuesday. I'm honouring his wishes.'

'And your name, mate?'

No point in lying. 'Henry Herbert.'

'How do you spell that?' He's got a clipboard out now, taking some notes. Maybe he's starting to believe me, or perhaps he's just going through the motions of paperwork.

'Just how it sounds,' I reply. 'Hen-ry. Her-bert.' It's not the hardest name to spell.

Another voice calls from the building's depths. In a few seconds, its owner appears beside the bear, puffing. He's at least six inches shorter than me, his muscles fighting through a layer of middle-aged fat. He has ice-blue eyes, their mystique somewhat lessened by the dark rings below them. The man slaps a hand on the bear's shoulder, then disappears through the doorway. The side door clicks open. He bursts into the lobby, beaming an extra-wide smile.

'Henry Herbert? I can't believe it's you!'

He runs his hand through wiry blond hair, then holds it out towards me. I shake it, then he pulls me in for a hug, patting me on the back. He pulls away and I still have no idea who he is, his facial features familiar yet distorted with age.

'You don't remember me, do you?' he asks, sensing the confusion. 'Gary? Gary Winters?'

I nod as if I'm placing him, but I can't. I'm trying to visualise the people I trained with at the police academy, but he doesn't look familiar.

'Come on. We played basketball together almost every lunch? Alistair, Steve, Joey, all the guys.'

Every lunch? Shit, he's talking about high school. My stomach lurches. I've pushed all memories of high school deep into a vault I've never tried to unlock.

'I haven't seen you at any reunions,' he continues. 'You missed the big two-oh.'

'Yeah, I've been busy.' I need to leave. My uncle's death has already started digging up the past. This is widening the shovel.

'Busy for over twenty years? Doing what, mate?'

'Well…' I could tell this man anything. I still don't remember him. I don't have to impress him with accomplishments, but that's the trap. That's why I've stayed clear of reunions. There's a need to impress, to tell some grand story about how I got through the depression of my father's death and became rich and famous or invented a cure for something, as if teaching over two hundred children along with countless other jobs means nothing.

Maybe I can use my actual past to my advantage, connect with someone who remembers me. 'I trained as an officer when I first left school.'

'You did? Up at Joondalup?'

'Yeah.'

'I took a gap year,' Gary admits. 'I went overseas, then the year became two. When I returned, I went to Joondalup myself. My favourite was Senior Constable Kirino. You have her?'

'Yeah. Young. Tough as nails, but a skilled teacher.' I try to smile. 'I left the force after two years, though.'

'Oh?'

'Some things happened. Injuries. No need to get into that. I did some odd jobs afterwards. Then I've been a teacher for the last decade-ish.'

'You don't say. Impressive.'

I'm not sure whether he genuinely thinks it's impressive, but I don't push. And I don't tell him I'm no longer a teacher. There's a slight pause, as if that's what he's expecting me to do, to continue telling my tale. When I give him nothing, he points to his uniform and smiles.

'Took a country posting, secured my career. First some small towns, then Albany, then I ended up at Margs. Can't really call this country, though, can I? It's paradise.'

I raise the photograph, trying to end the catchup while still making him feel important. 'Your friends in there think I'm some kind of creep, but I'm onto something. I need you to check a case. The name's Harris, Charlotte. Car crash. Local area. I need to see if she's connected to a Lillian, last name unknown. It's for my Uncle Graham.'

'I *knew* Graham was your relative. There's only a handful of Herberts around. He used to sell typewriters at the markets, right?'

There's a thump on the panes. The bear holds a clipboard into view.

'Ah, wait just a second.' Gary disappears into the off-limits zone.

As I wait, an older, rake-thin man enters the building. He strides to the counter, rapping on the Perspex. 'Some punk's broken into me car,' he complains the second he's got the woman's attention. 'Took me CDs and everything.'

The man's so fired up, part of me wants to stay and listen to how the case unfolds. But Gary appears again, clipboard in hand, and motions for me to join him outside. We leave the building and walk around its side. When no one appears to be listening, Gary hands me the clipboard and a pen. 'You gotta mobile?'

'Sure.'

'Write your number down here. And where you're staying.'

I hope that giving away my number will not lead to an onslaught of catchup texts, but if it's how I'll get the law on my side, I'll grin and bear it. 'Is someone going to help with those women?' I ask, scribbling my details.

'I promise I'll call by tonight, give you an update on whatever I find.' Gary takes the clipboard back. 'And Henry, it's good to see you again. Sorry to hear about your uncle. Times like this, it's good to rely on friends and family.'

'Sure,' I say.

Trouble is, I no longer know who to rely on.

CHAPTER ELEVEN
WORDS POUR OUT OF ME

I ease my car into Uncle Graham's property, cross the rock bridge, pull up outside his house. All the while, I'm expecting Uncle Daniel or his mates to burst into view, ready to do something far worse than shove me. They don't know I'm still pursuing Lillian, though, so perhaps I'm overreacting. Unless they saw me at the police station. If they didn't, they'd expect me to return here, prepare for the eulogy. It's Friday, and the funeral's not till Tuesday. Plenty of time. Plenty of time to check on me, too.

There may be a simple explanation for why my family wants to cover up Lillian's existence. Maybe she was Uncle Graham's ex-lover, and their split was far from amicable. Maybe my uncle wanted to make amends on his deathbed, but my family thinks otherwise, desperate to keep the woman in the past. A simple explanation, unlike the darker ones creeping into my thoughts.

I exit the car, listen for would-be intruders. There's just the shrill laugh of a distant kookaburra. I stand at the front door, my hand hovering by the lock, unwilling to slide in the key.

Uncle Daniel was here, looking for me. Did he have his own key? What will I find inside?

I find myself walking to the shed. I want one last look at Uncle Graham's collection before I leave his property for good. Maybe I should take some typewriters, learn to repair them myself, sell them at markets in Perth? Arty areas like Mt Lawley and Leederville where people would spend big on a perceived trend.

I draw back the shed door. It's clear that Uncle Daniel has been inside. There are no more vehicles by the entrance. Two typewriters are on the floor, in pieces. Did breaking the padlock lead to this, or would Uncle Daniel have let himself in anyway? I don't know what message he's sending, but the sight of the typewriters rattles me in a way I don't expect. How callous of someone to come along and disrespect the property of a deceased person; let alone, when that person is part of your family.

Just what kind of family am I part of?

Have I always wondered this? Has avoiding them for so long avoided an answer?

I pick up the typewriter pieces, put them back on the bench. Then I grab an intact machine I like the look of. It's metallic grey with a silver name plate that says *Royal*. A reminder of my uncle, since I don't know what's happening to the Lillian model. I look around some more, catch sight of a framed picture hanging above the bench. Only, it's not a picture. It's money, preserved behind glass. A hundred-dollar bill. I wrench the frame off a crooked nail, a smile building. It's another item from my uncle's list, right there in plain sight. How did I miss this before? Too many things to spot, I guess, my fixation on the Lillian typewriter.

I leave the shed, put the *Royal* and the frame into my boot, tell myself I'll come back for the other machines if I still have the urge to restore them. Now for the rest of the list items. I approach the front door of the house as if it's booby-trapped, as if Uncle Daniel has escalated his warn-and-shove approach to gas-leak-and-explode. I ease the door open. Sniff the air. Nothing happens; still just the same stale aroma. I step over the threshold. Everything appears to be the same. Maybe Uncle Daniel went into the shed first, while he messaged me, taking off the instant I replied I was in town.

I re-box the items from Uncle Graham's list; put them in my car, plus the Lillian typewriter. Then I grab a few tubs from the spare rooms, ones I haven't rummaged through. I even spot one full of Lego. My wife will use it at school once I find the mini-figure. Give kids Lego and you don't have to worry about teaching them all day. Engineering, problem-solving, mathematical geometry: sorted.

I get in my car, swing the vehicle around, start heading for the rock bridge.

Brake.

Something replays in my mind, the angry guy in the police station saying somebody's broken into his car, taken his CDs. I'd wondered what kind of criminal outfit made a living off dinosaur technology. But if that guy had CDs in his car, maybe Uncle Graham did, too? I need to find the music for his wake, and I'm yet to see a single disc. I hadn't even thought to check his vehicle. Assuming it's there, in the closed garage to the right of the house.

I park the car, walk back to the house. The unlocked garage door swings upward. There's a brown Kingswood within. Uncle Graham's had it forever. Not sure why Uncle Daniel didn't take this vehicle, but I'm thankful he overlooked it. The door's unlocked, too. The vehicle's had a bit of an upgrade: grey leather seats and shiny wood panelling, a stereo system with an LCD screen. Had my uncle taken to restoring cars, too? I could have thrown him a bargain for the stereo, got him a more reliable brand.

The car keys are amongst the coloured assortment Aunty Janice had left me. No shed keys, but car keys? I fire up the engine, surprised to hear it roar to life. I check for signs that someone's driven it recently, find nothing besides a driver's manual and a sick bag. Not even one tiny scrap of rubbish. I play with the stereo controls, eject the CD in there. A Verbatim disc pops out, coated in black to look like a mini-vinyl record. There's a bright orange strip around its centre. On it, someone has scribbled: *music for wake*.

My mad rush for self-preservation is helping cross a few items off the list.

I kill the engine, shut everything, return to my car. Then I'm over the rock bridge for what I hope is the last time, racing towards my new sleeping quarters. Along the way, I vaguely remember something about a check-in time, then panic that I'm early, but a text pings through informing me the keys are waiting on the table outside cabin five. I smile at the timing. Things are starting to go well for me, ignoring the morning's horrible event.

The studios are just off Caves Road. I pull onto Carters Road and find the entrance to my left. A quick roll up a gravel driveway and there's a sign, directing me down a track between thin trees and thick scrub. I'm disappearing already, lost to the wilderness, even though the town is less than ten minutes away. Two small buildings appear, little portable houses overlooking a distant paddock. There's a big gap between each building— they're separated enough to ensure I won't hear anything from a potential neighbour, although there are no cars out the front of either. I pull into the driveway of number five, the first building off the track. The second I step out of my car, a melody of cricket chirping and bird tweeting assaults my senses. Nature owns this place; I'm just visiting.

The studio has one wall covered in corrugated steel, another in rammed earth panels. I walk up a timber ramp and open a matching gate, stepping into my new hidden world. There's a small verandah with a little table, two chairs, and a Weber barbecue system. On the table is a small pot, a plant contained near its free-range cousins. Nestled against the pot is a brass key. I take it and open the studio's sliding door. There's a long stretch of windows around two sides, a lot of glass to see through.

The studio has everything I need: leather couches, coffee and dining tables, an extended kitchen bench with a stovetop and plenty of cupboard space, a huge bed, a television and stereo, some books, magazines and board games, and a large bathroom with a shower and spa. The owners have even left a complimentary bottle of red wine, with two glasses. My wife is going to take one look at this place and kill me, knowing I've spent too much. Once she's killed me, she'll agree I picked a great place given the short timeframe. Besides, hotels in Perth are far more expensive. By comparison, I've picked a bargain.

There's work to be done. I unload most things from the car, place them on the floating-timber flooring, beside a couch. I load food into the fridge and cupboards, then find the bag I'd arrived in Margaret River with, the one filled with my clothes and other essentials. Satisfied I've unpacked enough, I make quick use of the shower, relishing the thought of dirt and sweat and beach sand washing away.

I know I'm imagining it, but I swear there's a big bruise on my back. The beads of water sting the area. I try to touch it but can't tell what's going on there—I need a mirror. My hand drifts to my side, rubs a gnarled scar I know I'm not imagining. If I closed my eyes, I could still see my attacker lunging for me with their knife, digging it deep into my flesh. It was the catalyst for leaving the police force and, when I found the courage, to become a teacher. I was trying to help kids break the cycle, but many parents wanted me to focus solely on grades rather than personal growth.

I try not to dwell on the past, allowing the simple act of showering and changing into fresh clothes revitalise me. A sandwich helps, too. I devour two of them at the little table on the verandah, watching a family of kangaroos laze about on a distant strip of cleared land.

I check my phone. There's one bar, then a drop in service; thirty seconds later, three bars. I call my wife. It goes straight to her message service. Idiot, she'd be teaching a class, just like yesterday. I leave a brief message, fumbling over my words, not sure what to say. In the end, I tell her I miss her, that my family is crazy and that maybe it's a good idea she stays in Perth. When I finish the call, the phone's signal flashes to No Service. I don't know if my message got through.

I bring my plate inside, wash the dishes. Then I sit on the leather couch, reach around and grab the box, placing it on the coffee table. Time to focus. While I wait for Gary's call, maybe I should do the obvious and use the items to help with the eulogy? I stare at the box a little longer, find the notepad and pen I bought at the supermarket. No need for the items yet. A few memories have already resurfaced, my meeting with Gary stirring the teenage years I'd worked hard to repress.

Words pour out of me, things I never got to say to Uncle Graham. Time becomes a blur. Shadows creep into the studio, the sun lowering.

My phone rings. I assume it's my wife.

'Henry?' It's not Lucy.

'Hi, Gary. What's up?'

'I need to talk to you, mate. I've got some information.'

'Okay, go ahead.'

'No, not on the phone. Can we meet tomorrow?'

Fuck, I hate that approach. It's the same with doctors. If it's essential information, why can't they give it over the phone? Now I won't be able to sleep. I'll mull over the infinite possibilities of what he'd like to tell me. 'Can't you give me anything now?'

'Sorry.'

I sigh. It was worth a shot.

'But we can keep it out of the station,' Gary says. 'Do you want to meet for coffee?'

I can't imagine sitting with this man for an extended time. Not just yet. Then I remember the ad in Coles. 'There's a Farmer's Market, tomorrow morning.'

'I know the one. Should we say eight?'

'Sure? Call me when you're there.'

Gary bids goodbye and hangs up. I stare at my notepad until the words blur together.

'What's he going to say about you?'

My phone pings, telling me I have a voice message. Then another box pops up, informing me of a missed call from my wife. Service must have returned right before Gary's call, everything catching up. I almost ring my wife straight back, but something makes me listen to the message first, while I still can.

'I guess I miss you, too. Been a long week here. A lot of writing samples to analyse, as if a weak sentence structure will ruin these kids forever. God forbid we analyse imagination! I'll call you in the morning, okay? I'm at Sarah's now. We're just getting her kids to bed. Sarah's got her friend to help on Sunday so surprise, I'll be down in Margaret River in the evening. I'm not staying away. I've always known your family's crazy. You're pretty crazy yourself, especially the last couple of days. But you've got a lot going on, and, well, I'll show you I'm not mad at you when I get there. Take care.'

My finger hovers over the phone's keyboard. Should I message Lucy, implore her to stay away from Margaret River? I don't want her drawn into this. But if we stick to my plan, she'll be safe in the studio, won't she? After the markets, we can stay hidden until the funeral. I text Lucy the change in accommodation details instead. I know it's selfish, but the need to have her beside me overpowers the urgency to keep her away. We'll work everything out when she arrives.

I stare at the notepad again. That's me done for the day, my attention torn between thinking about my wife's impending visit and the possible bombshell Gary might drop.

Despite trying to assure myself it's safe here, as the sky darkens, I imagine too many wild situations, the worst being my family swarming the studio as if they're a tactical team. I find the CD I'd taken out of Uncle Graham's car, put it in the studio's stereo unit and start it up. Then I hunt down the bottle of red wine the studio owners left for me. I shouldn't be drinking when I need to be alert for my uncle's invasion, but it's precisely that thought that makes me reach for a glass.

Before this trip, I wasn't the biggest drinker. Look at me now. Soon I'm sitting on the couch, gazing out at a black void masking the wilderness beyond, listening to unfamiliar music that's at least as old as me. I stop worrying about tactical teams, awful families, endless possibilities, and dinner, long enough for my body to put the wine glass down, wander to the bed and sink against its covers.

I think I hear my phone ping again, but I don't care. I let the darkness take hold of me, hoping it'll provide pleasant dreams.

CHAPTER TWELVE
REVISIT A TRAGEDY

As I wake, my brain struggles to process where I am. It's the third place I've woken in as many days. It's still dark outside, but it seems I've left a downlight on in the kitchen nook. I find and check my phone—five-fifteen in the morning. I used to wake up this early every day for school, despite the consensus that teachers put in a meagre eight to three effort. There's a text message waiting. I bring it up.

I come 4 a visit. Were Ru?

Uncle Daniel, sent at nine-seventeen last night. I force a dry chuckle at the thought of him going into Uncle Graham's house to find nothing but tubs and scattered junk. But I swallow the sentiment with the fact that he turned up. Had he found out I'd gone to the police? Was he with his Māori friend? I wonder how long he stayed, waiting. If he's figured out I've gone somewhere else, he'll be looking for me.

And I'm meeting Gary at a very public market.

I consider texting Uncle Daniel back, creating a cover story like being out at the brewery all night. There's no point lying, though. The details could unravel; he could ask to see me this morning. Better to ignore the text. That's what we tried to tell students about social media bullies. Don't respond to them. Take screenshots of their comments to build a case. I should follow the advice.

Perhaps I should call Gary, then? Cancel our meeting. I can't, though. I *need* to know what he's got for me. Besides, a public market makes for a lot of witnesses, should anything go wrong.

I'm wide awake now, despite the time. I change, forgoing another shower, then make some toast and eat it on the verandah. Ice laces the outside air, every part of my body jittering as if I've had an energy drink. Using the energy, I unload the tub of Lego from my car, take it to the dining table inside. Years ago, I would have thought Uncle Graham has amassed a ridiculous amount of Lego for someone without kids, but lots of shows have documented a thriving adult fan community. So… typewriters, cars, Lego. My uncle was busy building things, keep his ageing fingers dexterous.

I empty the tub's contents across the dining table.

'Where are you, Indy?'

It takes a good twenty minutes to find him, grinning back at me under his plastic fedora, dotted stubble painted on his face. I remember the first time I watched *Raiders of the Lost Ark*. My mother had gone to work, so Uncle Graham had rented the videocassette and created a cool tent around our couch using bedsheets and chairs. While munching on a bowl of popcorn, I'd marvelled at Indy's heroics as he risked his life in the jungles of Peru. I'd asked my uncle if people like that existed in real life.

He'd said of course. Then he'd pointed out that Indy almost died scavenging a treasure that someone else took, anyway. The criminal indecency had outraged me, spurring my first thoughts of joining the police force.

I head over to the coffee table, humming the Indiana Jones theme tune, and unpack the items from my uncle's box. Then I get the list, scratch out what else I've found.

> *Photo album #1*
> *Photo album #2*
> *Photo album #3*
>   * use these for images of my life*
> *Photo album #4*
> *Akubra Hat*
> *CD - labelled 'music for funeral'*
> *CD - labelled 'music for wake'*
> *Book - The Secrets She Keeps - Robotham*
> *Book - Australian Ghosts*
> *Flask of Limeburners (Roland has plenty)*
> *Indiana Jones Lego Minifigure*
> *Typebar with Letter C*
> *Movie Poster - Back to the Future*
> *DVD - The Castle*
> *Framed $100 Bill*
> *Shark tooth necklace*
> *Compass from Pop*
> *Find Lillian*

Down to one item. Not bad at all, except it's the most important one on the list. The thought stops my humming. Still, it's only

Saturday morning. I could get the information I need by breakfast, follow a lead to Lillian by lunch. I try to convince myself it's true as I scrutinise the items. I don't know why Uncle Graham had an Akubra hat. It's an Australian version of Indy's fedora, leather from a cow or kangaroo, a shark tooth strapped on the side. Did my uncle wear this out fishing? Did he fish? Or did he wear it on treks through the forest? Is it something lots of locals wear? Maybe it was part of his image at the markets: the Akubra-wearing, typewriter-fixing guy. Crocodile Dundee's cousin.

I move my attention to two books. Perhaps I can read them over the weekend? No, I don't speed-read. I like to work through the prose with a slow cadence, enjoying the words. The books are quite different, one a crime novel from an Australian author and the other a so-called non-fiction book on Australian ghosts. I recall Uncle Graham reading blockbuster bestsellers from authors such as Matthew Reilly and James Patterson. Movies in book format. Maybe he branched out, discovering some new favourites?

The movie poster relates to one of Uncle Graham's favourite films, *Back to the Future*. I know that for sure. He loved everything Michael J. Fox. Then there's the DVD of an iconic Australian movie, *The Castle*. Why didn't Uncle Graham want the DVD of *Back to the Future*, choosing a poster for one movie, a disc for another? I grab the DVD anyway, put it by the stereo. There's a player underneath the television; I'll put it on later.

The call of the photo albums is stronger for now. I open the one labelled #1, see my image plastered across numerous pages. Younger me, not a care in the world. Holding a fishing rod on a jetty, next to my dad and Uncle Graham. Playing with Scalextric cars post-Christmas. Taking over the lounge room to set up a game of Mouse Trap, leaving a plastic minefield my mum is stepping over. All of us at the dinner table—mum, dad, Uncle Graham, Aunty Janice, Uncle Roland and I—eating a Sunday roast like it was a tradition that would last forever.

There are photos of places around Western Australia, captions beneath labelling them. Some sites are foreign to me, while others stir memories long forgotten. I recognise infamous attractions like Dizzy Lamb Park and Atlantis, the West Aussie versions of Universal Studios and SeaWorld. Both no longer exist. There's also a place in Mandurah that had mini-golf. One hole had a dinosaur statue. We used to visit these places often when I was little, then stopped.

Of course, I know why we stopped.

For the first time in years, I wonder what life would have been like if my father hadn't died in that crash. Would Aunty Janice, Uncle Roland and all the others have dispersed across the land? Would Uncle Graham have followed, or stayed in Perth? Trips to themed attractions and Sunday roasts might have remained part of the norm, my family remaining relatively normal. Refraining from lying to each other, threatening each other.

I close the photo album, unable to look at any more images. I hurry out of the studio, turning off the lights, locking the door. Next thing I know, I'm on the road, driving into town, heading for the markets. I pass the main shops, move up the hill beyond them. Over the crest, I see a row of parked vehicles on the dirt. Makeshift market parking. I sneak the car into a gap between two Utes and kill the engine.

Time to find out why my family's acting insane.

A group of people pass me, swinging cloth shopping bags. I follow them over the road to an Education Campus. The faint sound of music creeps toward me, followed by chatter and the distinct aroma of frying bacon. The campus buildings give way to a grassed area, revealing the market. There seems to be a wide variety of stalls, most food related. I work my way around them, cautious of who I might bump into but hungrier with each vendor I pass. Before I know it, I'm buying a loaf of bread, natural yoghurt, jam. I'm swept up in the good vibes and delicious food and don't care that I'm spending far too much on things I could get cheaper at the supermarket.

Halfway into a piping-hot, vegetarian breakfast wrap, my phone rings.

'Henry? I'm here a little early.'

I chuckle. 'So am I.'

'Excellent. There's a little information stall in the middle, selling recycled bags.'

I finish my wrap and meet him at the stall. Gary's out of uniform, in a tracksuit with a beanie, warding off the morning chill.

'We're meeting at the information booth, and you're about to give me information.' I shake his hand. 'Cute.'

'I'd thought you'd like it. You were always funny at school.'

'Really? I wouldn't have thought so.' Especially since I was dealing with my father's death.

'I've bought you a bag,' he says. 'Calico. Better than plastic.'

I don't want a bag. Gary sees my reluctance, places a hand on my shoulder and guides me back into the throng of vendors and shoppers. We work our way around a strip of craft stalls. There's an empty one halfway along, probably Uncle Graham's.

Gary shoves the bag into my hand. 'It has some notes for you, inside.'

Ah, I get it now. Idiot.

'You need to know, Margaret River Police Force has your back.' Gary leads me to a coffee cart, orders two flat whites, no sugar. 'To an extent. You might've uncovered something, might not. But for now, it's enough to warrant a little overtime on my part. On the record, I'm only supposed to share what a member of the public may know. But as a fellow survivor of our high school, I figure you've earned a couple of additional notes.' He gets the coffees and hands me one, gestures for us to keep walking. 'Your uncle's stall isn't here today. I guess his partner thought it best to keep away, though quite a few locals would've come to pay respect.'

'It seems many people knew my uncle,' I say. 'More than I did.'

'It's different to the city. You can't live in a smaller community without people noticing you. Or at least talking about you.'

'Then why was everyone tight-lipped about Charlotte Harris?'

'No one likes to revisit a tragedy.' Gary taps the bag with his spare hand. 'It's all in there. Hit and run accident. Night-time, no witnesses. Case that went cold, minimal resources used on it. Bad enough, but the woman was pregnant.'

'Pregnant? Did the baby—'

'It survived. That's all I've confirmed for now. There's conflicting information about what happened to her, and why. I've arranged for you to meet with the foster parent for now. She can decide how much she tells you. Can you get to Busselton today?'

'Just me?'

'Got a few errands to run here.'

'What time's the meeting?'

'Not fixed. You need to be there by the end of the working day. She's an old dear, volunteers at the jetty.'

Gary and I shake hands, go our separate ways. I head straight for my car, calculating how long it will take to arrive in Busselton.

I hop into the driver's seat and lock the doors, slide the coffee into a cup holder then tip the bag's contents onto the passenger seat. It's a Manila folder, containing case notes typed and summarised for my benefit. There are some other pieces of paper, too: a certificate, a clipping. I read the summary first. Reread it, my hands gripping the paper so hard the sides crease.

Charlotte Harris was pregnant when she was in the accident. She made it to the hospital, the birth induced before she passed away.

The baby's name was Lillian.

CHAPTER THIRTEEN
THE REAL DEAL

There's no time to pay attention to the scenery between Margaret River and Busselton, my focus on the road ahead and the meeting that's about to take place. I arrive at Busselton in under forty minutes, park in a car park right near the jetty. Before rushing out to meet the foster parent, I take one last glance at the folder Gary's given me.

The woman's name is Leonie Haynes. She's eighty-three years old. Gary hasn't supplied a photo. The few details about Lillian are in the form of a photocopied birth certificate. Someone has redacted her birthdate; not sure why. They've left the parents' names uncovered. Mother: *Charlotte Harris*. Father: *Unknown*. There should be a foster carer note attached, court orders and reasons Lillian ended up with Leonie, but there's nothing. Charlotte had parents. Jock said they've left the country, so there must have been a reason they left without Lillian. Either Gary couldn't access that information yet, or I'm not allowed to know. He said Leonie would decide how much she tells me, which doesn't fill me with confidence. There are some more notes about Charlotte's car accident. I've skimmed them, but I want to hear everything from Leonie first, then compare summaries. I slip the pages back into the folder and slide it under my seat, a habit to keep things out of sight from would-be thieves.

I get out of my car.

There's a waterfront café-slash-pub beside the car park, a waft of bacon, eggs, and coffee tempting me. I walk straight past it to the jetty, though, head for the distinct blue and white buildings that mark its start—the Interpretive Centre. I wait in line as the lady at the counter speaks briskly to a couple, assuring them their entrance fee goes towards the cost of restoring and maintaining the jetty. It's an attraction the town needs for its tourism, a one-point-eight-kilometre record-chasing construction. The couple happily pay the fee.

'I'm looking for Leonie,' I say as I'm called forward.

'But why do you need to see her?' the lady at the counter says, as if she's the gatekeeper to Leonie's social life.

'I've got a meeting arranged with her.'

She eyes me suspiciously. 'Think she's on the train. You'll have to wait.'

'Okay. Do I pay to get on the jetty, or—'

'Just wait over there, by the railing.'

I mutter my thanks and wait as instructed, the train in sight. I'm lucky, an older man tells me, trying to strike up a conversation. The train takes about forty-five minutes to get up and back, so I've avoided a long wait. I ask him if he knows Leonie. He tells me she's worked for BJI longer than him. She's part of the jetty, now. Sensing my confusion, he explains that BJI is Busselton Jetty Inc, the organisation that runs the place, like I should speak in acronyms. Like I'm back in education again.

The train pulls up. Two volunteers step off, no tourists. The older man gives a tall woman the heads-up. She's wearing a blue sweater vest. She approaches me, her stride fast, purposeful. As she nears, she slows down, takes me in. She's wondering whether to backtrack, her eyes widening just enough to give her thoughts away. I don't know what Gary told her, but she realises I'm not an officer.

I plaster on a smile, introduce myself and offer my hand to shake.

'Sergeant Winters said you'd be stopping by,' she says, her handshake weaker than her stare. 'This about Lillian?'

I nod.

'You know, I've been out in the sun too long. I'd like an ice-cream.'

'Do they sell them here?'

'You're in luck. There's a stand round the side of that building over there.' She points to the café-slash-pub near the car park. We head in that direction.

'So, Lillian's your foster daughter?' I ask.

'How do you know Sergeant Winters?' she replies, unable to hide the concern in her voice.

'We went to school together. I also became an officer for a while, too. Now I'm a… teacher.'

Her body seems to relax. 'And your concern for Lillian has something to do with your uncle, Graham?'

'Yes. Did you know him?'

'My husband goes from market to market selling his chilli jams. Something to do in retirement, bless him.'

I sigh. Why didn't I talk to him instead? Had I walked past his stall?

Leonie pats my arm. 'He's away at the moment, in Singapore visiting our son. Won't be back for a few weeks.'

'My wife's from Singapore,' I say, hoping to spark a connection. 'Which neighbourhood does your son live in?'

'Tampines, I think.'

'Her parents live in Bedok. That's pretty close.'

'I wouldn't know, haven't visited yet. My son moved there two months ago. Work paid for it.'

'Oh.' So much for the Singapore connection.

'It devastated my husband to hear about Graham. He always talked to your uncle. Said he was a good man.'

'You never met him?'

'A couple of times.' She doesn't elaborate. She studies the tubs of ice-cream for a while, then says, 'I'll have mint chocolate chip, thanks. In a bowl. Can't eat the cone these days, it's as tough as cardboard. Tastes like it, too.'

I order for the both of us, two of the same, and after a brief pause, we walk along a path beside the beach, the ice-cream a relief against the sun's increasing blaze. Wasn't it cold a couple of hours ago? I don't know how Leonie is wearing a sweater vest, but that's the least of my concern.

'Lillian's your foster daughter?' I try again.

'My husband and I provided home-based care for her. Poor angel.'

I assume she's referring to the loss of her mother at birth. 'Was she your only child?' I ask, cringing as I realise she's already mentioned a son.

'Oh, no. Leonard and I had two children together. They've given us three wonderful grandkids, one great-grandkid. We've cared for a few others along the way, too. At the time we had Lillian, we had another foster child, Tiffany. So back then, there was my husband and I and four kids. One big happy family. Oh, it's not like I had a house full of babies. My son and daughter were in their twenties, almost ready to leave the nest. They helped a lot with Lillian and Tiffany.'

'If you don't mind me asking, why didn't Lillian's own family look after her?'

'If you don't mind me asking, why are you prying into Lillian?'

'I thought you knew. Uncle Graham left a note, asking me to find her.'

'Then why worry about details? Why not just ask where Lillian is?'

I almost choke on a minty mouthful. 'I was leading to that.'

'In my experience, there's often little time to beat around the bush.'

'Okay. Can you tell me where Lillian is?'

Leonie holds up an empty cup. 'This ice-cream was good. Not too much sugar.'

'Please? I need to find her.'

'She doesn't want to be found.'

I resist the urge to scream. Leonie finds a bin and slides her cup into it. Then she turns, heading for the jetty. I slam my cup into the bin, catch up. 'What can you tell me about her, then?' I ask, my questioning going around in circles.

She licks her lips. 'I can still taste the mint. Not that artificial stuff, it was the real deal.'

'I've travelled all the way…'

Leonie pauses, pats my arm again. 'What do you want to know?'

'Well, she exists, right?'

Leonie nods.

'Then why would Uncle Graham want me to find her if she doesn't want to be found?'

'I can't speak for your uncle.'

'You must have an idea why?'

Leonie pulls back, her shoulders sagging. 'It's grand you're trying to satisfy your uncle's wishes, but I can't help you.'

'Then why did Sergeant Winters send me here?'

She sighs. 'When's your uncle's funeral?'

'Tuesday.'

'In Margaret River?'

'Yes.'

'Do you have a mobile phone?'

'Sure.'

'Can you write your name and number? My grandson bought me a mobile, bless him. Started teaching me how to use it.'

I reach into my pocket, draw out a pen and a folded note that used to be a shopping list. I scribble my details on a corner of the note, rip it off and hold it out. Leonie takes it, hides it against her palm.

'Can I ask you more about Lillian?' I try.

'I have to get back to work.'

'Just something. Anything.'

'I'm sorry.'

'Do you have a photograph of her? An address?'

'Everything okay, Leonie?' Another vest-wearing volunteer appears beside us, arms folded.

Leonie nods, slipping my note into her vest pocket. 'Thank you for your visit, Henry.'

'Sorry to waste your time.'

'Oh, you didn't waste my time. I got a free ice-cream.' She winks, then heads off with the other volunteer.

Leaving me standing at the jetty's edge with a thousand questions rolling through my mind. A key one springs forth, and I shout, 'What about her surname? Is it Haynes? Or Harris? Or something else?'

Leonie doesn't appear to hear me. She disappears into the visitor's building.

I do everything I can to keep myself from screeching in front of everyone. I've taken a decent chunk out of my day to find out little more than Gary's notes revealed. Did Gary know this was going to happen? Was this all just a test? I've given Leonie my details; maybe she was gauging me, seeing if I'm worthy to meet Lillian. If that was the case, did I pass or fail?

I saunter to my car, sit behind the wheel. What do I do now? Maybe I accept that I've done all I can to find Lillian, since she doesn't want to be found. Perhaps I go back to the studio, finish writing my uncle's eulogy. Grab a wine or two, watch a movie, relax. Wait for my wife and spend the weekend hiding, like I should have done all along.

A message pings on my mobile. The sound makes me smile. Leonie's reconsidered. I pull out my phone and bring up the text. My smile falters. It's not Leonie.

u still not back at tha farm?
Did u pull an all nighta?

Uncle Daniel. I consider a response, my finger hovering over the on-screen keyboard. Another message pings through.

Wait, I no where you've been

Three dots pulse on the screen, then a picture box appears. I click on the image. It's a photograph of me. At the market.
Ping.

And I no where u r now

More dots pulse on the screen. A second image appears. This time it's of my car. In a parking lot, Busselton Jetty in the distance.
Ping.

Where u going next?

I reach for the key, try to turn it in the ignition. My hand's shaking so much, I abandon the effort. Instead, I lurch out the vehicle, look around the car park. The photograph was from the rear. I scan three rows of vehicles. Most spots are empty. There's a young guy in a white Commodore with his head tilted back on a headrest, fast asleep. There's a woman in a green RAV4 flicking her fringe, looking at her reflection in the rear-view mirror. And in the furthest row, in a black 4WD, there's a huge Māori bloke waving. At me.
Lynden.
Fuck this. If Uncle Daniel's sent his messenger to monitor me, I'm not sticking around. Maybe I can lose him around the streets

of Busselton, then head back to Margaret River? I hop in my vehicle, thump the steering wheel.

'Steady on, mate.' The voice makes me jump back in my seat. 'The stress'll kill ya.'

Uncle Daniel is sitting beside me, front passenger seat. He slipped in, and I didn't even hear him.

'You're gonna give me a lift, okay, Henry.' He clicks on his seatbelt. 'We've got things to talk about.'

CHAPTER FOURTEEN
WATCH YOUR SPEED

I should have screamed for help. I should have fought my way out of the car, or taken whatever beating was coming my way. That may have increased my chance for survival. But I froze, told myself it's just my uncle, that whatever talk we're about to have will only end with another string of verbal threats. Maybe another shove. He's family. Family gets angry with each other, but they don't hurt their own.

Fucking stupid.

All my training wasted.

Common sense has kicked in too late. Now we're driving back to Margaret River. Well, *I'm* behind the wheel. Uncle Daniel is watching like a demonic driving instructor, his eyes tracking every movement of my hands. Maybe he's expecting me to reach over, karate-chop his throat or face. The thought has run through my mind.

'You know, you're not supposed to have your hands at ten and two,' he says, relishing the role. 'We all used to learn that, but it's bullshit. Power steering means we can rest our hands lower. Plus, if your airbag goes off, those high arms could do you more damage. I heard a guy decapitated himself once. Decapitated, with his own arms. Fucking crazy, right?'

I lower my hands to the sides of the steering wheel, then glance at the rear-view mirror. A few cars behind us, Lynden's 4WD swerves into view. Tailing us, but not too close. He must have done that the entire way to Busselton. I was so focused on my meeting with Leonie, I hadn't noticed.

'What did you want to talk about?' I ask. Time to get it over with.

'Just wanted to know what you were up to. Came to see you last night. You weren't at the farm, though. Again.'

'So, you followed me all day?'

His chuckle is so dry it makes my skin crawl. Not for the first time, I wonder if there's a screw loose in Uncle Daniel's brain. I don't know enough about him to tell. Out of all my father's relatives, he's the one I've seen the least. He left home when he was young; I know that. Aunty Janice always said it was the biggest mistake he'd ever made. He worked in the mines, a FIFO life of excessive money he siphoned into drugs and alcohol. They let him go when the mine dried up. That's all I know. Every family gathering, he'd just say he was keeping busy. Nobody ever asked him to elaborate. Given his amusement at threatening a relative, maybe I don't want to know what work he was keeping busy with.

'How did you find me?' I prompt.

He chuckles again. 'Absolute fucking luck. There's a chick I like at the markets. Got there nice and early to see her play some music. I'm sitting there, watching her, having a coffee. Lo-and-behold, I see you over at a stall, looking at bread or something. I hid behind a crepe van, called Lynden, waited for you to leave. And here we are.'

I try to retrace my steps, scanning my memory. The excitement of the markets got the better of me. My uncle's absolute fucking luck resulted from my foolhardiness.

I try to tell myself that if Uncle Daniel was hiding, he might not have seen me talking to Gary. He might not know what prompted my trip to Busselton.

'I can't believe you'd show up at the markets,' my uncle echoes. 'The most popular fucking place on a Saturday morning, and you're there. I thought maybe you were trying to hide from me, but you can't have been unless you're fucking stupid.'

I sigh. Fucking stupid. Confirmation from my crazy uncle, it means a lot.

'I was hungry,' I reply, trying to create some normalcy to my visit.

'Well, they've got great food there. Great chicks, too.' Uncle Daniel takes his mobile out, types something. 'Keep driving to Margs. I'll tell you where to go when we're closer.'

'Where *are* we going?'

'Somewhere I can keep you till the funeral.'

'You're kidnapping me?'

'Just keeping an eye on you.' His phone pings. He types a reply.

My left hand slips off the steering wheel. It takes tremendous effort to lift it back. I have to do something to get out of this, to tighten the screws in my uncle's brain. 'So, you thought I was returning to Margaret River?'

'What?'

'I wasn't. I was on my way to Perth.'

'What do you mean?'

'I've had enough of this shit. You were right all along. Fifteen years without seeing Uncle Graham, what the hell was I thinking? Aunty Janice can do the eulogy, like she wanted.'

I can see my uncle calculating it, deciding whether Busselton was just my first stop on the way back to Perth. 'Then who'd you buy an ice-cream with?'

'My grandma,' I say, even though she died long ago.

'She's not *my* grandma.'

'Two sides to my family, idiot.'

'You're the fucking idiot. And I call bullshit. Maybe I should ask the old bird myself.'

'No!' I grip the steering wheel hard.

Uncle Daniel chuckles. 'I think I'll just keep you out the way, anyway. Just to be safe.'

'So you *are* kidnapping me?'

'You're not a kid. There's no ransom.'

'It doesn't matter if you're a kid... Abducting, then.'

'Just shut up and drive.'

I'm happy to sit in silence. The speed limit is a hundred and ten, but my right leg won't push down hard enough, my grip loosening on the wheel. I'm struggling to reach eighty. There's a line of traffic building behind us, desperate for the overtaking lane. I can't understand why Uncle Daniel is doing this, why he's risking so much. If he's keeping me out the way, does he think I'll go to the funeral, do the eulogy as if everything's normal? Does he think I'll forget about everything, return to my life in Perth and leave him be? Or has he calculated this? Has he decided to silence me for something he thinks I know? If so, there's no coming back from this approach. I need to do everything I can to get out of it.

I consider my options. One has me racing ahead in the car, trying to lose Lynden the second we get to a suburb with more than one street. It could work, but the fact that he tailed me before says he's a better driver than I gave him credit for. Besides, my uncle could just message our location. Another option has me swinging my car into an oncoming one, or swerving off the bank into a tree. I try to picture myself distracting Uncle Daniel, reaching over and unbuckling his seatbelt, swerving into something while he's unprotected. I'd kill or disable Uncle Daniel. But I'd end up in the hospital, too. At the very least. And if there's another car involved, I'd be responsible for their lives, too. I can't do that, despite what he's doing to me. That option is a last resort. The only other one I can surmise is going along with Uncle Daniel's plan, for now, looking for more ways to escape later. The rest of my family would expect my appearance soon, to help prepare for the funeral. Mum's arriving on Monday. Aunty Janice will have another meal in her honour, inviting me. And Lucy's meant to arrive tomorrow. She's going to turn up to an empty studio and wonder what the hell has happened.

'How much further?' I ask, turning into a new stream of traffic. I risk a glance in the rear-view mirror. Lynden is yet to find a space to join us. Maybe this is my moment. Maybe I should floor it. I tense my leg muscles and press as hard as I can on the accelerator. So much for the third option.

'Head back to town, then keep going,' Uncle Daniel says. 'It's about fifteen minutes further south.'

The steering wheel shakes in my hands. Or maybe my hands are shaking on the steering wheel.

'Watch your speed, hey. Don't want to attract the cops.'

Maybe I do, though. I push harder on the accelerator. A message pings on Uncle Daniel's phone.

'Lynden's way behind,' he says. 'Slow down.'

I can take this guy. He's old. 'You had your sixtieth yet, Uncle Daniel?'

'What?' He types something on his phone. 'Boy, I'm the youngin of the bunch. Fifty-seven and proud. Don't talk to me about my sixtieth.'

He's not that old, but far older than me. Someone his age shouldn't be pushing me around. Mum reared me to respect and fear my elders, in equal measure, but there comes a tipping point when physical prowess swings to the juniors.

There's a long stretch of cleared land to my left, bounded by a wire fence. Maybe I could pretend to lose control and veer into that? With such a heavy stream of traffic, there's a chance someone could stop and help, get me far away from my crazy uncle and his henchman.

I drop my left hand, pulling the steering wheel.

Something presses into my side. I tighten my grip on the wheel, steady the vehicle, and look down. My uncle is leaning over the centre console, a dark object in his hand.

He sneers. 'You'd better get me there in one piece, or I'll see how many times I can stab you before you bleed out.'

The words rip the air from my lungs. My foot slips off the accelerator. I could give him an answer to his sick threat—seven. Seven stab wounds almost bled me out after a drug bust gone wrong, the catalyst for leaving the force. That's why knives and I don't mix. That's why the sight of one now is freezing every limb in my body. Does Uncle Daniel know this? Probably. Aunty Janice would have kept him in the loop while I'd recovered. So, he's using my fear against me. A proud day for the Herbert family.

I still can't move. The car keeps drifting towards the shoulder. I know the threat is stupid. If he stabs me, the car will crash, injuring us both. But the thought of the blade piercing my skin robs me of all control.

'I'm serious,' Uncle Daniel snaps.

I force a nod.

'Straighten up now.'

I gasp for air. Blink away the past. Feel my arms again, realign the car. Focus on the road. Keep going at the reduced speed. Keep myself from sinking into despair.

'Good lad.' Uncle Daniel withdraws the blade.

We pass the town's main strip, ignoring the tourists and locals going about their carefree day; pass the campus that housed the Farmer's Market; pass what looks like the final stages of a new highway; pass row after row of trees growing in size and density. Then we're turning left, winding along a bumpy road, the trees whipping past and confusing my sense of direction.

My uncle shouts, pointing to a dirt track. I slow down, swerve left onto it, drive through a clearing in the forest then through an open gateway. The car shudders along an even clay path. Beams of sunlight strobe through the tall treetops. I slow right down, but Uncle Daniel taps the windscreen with the blade, directs me onward until the trees fan into a large circular clearing, revealing a two-storey stone and timber cottage. Uncle Daniel taps the windscreen again, instructs me to pull up beside a single-cab, decades-old Ute.

The second I kill the engine, my uncle digs the tip of the knife into the dashboard and traces a line along the side of the glove box. He stares at the resulting indent for a second, then leans towards me, his face twisted in a snarl.

'I know you're showing the photograph around.'

I don't reply.

'I asked you not to. We're going to talk about that real soon.'

He pulls back, kicks the car door open, jumps out. I take a long time to follow. My uncle doesn't seem to care; he's already heading for the cottage. I hang onto the door and check my surroundings. It's a set lifted from a horror movie—the isolated cottage in complete disrepair. Cliché, but no less terrifying.

The unmistakable aroma of a wood fire reaches me. It's not cold enough for a fire.

I glance at the Ute. There's a splatter of blood on one of its drop sides.

I'm snapped to attention by the crash of a screen door. A rake-thin man emerges from the cottage to greet my uncle. He's a couple of inches taller than me, but that's not what draws my focus. He's got a long wooden-stocked rifle in his hands.

First a knife. Now a gun.

My knees buckle. I tighten my grip on the car door. There's no coming back from this approach. The speed at which my uncle switched from implied threats to psychotic-killer intimidation means I am fucked. The kicker is, I don't know why.

CHAPTER FIFTEEN
THE UPPER HAND

I will not go easily. I drop back into my car, close the door, lock everything. My uncle and the man are chatting away, laughing as if this is all just a joke. I glance at the rear-view mirror. Lynden's approaching. There's no way I can drive out, the lone path blocked.

I've still got my phone. Uncle Daniel didn't even bother asking for it. I dig it out of my pocket. Three bars of service. Forty per cent battery. I lean forward, my head on the steering wheel so it appears I'm wallowing in defeat. The screen glows on my lap. Should I call someone? I can't use the speaker function, and I'd be stupid to hold it up to my ear. How do I communicate without drawing attention? I should have downloaded one of those hiking apps I've read about, that pings an emergency location. But I didn't because I never thought I'd need one. Text someone, then? My wife? She could get help, but I have no idea where I am. It would just send her into a spiralling panic, and this moment shouldn't be her last memory of me. The police, then? Gary?

Maybe he could tap into my phone, somehow? Track it, send a squad of Margaret River's finest to storm the cottage. But that could quickly go south. My uncle and his mates would take me hostage for real, and I'd be disposable. Someone better, then? Who? I have little time to decide. I'm sure they're coming closer to the car.

It hits me. I type a message, send it. Shove the phone back into my pocket. Seconds later, there's a rap on the car window.

'Coming out, Henry?' Uncle Daniel is grinning ear-to-ear. 'May as well check your new digs.'

Shit! I could have used the Maps app to share my location with Lucy or Gary. They didn't need to hack into my phone for that!

Uncle Daniel slaps the window. 'Come on, Henry!'

Too late. I've been working with electronics and there's so much I keep forgetting and it's going to get me killed.

Uncle Daniel slaps harder. 'Out!'

I groan, unlock the door, step out. I have to rely on the text I sent, hope it works the way I imagined.

Uncle Daniel backs away from the car, as if expecting an attack, then chuckles. He seems to laugh a lot. Maybe it isn't just a screw loose in his brain. Maybe drugs are fuelling him, some stimulant killing anxiety and making everything amusing.

'That's Reg,' he says, pointing to the man with the rifle.

Reg is making his way over, rifle aimed at the dirt. He looks older than he probably is, with a shock of silver hair beneath a baseball cap, his wiry frame complemented with wrinkled, bronzed skin. Someone who's spent a lot of time outdoors.

There's a squeak of brakes behind me.

'Looks like Lynden's finally here.' My uncle waves, then morphs the gesture into a middle-finger salute. 'Took your fucking time, Lynden. What if this guy got the upper hand on me?' He smacks my arm, chuckles even more.

I rub my arm. 'You've involved a lot of people just to keep me out the way.'

Uncle Daniel looks at me for a long time, trying to wrap his brain around what I said.

'Give me your car keys,' he says in response. I hand them over as he points to the cottage. 'Let's go.'

A meaty hand clamps onto my shoulder. Lynden. It pushes me along before I can react, bones jarring with each step. Reg heads to the Ute, his path marked by the crunch of gravel. The cottage looms ahead, looks even worse than I thought. Massive cuts of red rock form the walls of the bottom floor, their surface blackened with moss or mould. The upper storey is timber. Each plank's grey, painted surface is a flaking mess. There are windows up there, all boarded up. Below, there's a black screen door that Reg first burst out of; I can see the shadow of furniture beyond it. What looks like a water heater is nestled near the entrance, covered in rust as red as the earth. There are two plastic chairs beside it, cigarettes squashed around them.

Beyond the cottage, there's nothing but dense forest. If a helicopter flew overhead, it would miss it on the first pass. That's the point, though, I guess. This is a hideaway. Which begs the question: Besides me, what else are they hiding here?

Ring, I think, feeling the weight of my phone in my pocket. *Ring, dammit!*

Uncle Daniel thought to ask for my keys, but he still hasn't asked for my phone. Is that the influence of drugs, or just plain carelessness? Maybe he assumes there's no service. The signal was strong enough when I sent the message, though. Much stronger than at the studio, a phone tower probably nearby. I just have to find a chance to slide the phone out, share my location.

We're metres from the screen door. It bursts open again, held outward by another person. 'Dan the man!' the new guy yells. 'Been hunting, my brother?'

We reach the door. My uncle and the man exchange a fist bump.

'This might be a catch and release,' Uncle Daniel says. 'Gotta wait and see.'

'In that case, beers all round?'

'Fuck yeah,' Lynden mumbles behind me.

I'm shoved past fist bump man at the door, crossing the threshold. He's younger than the rest, closer to my age. His podgy face shines with sweat, his distended belly suggesting he's had a few too many beers a few too many times. I ignore him, look around the cottage's interior. The air is stale, lingering with smoke and an onslaught of body odour. There's a soft hum coming from something. Someone's wedged three couches into a U-shape, taking up most of the space. There's a pile of clothes and rugs over two of them. We squeeze around to get to a tiny dining table near a dish-covered sink. Uncle Daniel pulls out a chair and tells me to sit. I oblige. The others continue out through a rear screen door, their heavy footfalls thumping against timber decking. Something snaps and cracks and I take a while to attach it to the fire I thought I'd smelled earlier.

Lynden's outside, beside the screen door. He reaches down and swings open a bar fridge, pulling out a six-pack of beer cans. He makes some classy joke comparing the beer to a woman, then throws the cans to his mates. Laughter starts, aluminium smacked together. Uncle Daniel leaves me, hurries outside, shouts at the others to give him a drink. I'm sitting on my own, treated like the guest nobody wants, which I guess I am. Maybe Uncle Daniel's not on drugs. Maybe he's just a crazy arsehole.

I could grab my phone now, send my location. Check to make sure my message went through. I slide a hand into my pocket. Pause. Lynden's at the door, staring straight at me. He swigs his beer, eyes never leaving mine.

I can't look at him. I turn away, take in the surrounding details again. There's a staircase along the opposite wall, leading to the timber-framed upper level. Maybe I should creep up there, see if anything's interesting? Maybe there's a hidden utopia, a well-decorated master bedroom with a king-sized bed and gigantic television, complete with a clawfoot bathtub and spa. Perhaps they've stacked the place floor to ceiling with bricks of cocaine or other illegal substances. Or maybe a prisoner's chained up. Lillian or someone else related to Charlotte, to the photograph my uncle's obsessing over.

I glance at the front screen door. I could find a chance to slip out, leave my car, run into the bush and head back to a major roadway. Draw someone's attention, head straight for the police. How long would it take my uncle and his mates to notice I was gone? Two six-packs of beer? A carton? No, Reg is out the front. Maybe he's got his rifle trained on the door, awaiting such a bold move.

I stand to go and look.

'Sit down!'

Everyone roars with laughter as I slump back onto the chair. I see their game. Talk and drink and be merry, but watch me like a hawk. Fine. I'll wait. They'll slip up.

Except the more time that passes, the less confident I feel about getting my phone out. Everything's slipping away—my pride, my male ego, being an equal amongst adults. In my uncle's eyes, I'm still my father's young boy. Someone who'll sit and be quiet and do what he's told. Maybe he truly thinks he can hide me here for a while, scare me, then send me home thinking twice about ever crossing him; scolded into behaving.

He's yet to ask me anything about my adult life. I don't even think he remembers I'm married. He could look at my ring finger, see it plain as day, but he's said nothing about my wife. He didn't include her in any earlier threats. We'd invited him to the wedding, on mum's insistence, but he never turned up. Maybe this is the positive point I can hang onto, something that could work in my favour. He might not know my wife is coming down to Margaret River; or that I'm expected to appear for more than the funeral.

The screen door opens.

'Get up,' my uncle barks, pushing past Lynden. 'Grab your shit.'

'What shit? I have nothing.'

'Ah.' He burps. 'Right. Come on out here, smart-arse. I'll tell you what we're gonna do.'

I stand, glance at the front door. Could I still run for it? Reg might be asleep in his Ute, or distracted, cleaning the blood off its tray.

'Hurry up, or Lynden'll steal the last beer.'

'Too late,' a voice calls out.

'Fucking bastard!'

Uncle Daniel waves me onto the back decking, steps up to Lynden and smacks him across the back of his head. Lynden stares at the much-smaller man as if deciding how to break him, then smiles, cracks open the beer can and sips from it. Relishing the moment in front of my uncle.

'Absolute fucking bastard,' Uncle Daniel mutters again, turning to me. 'We've decided we should go out in Reg's Ute, have a friendly word.'

My first instinct is to ask why we can't talk at the cottage. I don't want to know why they need the Ute.

'I'd love to go back into town, if we're headed that way,' I try, confidence wavering in my voice.

They all chuckle. My uncle parrots me in a high-pitched voice, and the podgy-faced friend joins in.

'People are expecting me,' I try. 'You know, for the funeral.'

'*For the few-na-rall. Blah, blah, blah.*' Uncle Daniel does a stupid little dance that looks like he's had an electric shock, then backs away, amused with himself. 'No one's expecting you. Janice doesn't even think you can string the words together for the eulogy.'

A phone rings.

My body sags with relief until I realise the sound isn't coming from my phone. Uncle Daniel fishes his mobile out of his pocket.

'The fuck?' He points to the phone. 'Fucking ESP or something. My sister. Be quiet, okay.'

I wait, breath held. Aunty Janice was supposed to ring me, was supposed to reply to my text. Why is she ringing Uncle Daniel?

'Hey, sis... Oh, he did, did he... Yeah, he's with me... He wrote that?' Uncle Daniel stares daggers at me. 'I didn't want to impose, but... Fine. We'd love to come for dinner tonight... No need for a lift. He can take me... Early dinner? Sure.'

My uncle ends the call, all amusement drained from his face. He's trying to figure out when I invited us over for dinner at Aunty Janice's, when I brought a third party into the mix. A third party who needed to know where I was, for the funeral and its preparations. I hope he remembers the joke he'd made to Lynden. Now I really do have the upper hand on him.

Uncle Daniel kicks a nearby beer can off the decking, gawping at his mates. No one offers support. We stay frozen in time until a smile creeps back onto his face.

'Well played,' he offers. 'But dinner's hours away. First, hand over your fucking phone. Then we'll go for that drive.'

CHAPTER SIXTEEN
LIKE A GAZELLE

I'm wedged between my uncle and his podgy-faced friend in the Ute's single cab. The friend is driving. My uncle is busy texting away, the screen tilted so I can't see it. Reg sits in the tray behind us, one hand on a rail, the other on his rifle. I'm waiting for the rifle to go off, booming to life against the bumpy track. Of course, that doesn't happen.

We're close to the cottage. We'd just returned to the main road, turned left, driven for about three minutes then turned left onto another dirt track. About twenty metres in, there was a rusty gate blocking the path, tall trees acting like the rest of the perimeter fencing. The rust on the gate was for show, though, old material fastened onto a new steel frame that Reg easily opened. We've coasted along the continuing path for a few minutes, taking its twists and turns through the gaps of Ghost Gums. It's an endless stream of white trunks and wispy green canopies. Any other time, I'd marvel at the sight. All I can think about is where we might be going.

The track is descending. We'll come to the bottom of a valley, or the banks of a river, I'm sure of it. What will my uncle do with me there? I thought I'd got him, contacting Aunty Janice and setting up a dinner date. That way, I *had* to make an appearance. If all things went well, I could have made a break for it at her house, returning to my studio and staying hidden. But the way Uncle Daniel had agreed to the dinner date over the phone, how that smile had crept on his face, it's obvious he knows how to flip the situation in his favour. Given our remote location, and the man in the back of the Ute with the gun, I'm thinking I might have an accident before dinner.

And I still don't know why. For asking about a photo? It makes little sense.

'You come out here often?' I try, my question directed at either of the cab's occupants.

'Whenever we want,' the pudgy-faced driver says. It's supposed to sound menacing, but I'm anything but threatened by him. He's the anomaly of the group, the hanger-on they must keep around for some petty reason. Money? Access to someone? Laughs?

'What do you do here?' I ask.

'Shoot stuff.'

Uncle Daniel chuckles, keeps texting.

'That it?'

'And fish.'

'I didn't see any fishing gear.'

'Then I guess we ain't fishing today. Put two and two together, Einstein.'

We approach a fork in the track.

'Dan? It's right, ain't it?'

My uncle looks up. 'Yeah. Left's to the river.'

He keeps texting. I try to glance at his screen again, see who he's talking to, but it's still angled away. It's likely Lynden, who stayed back at the cottage to keep drinking beer. We're minus the muscle, but there's still three of them against me, and one has a rifle.

The Ute goes down a steep stretch of gravel, branches scraping against its sides. I hope Reg is getting a few to the face.

'Almost there,' Uncle Daniel says, slipping the phone into his pocket. 'You ready, nephew?'

'Ready for what?'

He chuckles again, relishing in the absolute fuck-all he's giving me.

The land evens out, the gap between bushes widening, tall trees becoming shorter, thinner. Moments later, we're on grassland, an enormous field stretching into the distance.

'Stop here,' Uncle Daniel says, pointing to a pile of logs to our right.

Podgy-face pulls the car over, kills the ignition, takes out the keys.

My uncle double-taps my leg with claw-like fingers. 'This is exciting. Everyone out.'

They lead me onto the field. Somehow, the air is freezing here. We're in the middle of a sunny day, yet I could exhale a cloud of ice.

'I'm going to ask you again, Henry,' Uncle Daniel says, barging his way ahead of us, 'who was the ice-cream lady you saw in Busselton?'

I keep from sighing with relief. This is what he wants to ask? I've already rehearsed the lie. 'I told you, my grandmother.'

'Why have I never heard of her?'

'Have you ever met my mum's side of the family?'

'That's not the point. What's the bird's name?'

'What's it matter?'

'You got her number?'

'She hasn't got a phone. Scared of modern technology. That's why I had to drive to see her. Mum asked me to visit while I was down here.'

I know Uncle Daniel's trying to expose my lie, but I've had long enough to think about every question-answer scenario. His friends aren't helping, either. They're looking over at the expanse before us, their eyes avoiding the confrontation despite helping take me here.

'Why are you doing all this?' I ask.

Uncle Daniel takes his time to answer, kicking at the dirt. 'Did you know I've been to prison?'

'I hardly know anything about you.'

'Yeah, I guess you don't. The family doesn't wanna talk about it. It's part of my life I don't want to revisit, either.'

Reg peels away from us, crouches, and brings his rifle up, aiming at something across the field.

'Doesn't mean I've gone square, though, Henry. Secret is, learn from the time you got caught, don't get caught again. Like a gazelle, always running from the lion. Keep running, you'll never get caught.'

'Is that any kind of life, though? To keep running?'

A shot cracks, echoing around us. Reg stands. About fifty metres in the distance, a tuft of grass kicks up a foot away from a rotting tree stump. Reg winks at me, nodding towards the stump, as if his aim was supposed to scare or impress me.

'I've heard the lion-gazelle story,' I continue, trying to appear unfazed. 'Thing is, if the lion gets up a bit earlier than the gazelle, and starts running first...'

'I'd stopped running, Henry! I'd slowed to a walk. No one gives a fuck what we do out here. Everyone's too busy worrying about keeping tourism alive to care about us.' Uncle Daniel holds his hand out, gesturing for the rifle. He swaps places with Reg, forgoes the crouching and lines up his shot. There's a crack. A tuft of earth flies up two metres from the stump. Reg tries to withhold his amusement.

'I don't care what you're doing,' I lie. 'I was just trying to honour Uncle Graham.'

'Oh, that's the rub. You dig around about one thing, you're gonna dig up other stuff, too.' He holds out the rifle for me to take. 'Go on, have a crack.'

I hesitate, but he seems serious. He slides the rifle into my outstretched hand. I grip the stock. If I knew how to, I'd swing the weapon round, take him out, bat away the others. But they could have shot me, and they haven't. Now they're handing over the one thing that can assert control. Why? What am I meant to prove by shooting at a stump?

Fuck it. I take a knee, bring the sight to my line of vision. Take a deep breathe. Aim. Exhale slowly. Fire.

A sliver of bark jumps off the edge of the stump, followed by a tuft of dirt behind it. Podgy-face gasps. It's not like I hit the stump in the middle. I hadn't felt the wind or calculated the distance with any accuracy. I hadn't used the scope before, either.

'That good enough for you?' I say, handing the rifle back to Reg.

Uncle Daniel has his phone out, held sideways. Was he filming me? 'Not quite. You didn't hit it square on.'

'He got closer than you,' Reg chuckles.

Everyone pauses, watching as my uncle calculates his reaction. Again. He puts the phone away, points to the right of the field. 'Well, we haven't finished yet. There's one more round. The second level, or something like that.'

He waits for me to understand. My thoughts backtrack to why I guessed we were here. Maybe I'm about to become the next target. They'll give me a running head start across the field, then take shots. The human becoming the prey. Maybe my uncle has warped his own stupid story; I'm the gazelle now, and he's the lion. Or a bullet's the lion. Nothing can outrun that. Then they'll load me in the back of the Ute to join the rest of the blood splatter. Or bury me near the tree stump.

'Can't you spot em?' Uncle Daniel asks, pulling me from my thoughts.

He's still pointing. I follow the direction, scan the field. I'm expecting more friends, hunters ready to chase after me. But in the distance, well over a hundred metres away, is a group of kangaroos. A mob, I think you call them. Some are already hopping around, disturbed by the gunshots. Others are still sunning themselves, disregarding our intrusion.

'Are you a betting man, Henry?'

I shake my head. 'I don't believe in free money.'

'It's not free,' podgy-face interrupts. 'You make a series of calculated decisions on the outcome of something, and if you're correct, you reap the rewards.'

'For something someone else did. That you had no control over.'

'Geez, you'd be fucking fun with a group of mates at the pub, wouldn't you?' Uncle Daniel shakes his head. 'Besides, not every bet is for money.'

I sigh. This is where he tells me I'm betting for my life.

'What are we betting for, then?' I ask anyway.

He gestures to Reg, who hands the rifle back to me. 'See, I know you're showing that photo around, even after I told you not to.'

I don't respond, even though I want to ask how he knows this.

'And I think you're full of shit about that old bird from the jetty.' He holds a hand up before I object. 'So, my deal is, you shoot a roo, I give you the benefit of the doubt. I believe it was your grandma. I'll give you one final warning about the photo, cause now you know what's waiting for you if you don't listen. Sure, I'll still follow you, but you get to go back to wherever you're staying, not my place. We handle this after the funeral. Bury Graham properly.'

'And if I don't shoot a roo?'

'We go back to my place. I get some answers the fun way. Lynden helps, with his fists.'

The rifle almost slips from my grasp.

'You like the sound of that? You have three shots.'

'You're not giving me much of a choice.'

'Sure I am. There's a sensible choice or a fucking stupid choice.'

'Where do I shoot from?'

'Right here.'

There's no point sighing, no point trying to weasel my way out of this. I've gone along with my uncle's game. It's too late to stop now unless I want to go straight to the beating.

Twice before, people have beaten me badly. The first time, I was sixteen, out late with a school friend at a party, the kind where parents are absent and half the suburb's youth are attending. The friend was trying to impress a girl he liked, got a bit too drunk and talked shit to someone. That someone was the girl's older brother, and he wanted us gone. He and two of his goons started pushing my friend around. I stuck up for my mate, ended up with a broken nose and fractured ribs as my reward. The second beating, I was a police officer, called to a domestic dispute. We discovered a FIFO worker arriving home to treat his woman like a punching bag. In front of their four-year-old son. While my partner was taking the woman's statement, arranging for her care, a group of the worker's mates appeared out of nowhere and started treating me like the punching bag. They hospitalised me for a week. Six months later, I was back in Emergency with the stabbing. Recognising mortality.

I'm recognising mortality now, too. I don't want a beating again, but I also don't want to kill an innocent creature. Something shouldn't die to save me. It has to, though, doesn't it? Someone else will shoot it one day, anyway, right?

I crouch on one knee, line up the shot. Gauge my distance to the kangaroos. It's much further than I'd first thought. One hundred and fifty, two hundred metres? It's a big range. I aim where I think I should and take the shot.

A clump of earth lifts a good twenty metres in front of the mob. The kangaroos raise their heads, as if to see what the noise is about. More start hopping around, heading for the trees.

'Come on, Henry,' Uncle Daniel says. 'That was shit.'

He's right. I used to be better at this. I lift the rifle a tad higher, slow my breathing, focus. The second shot is closer. All the roos take action now, panic flicking them into self-preservation mode.

'You'd better take that third shot, Henry. Look, you've got two roos just standing there.'

This is ridiculous. I can't shoot a kangaroo. It's a family over there. They're at peace in this area, comfortable enough to come out during the day. In the bushland around Perth, kangaroos hide until the safety of night, desperate to avoid cars and humans. If I take one of these kangaroos out, I could create the same kind of connection. Alter their lives forever.

'You're making me a fucking lion, Henry! Is that what you want?'

I stand, lower the rifle.

'You want a beating?'

I watch the kangaroos disappear into the growth. One remains, a blur against a patch of grass.

'If you don't at least try to make that last shot, I'll get Lynden to stomp on your balls first, crush them like a can of beer!'

That's a powerful incentive to continue. I lift the rifle again, my arm less shaky. I aim a good foot above the kangaroo, then swing it to the right, adjusting for the wind that made me miss the stump. My vision flickers on the kangaroo. I swear it's stopped to stare straight at me, like it knows what I'm about to do. Just before I shoot, a tiny joey comes back out of the bush. Heading towards its mother. I'm about to kill a mother.

'Do it, Henry! Do it!'

I try to think of it as a pest. Elsewhere in Australia, people make it their job to cull kangaroos. It might not be any different here.

I close my eyes, drown out my uncle, and squeeze the trigger.

CHAPTER SEVENTEEN
JAMES BOND

We pull up at the cottage. Uncle Daniel yanks me out of the Ute. I glance back at its tray, at the two legs sticking out of it. Two rigid legs. The three men direct me into the cottage like sheepdogs herding cattle. Lynden's waiting for us.

'He failed,' Uncle Daniel says.

Lynden launches a fist towards me, mind-bogglingly fast for someone so large. I don't even have time to flinch. His fist connects with my jaw. I stagger and fall against a couch.

'You idiot!' Uncle Daniel screams. 'We've gotta go to dinner tonight. Anywhere but the face!'

I roll off the couch, trying to get away. My head's already dizzy, the room multiplying in size. I don't even see the next set of punches, quick jabs to my arm, chest, arm.

The others are laughing again. I hear Reg enter the room, ask where they want the kangaroo he ended up shooting. Uncle Daniel ignores him. Instead, he asks me, 'Who's the old bird at the jetty?'

'My grandmother.'

Lynden leans over me. Jabs my chest, arm, chest.

'Who?' Uncle Daniel says.

'My—'

Jab, jab, jab.

'Who?'

I shake my head. Lynden drives his knee into my chest, striking me so hard, I'm lifted off the floor, back onto the couch.

Uncle Daniel sits beside me. 'I'll pay her a visit, I guess.' Reg and podgy-face leave the room, returning to the rear decking. As if they've seen this a hundred times before. 'Did you show her the photograph? You should just tell me now.'

'I just bought her an ice-cream.'

Uncle Daniel nods to Lynden.

Lynden tries to do a roundhouse kick, but it's so off-balance he hits the couch instead of me. He grunts, lifts a booted foot, and stomps down on my right thigh. The force jolts through my body, the crushed muscles sending signals of instant agony. I howl, push down on my leg, rock back and forth. Anything to distract the pain. Lynden steps back, watches, smiles.

'This is just a teaser,' Uncle Daniel says. 'You wait to see what we'll do tomorrow. No dinners, so we can target the face.'

'Then how will I give the eulogy?' I manage, spittle flying from my lips.

Uncle Daniel pats me on the back. 'You're such a smart-arse. Is that why you got the police involved?'

'What are you talking about?'

'The police. You were talking to one of them at the markets.'

I close my eyes. This is what he's been leading to. He saw me with Gary.

'I wasn't—'

'He was out of uniform, but I've seen that pig around.'

'It's Gary. I went to school with him. High school. We were catching up.'

'You mean you weren't showing him the photograph?'

I look up at Lynden. He's waiting. 'He saw me in town,' I offer, 'told me to catch up. Then we met at the markets, had a coffee.'

'Then you drove to Busselton, on a whim?'

'To meet—'

'To meet your grandma. Wow, it's one big fucking day of reunions.'

Uncle Daniel nods to Lynden, who raises his boot to stomp me again. Last second, he changes his mind, kicks out at my chest. My head snaps back, clunks against the couch's wooden frame, and it's lights out.

When I regain consciousness, I find myself alone. There's a packet of frozen peas beside me on the couch. For my head, I guess. Some repressed part of my uncle showing he cares. I try to get up, shuffle against the couch cushions. Everything hurts. My head feels like it's nursing a hangover. There's a soft hum echoing through it. My arms tremble, and Lynden only jabbed them. And my chest is so sore that with each breath, sharp stabs ripple through my body. My thigh's the worst, though. The top half of my leg feels ten sizes bigger.

At least I'm not that dizzy. I guess that's a consolation.

I don't know how secret agents like James Bond can take repeated beatings then rise to take on the world. Every part of me is in agony. And for nothing, my uncle getting no solid information out of me. Which means the beatings will worsen, as he'd promised. Which means I need to do everything I can to escape at dinner.

What would James Bond do?

I hear laughter outside; the loud crackle of burning wood. Smell the unmistakable waft of cooking meat. Don't let it be the kangaroo. I'd missed it on purpose, but Reg had ripped the rifle from me and finished the job. The joey had jumped away, motherless.

I try to divert my brain from the pain in my body. Focus on the stairs. There's a lingering need to see what's up there. James Bond would do that, explore the villain's lair. Besides, I think my uncle's hiding something, which is why he fears the photograph drawing unwanted attention. But what's the connection?

It takes considerable effort to wiggle my legs into working, to push my body upright. Lynden stomped my thigh once. Just once. I tell myself this until the muscles cooperate. My chest burns. If the pain doesn't go soon, I've fractured a rib. Again. I wait, standing, a warm rush passing through my head. Nobody calls for me to sit down; I'm no longer worth their attention. I shuffle around the couches, reach the staircase. Still, nobody's called out. I take one riser at a time, gripping a flimsy railing, ready to hurry down if I have to. If I can.

The hum in my head is getting louder.

There's no door at the top landing, which baffles me. Once someone's in the cottage, they have access to everything up here.

Maybe there's nothing, then? Maybe it's just a master bedroom like I'd envisioned.

Except it's not a bedroom. I reach the landing, see a small office desk a metre into the area. On top: some files, an empty coffee mug, and a plastic machine that looks like a money counter. It's absent of money. Beyond that, at least eight white boxes, each around six feet high, a metre wide and deep, creating a grid across the room. Industrial-style steel fans run along a gap between them, turning at a slow pace. The hum's not in my head. It's coming from the fans or the boxes, the noise louder up here. Despite the fans, the room is much warmer than downstairs. My immediate instinct is that the boxes are full of drugs. Cables run to each one. For lights? Maybe each box houses an indoor hydroponics set? I saw a few of those during my time as an officer. None with this kind of setup, though. All that's missing are the bikini-clad girls in surgical masks, cutting the product and piling the money.

I have to stop myself from laughing out loud. My uncle and his mates, having girls like that? Heaven help the person who'd want to be intimate with any of them.

Drugs don't connect with what I see, anyway. Given the hum, if I had to put money on it, I'd say someone has designed crude servers, racked equipment hidden away. A few guys at work talk about this sort of stuff all the time. I pretend to understand. Cables feed into the boxes, hidden in spots by thick rugs, a fancy fire hazard. They disappear into the distant wall. I try to make it to the closest box but as I reach the desk, breathing becomes a struggle. I don't know if I can explore the room and return downstairs without collapsing.

There's a loud crash below. Glass shattering. Muted yelling, followed by uproarious laughter.

Preservation overshadows curiosity. I'll try to explore the room later, if I'm still here. I've seen enough for now. It already changes my entire theory on the dirt my uncle didn't want me to dig up. No drugs. No chained prisoners named Lillian. I almost marvel at the insanity of my uncle's mind. He's gone to all this trouble to keep me away from everyone, so I don't draw attention to him, but he's hidden me in a place that has its own secrets. Who the hell does that? Just how unhinged is he?

I'm halfway down the staircase when the rear door starts opening.

I can't make it down. I clench my teeth, push through the pain, and whirl around, so it looks like I'm ascending the stairs.

'What the fuck are you doing?' Uncle Daniel's voice booms.

I freeze as if he has caught me unaware. 'Um... I... I need the toilet.'

'Wrong way, idiot. Toilet's round the back.'

'Oh. I didn't...' I stare, waiting for him to prompt me down. When he doesn't, I turn and make sure he knows every step hurts.

I get back to the couches, lower myself on the closest cushion.

'Don't you want the toilet?'

'Don't think I can make it.'

'You need to piss or shit?'

'Piss.'

'Go out the front door, use the trees. We don't care.'

For some reason, Uncle Daniel comes over and helps me stand, then walks me to the front door. Is he feeling guilty about having his friend beat me? Has he realised he can't look at me the same after all this is over, assuming I'm still alive? Or is this just another part of his shifting personality?

'Stop groaning,' he barks as we step outside. 'It's not my fault. You shouldn't have missed that kangaroo.'

'It was a bet you knew you'd win,' I say.

He lets me go, points to a stump a couple of metres away. Luckily, I do need to urinate. Uncle Daniel waits for me to finish, then guides me back inside. 'Lynden got a mate to check your cadet file. You scored super high for marksmanship.'

'With a handgun.'

'Bullshit. You went in competitions. You missed on purpose.'

'The competitions were ages ago. You were going to have me beaten, anyway.'

He pushes me down onto the couch. 'Henry, I tried to give you an out. I'm still giving you an out. Your one job is to give that eulogy. After that, you need to leave your dad's side of the family alone, like you've always done.'

'What are you saying?'

'Graham liked you, but he was your last connection to us. We're all dead to you now.' He pats me on the shoulder. 'I don't know when you last ate. Fancy some kangaroo?'

It's meant to sting. A final insult, a one-two punch. I shudder, draw in the deepest breath I can manage. I need to show he hasn't fazed me, even if I'm crying within.

'No thanks, I'm saving myself for dinner. Don't want to disappoint our host before I'm dead to them.'

It's the best quip I can manage. As corny as James Bond.

CHAPTER EIGHTEEN
ALL MORALS OFF-LIMITS

It's just past five in the evening, the sky still radiant. We pull up at Aunty Janice's, ready for dinner. She's put out the welcome wagon again. There are four cars outside, more family. The last time I arrived here, the sight of the vehicles worried me; this time, it provides comfort. More people to keep me safe, to cause a distraction.

Lynden tailed us again. As Uncle Daniel and I step out of my car, Lynden pulls over beside the entrance road, almost into the thick growth, obscuring his vehicle from view.

I hold out my keys.

'Nah, don't need em,' Uncle Daniel says. 'Got that guy over there, just in case you try to drive off.'

I try not to smile at my uncle's mistake. 'Are you going to bring dinner out to him?' I ask to cover my amusement.

'He's got his protein bars and Red Bull. He'll be fine. The All Blacks are playing tonight. He's got his phone to watch them.'

He'll be distracted, then? I scan the path from Lynden's car to the house. Plenty of forest on each side. Lots of trees to hide behind. A few plans start to form.

'And if you think about telling my sister about what we've been up to…' Uncle Daniel pulls out his mobile phone, brings up a video '…Ian whipped this up.'

He presses play. The video shows me at the field, rifle in hand. Lining up a shot. Firing. Footage is spliced to show a kangaroo falling down, a close-up on the dead body, Reg's shot made to look like mine.

'Don't think people would like a teacher who goes around shooting roos,' Uncle Daniel says. 'Not even your police mate could help you, either.' He puts the phone away. 'We own you now. Welcome to the club.'

He chuckles, heads to the house's front doors, knocks on their oak surface. At least I know the reason for our hunting trip, aside from it being an excuse to beat me. Blackmail via a video out of context, the icing on their cake of manipulation. And just when I was beginning to think my uncle was somewhat compassionate.

A door opens, Uncle Roland answering. For a moment, he looks tired, but his face changes when he sees us, a broad smile forming. 'Daniel! Henry! So good of you to come.' He ushers us into the house. I try to walk as normally as possible, my muscles still aching. Uncle Roland doesn't appear to notice.

Everyone is sitting out the back, under the gazebo. A bright red tablecloth covers one of the tables, wines glasses and a cheese platter resting atop. Scanning the chairs, I recognise several faces from the other night—uncles and aunties I'd hardly seen before Uncle Graham's passing. They greet me with as much enthusiasm as before. Aunty Janice already has a glass of wine poured for me. Red. Roland directs Uncle Daniel to an esky full of beers.

'Before I forget,' Aunty Janice says to me, 'here's the details for Tuesday.'

She slips me a business card with the glass of wine. I read it. On one side, the funeral director's details are printed—name, address, phone number. One the other, Aunty Janice has handwritten the name of a church and a few times.

'You need to meet at this funeral director by ten on Tuesday. We head to the funeral together. In a limo. Bring Graham's possessions to the director; they're going to make a display for us.'

'Do I need to visit the director before the funeral?'

'I'm meeting with him on Monday. You don't have to.'

'Are you sure?'

'Trent helped digitise Graham's photos already. The director's got someone to put it into some kind of presentation. You just need to write that eulogy.'

'Sure,' I sigh. Write the eulogy, that's all everyone wants me to do. Even though Aunty Janice thinks I can't.

'Now, what have you two been up to all day?' she asks as Uncle Daniel returns with a beer.

'We went to the Farmer's Market,' I say, avoiding my uncle's glare. 'Then Uncle Daniel took me for a drive, showed me some local sights.'

Uncle Daniel nods, cracking open the bottle.

'That doesn't sound like Daniel,' Aunty Janice says. 'Are you sure he didn't just take you to the pub?'

Everyone laughs. I can't be bothered blurting the truth, since then I'd spend the night explaining the video. The dig has made

Uncle Daniel's face redden, though. He masks it with a swig of beer.

I sigh with relief as the conversation continues, the alcohol flowing. Uncle Roland wheels out a Weber, fires it up, migrating sausages from the fridge. I offer to help, drifting away from the others. I'm led inside, given a bowl of sliced onions and a tray of lamb cutlets to carry. Uncle Roland grabs a stainless-steel mixing bowl and tosses some gigantic prawns with olive oil and herbs.

I put the cutlets on the bench. 'Uncle Roland, did Aunty Janice say anything more about the photo I sent?'

He points an oil-soaked hand at me. 'She was on the phone half the bloody day about it. What are you doing to her? As if she didn't have enough—'

'I didn't think she'd be that dedicated. Tell her to stop looking. It's okay.'

'I've already told her. She hasn't. Maybe you could give it a go?'

'Did she find anything?'

'A few people thought the face was familiar. Got little more than that.' He finishes the mix, washes his hands.

I glance around, confirm we're alone. 'Can I ask you about Uncle Daniel?'

'What about him?'

'Is he...'

'Right in the head?' Uncle Roland chuckles as I nod. 'He drinks way too much with his mates. He can't hold a job. But he's relatively harmless. He's the drunk uncle every family seems to have. Janice told me there's no sense in changing him.'

'Has he ever been violent?'

'Not that I know of. He's opinionated, and a tad racist. Why?'

'Just some things he said.'

'Oh, he talks a good game, like he's some bigwig in the Department of Defence, but I think he's seen the most action in one of his video games.'

'He still plays video games?'

'Nothing much else to do with his mates when they're drinking all day. I'm amazed he didn't play any with you.'

I almost say I hadn't even seen any television in Uncle Daniel's cottage, then hold it in. 'He didn't take me to his house,' I lie, thinking that Uncle Daniel might have an actual house somewhere else, the cottage a secret. A carrot to dangle later.

'Ah,' Uncle Roland replies. 'Probably for the best. He's renting with a mate. It would be generous to call the place a dump. Now, what's say we take all this outside, continue the chatter over the barbecue?' He smiles, grabs some long tongs, a spatula, and the bowl of prawns, then motions to the door. 'Give us a hand with that?'

We head outside, continue the cooking process. Uncle Daniel wanders straight over, beer in hand, as if realising we were chatting about him, eager to halt any further conversation. I wonder which of his mates he rents with, and if it's a different place to the cottage. Before I can ask, Uncle Roland shifts the topic to cricket, and the second they name players and how the order of the batsmen is a travesty, I'm lost. I know nothing about cricket. Same with Aussie Rules football. Every Australian male is supposed to be a hardcore fan of the iconic sports, but I never saw the appeal.

I backpedal to the trestle table, unnoticed, and sit near Aunty Janice. She's talking about a recent trip down south, to Albany.

'Have you ever visited, Henry?' one of my relatives asks, bringing me into the conversation.

'This *is* a trip down south, for me.' They laugh. I try to join in, but it hurts. I clutch my side instead. 'Can't believe how quickly it drops in temperature around here.'

I've tried hard to hide the aftereffects of my beaten body, but everything is tightening up. Now that I've sat down, I don't think I can stand again.

'Do you need a blanket?' Aunty Janice asks, mistaking my discomfort. 'Or a beanie?'

'It's not that bad yet.'

'Then have some more wine. That'll warm you up. Leeuwin Estate, Art Series. One of my favourites. Absolutely worth the money.' Aunty Janice stares at the wine in her glass as if it's revealing the mysteries of life.

'You remind me so much of your father,' one of the other aunties says.

'Do I?'

'You've got his lovely, large eyes. And the same wave in your hair.'

'Is your mother coming down?' another aunty asks.

'Monday, I think.'

'She loved your father so much.'

'Enough to never remarry,' I say.

'There are more important things in life than having to be married,' the first aunty says.

'Or having a man,' the other adds.

'Oi!' the woman's husband interjects. 'I didn't think this would turn into a husband-bashing session.'

'We've got cheese, and we've got wine. What did you expect?'

The husband leaves to uproarious laughter, joining my uncles at the barbecue.

'You want to go, too, Henry?' Aunty Janice points to the barbecue. 'This is your cue.'

'I'm okay.' I shrug as if it's no big deal, happy to rest and recharge.

'Your Uncle Graham loved your mother, too,' another aunty continues. 'He stayed around to help care for you.'

I nod.

'I think he had a real soft spot for your mum, but she only had eyes for your dad.'

'June!' Aunty Janice exclaims. 'Naughty rumours! No more wine for you.'

'Maybe I need more wine. We can dish more dirt.'

'Oooh!'

Aunty Janice grabs the bottle, gives it a shake. Empty. 'Then I'll be right back.'

She gets up, heads to the house. Uncle Roland notices, retreats into the house with her, Uncle Daniel now in charge of the grill.

They're gone for a long time. I wait with the other aunties, but none of them seem willing to dish more dirt without the wine. Their last admission replays in my mind: Uncle Graham, a soft spot for my mum. Is that why he stuck around all those years? Was he trying to get closer to my mother? Was he trying to replace his brother? That can't be true. Our family's not part of some scripted TV drama, where they swap and replace partners at ratings time, all morals off-limits.

'We're back!' Aunty Janice announces. She's carrying two bottles of wine, Uncle Roland balancing two wooden salad bowls. Aunty Janice has a red flush across her face that I hope is from the wine. Uncle Roland puts the bowls on the table and retreats inside again. I assume he's getting more food, but he reappears with a cricket bat held high.

'See, Dan. You didn't believe me, here it is.' He slices the bat through the air as if he's striking an invisible ball. 'Won it at an auction.' He approaches me with it first. 'What do you think, Henry? Beauty, right?'

'Aw, Roland,' Aunty Janice calls out, 'Henry doesn't give two cahoots about your cricket bat.'

'But it's signed by JL. You know him, Henry? Justin Langer. I'm pretty sure he used to use it, too. He went to Aquinas College, you know. All the best cricketers went there. So did cousin Sam.'

'All the best... Like who?' Aunty Janice taunts.

'Like... I don't know. But I'm getting his hat next. And David says he knows someone who's got one of his jackets. I can have it all framed like you see in those collectible stores. Put it up in the man-cave.'

Aunty Janice sighs. 'Like a big kid. And always at the wrong bloody time. Roland, put the bat down and come and eat.'

Uncle Roland leaves the cricket bat against the rear wall of the house, near the door, then joins us. Uncle Daniel finishes the grill, getting the men to carry the plates of meat over. The sun has set, solar lanterns switching on. Time passes with a flurry of food, alcohol and chatter. I let it. No sense trying to escape too early. Plus, my body's not quite ready, and I'm enjoying some actual food.

And I'm learning more about Uncle Graham. The same aunt who'd suggested he had eyes for my mother also suggests he was a ladies' man at the markets, always having a few women chatting to him. Nobody can say whether he ended up with anyone, though. Uncle Graham liked to fly solo. I find something part-inspiring, part-depressing about that. An aunt acknowledged there were more important things than marriage, but the same woman was married. It's like a wealthy person saying you don't need money to be happy while splurging on things their poorer counterparts could never obtain. My uncle didn't end up with anyone, and he died alone. Who's saying he was happy with that decision?

Assuming he died alone. Assuming Lillian wasn't a secret, special part of his life.

Throughout the discussions about Uncle Graham, I've had my eye on Uncle Daniel. Watching. Waiting. He's the world's worst guard. He's had at least six beers, his voice becoming louder, slurring. If he forced me to return to his cottage now, he would either get aggressive, fuelled by the booze, or pass out before we returned. One of the other uncles is showing him pictures of a tennis star on his mobile phone. They're ogling her, making obscene suggestions my aunties are trying to ignore.

I excuse myself, saying I need the toilet, and head back to the house. Add a little sway to my step that draws laughter from Aunty Janice. I glance back. Uncle Daniel hasn't even noticed I've left. He's asking the uncle to *zoom in*. When all attention seems off me, I try walking properly again. I've nursed the same glass of wine all night; it's just my muscles that are acting drunk. I reach the house and grab the cricket bat off the wall, then go inside. The second I saw Uncle Roland leave it there, I'd worked on a way to use it. With the mention of video games, I'd thought of the ones from my childhood, of guiding a character trapped in a room with a gigantic boss. The developers always hid the weapon to defeat the boss, you just had to know where to look. Now, my gigantic boss is waiting outside, making sure I don't leave the dinner party early. Time to see how he reacts to the weapon Uncle Roland left for me.

I work my way through the house until I locate the laundry room. Like most laundries, there's a sliding door leading out the side of the house. I unlock it and ease outside again. From this angle, anyone looking from the gazebo would have their view obscured. Perfect.

I pause. Maybe I shouldn't do this. There's every chance I could fail, making the next beating from Lynden even worse. Perhaps I should just find a phone—I'm sure there'd be a landline somewhere—and call the police. I can fill them in on everything, get saved that way. But if I'm made to return to Uncle Daniel's cottage before they arrive, the police might not find me. I'm pretty sure the cottage isn't the place my uncle is renting, so he might not have it listed under his name. By the time the police uncover the right details, it could be too late for me.

I need to give this plan a chance. At least sitting down for an hour or two has recharged my body. Every muscle still aches, but there's no longer a sharp sting in my chest. My breathing's okay, too—thankfully, no ribs appear broken. I hurry as fast as possible around the perimeter of the house, through the cover of trees out front, heading for Lynden's car.

The darkness will hide me. The trees will hide me. I need them to, need the element of surprise for as long as possible. Because I'm surprised, too; never would I have pictured myself about to strike someone with a cricket bat.

I reach the car. I can see Lynden's gigantic frame. He's got his mobile phone centimetres from his face. It casts an eerie glow against his skin. I can hear a whistle, then a crowd cheering.

It sounds like they're all around me. I harness the sound to build the adrenaline I'll need.

I shuffle to the passenger side, crouched. He's cracked the window open a sliver, cigarette smoke wafting out. Between that and the loud game on his phone, Lynden's hardly trying to be inconspicuous. I scoop a handful of gravel, hurl it at the front of the car. Rock skitters across the windscreen. That's enough to make Lynden curious. The phone is silenced. He opens the door, eases his frame out. I keep low on the other side of the car. Imagine him looking around, trying to figure out what just happened, trying to peg the disturbance's origin. There's a crunch of gravel. He's moving around the door to the bonnet. I crab-walk to the rear, risk a look. Lynden's crouched near the license plate, looking back towards the house. This is my moment. I need to strike before he turns to the car. Before he discovers me.

No. I can't. I could put him in hospital, or worse. I don't think I have it in me.

As if desperate to send a reminder, my leg throbs, the muscles contracting. The man in front of me caused that pain. He took great pleasure in beating me. He's going to do it again.

I rush towards Lynden, the cricket bat held over my shoulder. He hears me at the last second. Turns. Throws an arm out. I swing the bat down, hard. It connects with his arm. There's a crunch. His body lowers, stunned. I don't waste time dragging the bat back in an arc; I just jab it at his face. He grunts like it's a minor inconvenience. I jab again. He tries to hold his arm up to stop me, but it hangs limply. I see an opening and wind up, take a bigger swing. My muscles are so sore, it's a pathetic attempt, a little tap. Lynden shakes his head, then tries to stand. I resort to a quick flurry of jabs. My mind screams: *Stay down stay down stay down.*

One jab connects with enough force to snap his head back. He drops, bouncing off the bonnet and thumping against the ground. But he's not done. Seconds later, he tries to push his body upwards, grunting through the pain. I panic, swing the bat high and arc it down against his back. He whimpers and goes limp.

Done.

I look at the bat. There's a long crack running through the middle, a few dark patches on the surface. I almost drop it, disgusted by what I see. I nudge Lynden with my foot. He doesn't move. Fuck. I haven't killed him, have I? It wasn't meant to go that far. The big bastard didn't go down when he was supposed to.

Before I can stop myself, I've run to the house's front door. Maybe I can get Uncle Roland to help me. He can at least call an ambulance before I drive to safety. I crack open the unlocked door and hear voices. People whispering but with raised inflections, a private argument.

'You were meant to stay away from him. What didn't you understand?' It's Aunty Janice.

'If my nephew wants to hang with me, he can.' It's Uncle Daniel.

'I don't know why you *forced* him into *hanging* with you, but it stops now. You're dragging him into a world he doesn't need to see, you utter fucking tit.'

'Oh, Miss Fucking Preachy.'

'Just lay off the beers. Time to go home.'

'Nah, Roland wants me to have some scotch.'

I close the door, back away. Run to my car, start it, throw the cricket bat in the back. I ease the car out of the property, hoping no one's heard the motor, then brake near Lynden's vehicle, wind my window down and peer outside. He's still on the ground. I consider calling an ambulance myself, but of course I don't have my mobile, and I don't want to touch Lynden's.

I hear a moan. The gigantic boss is moving, trying to rise from the ground.

That's all I need. I peel away, back onto the main road. I turn right, accelerate as fast as my shaking leg allows. There's no one else on the road. It's just an endless blur of lines guiding me from the wall of trees on either side. My heart's racing. I can't help but imagine Lynden getting up, roaring his way to my drunk uncle, the two of them giving chase.

I shake my head, trying to concentrate on the road. Trying to figure out where I'm headed. Without my phone's map, instinct made me turn right, had me drive in the direction I assume is north. Hopefully, that will lead to the studio. Please let my inner radar be working.

Five minutes pass. Ten minutes. I lose track of time, trying to stop panic from setting in. I turn right. Can't see any street signs. If this is Carters Road, the studio's entrance should be close. This can't be Carters Road. I keep driving, winding my way past the signage of two, three, four wineries. Maybe I should turn around? No, keep going forward. I check the driver's dash. There's a quarter tank of petrol. Plenty. I reach the end of the road and turn left. That will keep me heading north, won't it?

Headlights appear far behind me. I push down on the accelerator, but I'm still well under the speed limit. The other car is catching up. I can't bring myself to go faster. Every limb's shaking so much I fear the slightest extra twitch could swerve me off the road. The car revs behind me, flashes its high beams.

I grip the wheel, my knuckles turning pale. The car screeches past. Honks. It's not Lynden's car. It's some souped-up Ford, the driver angry I'm not breaking the speed limit, too. In seconds, the Ford's lights disappear into the darkness ahead, and I'm alone again.

I'm about to pull over—to catch my breath or throw up or pass out—when I catch sight of a landmark on my left. The Education Campus, where they had the Farmer's Market. Twelve hours ago, when the day was looking far more positive. I know where I am now. Can't help but whoop for joy.

Ten minutes later, I'm back inside my studio.

Crying myself to sleep.

CHAPTER NINETEEN
EVERYTHING SCATTERS

Clouds shift outside, shadows moving around the room. Something creaks above my head. My sleepy brain pictures myself back in the old family home, unlocking a memory. The creaks are from my father tiptoeing around the house, wooden floorboards reacting to each step. He's getting ready for work, putting the kettle on for a coffee and getting changed into his green overalls, splashing on a handful of Brut aftershave to drown out the forthcoming aroma of grass and manure. He's humming a tune. Something by The Beatles. He's clanking some cutlery around, looking for a knife for his jam on toast. I need to get up, need to pretend to go the toilet just to see him before he disappears for the day. Before he disappears forever.

I sit upright, rub the sleep from my face. No, I'm not in my old home, it's the studio. I hear another creak and start to panic, but tell myself it's the metal roofing, pinging as the new day warms. I relax. Smile. That was the first clear memory of my father I've had in a long time. All it took was having my life placed in mortal danger.

I get up, knock something. The cricket bat drops off the side of the mattress, clunking against the timber flooring. I'd taken it with me while hurrying in from the car. I shudder, picturing the way Lynden had fallen, the sickening smacks and crunch as I'd hit him. I've crossed a line, but I did what I had to do, right? I won't need to use the bat again. I'm safe now. But I nudge it under the mattress, just in case.

I boil the kettle, go through my morning routine, mirror my memory. Except there's no child to watch over me, to wonder where I go all day, to worry whether I'll come home. I try to shake a creeping sense of sadness, plan what to do next. Everyone from last night will wonder where I've gone. Uncle Daniel will be furious about my escape. Aunty Janice will be ready to scold me about leaving without proper manners. She's probably called my mother, who's called Lucy. And my mobile phone's at the cottage.

I have to contact a few people as soon as possible, Lucy and Gary a priority. I quickly use the bathroom, shower, change, head outside. There's no landline in the studio, but the visitor's information file says there's one at the front office. I pass my neighbouring studio, still absent of a car, and head up a hillside track. The front office is a more substantial building, more like an ordinary house. The walk has done my body some good, the muscles loosening. I'm greeted at a counter by a man in his late-forties, early-fifties. He's wearing jeans and a blue checked shirt, his blond hair cut short to hide its inevitable thinning.

'I'm Saul,' he says, reaching over the counter and offering a friendly handshake.

'Henry. I'm staying in Number Five.'

'Perfect. You enjoying yourself?'

'It's amazing. I'm just relaxing at the studio today, but I need to make some phone calls first. I've lost my mobile.'

'Can we help look for it?'

'It's okay. I lost it somewhere in town.'

'I'm sure it'll turn up. We've got a phone over there you can use.' Saul points to a red phone on a nearby wall shelf. It's so old it has a turn dial. I can't hide my shock; I haven't seen one of those since I was a little kid. He laughs at my reaction. 'Just kidding, that's a prop.' He holds out a cordless phone. 'There's a chair and table outside by the door, if you want some privacy.'

'Do you have a phone book?'

'Sure. Not sure why they still print them, but they're good for us. I'll go grab it for you.'

A minute later, I'm perched on the edge of a deck chair, wondering who to call first. Gary? It's time to get the police involved. Or Lucy? I need to alert her without alarming her, since she'll be leaving this afternoon. And since she might help me with something else before I call the police.

I can't for the life of me remember Lucy's mobile phone number. I always just bring it up in the *Favourites* section on my phone. When we were first together, I'd memorised everything about her. I could have speed-dialled her mobile number, her parents' home number, her work number, all off the top of my head. During our argument, she'd said I took her for granted, on occasion. It seems she's right.

I remember our home number, fewer digits. I call it, not expecting her to be there, ready to leave a message on our answering machine. Lucy picks up, though. The sound of her voice throws me.

'Hi… It's me.'

'Hi, me,' Lucy says.

'How come you're home?'

'Sarah's friend arrived early, took them all out to breakfast. I came home to pack a few things. I'm coming down today, remember?'

'Of course, I do. We're not staying at my uncle's place, though.'

'I know. I got your message and had a look on the net. Fancy studios.'

'So you've seen the price?'

'Why would I care about the price?'

Why *would* Lucy care? I always have it in my head that she obsesses over every transaction. At some point in our relationship, the perception just stuck.

'Listen,' I say, 'since you're home, can you get our iPad out?'

'Why?'

'I may have lost my phone.'

'In an hour?'

'What?'

'You just messaged back an hour ago.'

'I did?'

'When I told you I was coming down early? You had your morning coffee, yet?'

'No.' I'd boiled the kettle, never made the coffee. 'What did I say, in the text?'

'You said you'd meet me at your uncle's farm. I'm confused now.'

'Shit. Can you reply to messages even if the phone's locked?'

'I think so.'

'Seems like a glaring security issue.'

'Might be a new feature you didn't disable.'

'Yeah.'

'From a guy who works in a tech store.'

'I know.'

'Who do you think's got your phone, then? If they know about your uncle's farm—'

'It's Uncle Daniel. Don't go anywhere near him, he's fucking mad.'

'I don't remember who Daniel is.'

I'm not sure if Lucy's ever met him. 'Just ignore messages from my mobile. Come straight to the studio, don't go into town. I'll explain when you get here.'

'Is everything okay?'

'Not really, but I'm surviving.' I could just tell my wife that everything's gone south, that I'm doing the sensible thing and coming back to Perth. But things are in motion, and right now it's easier to believe we're better off hiding in the studio while I get Gary to help. 'Have you got the iPad?'

'Grabbing it now.'

I talk her through the steps to find my phone. The device appears, so its battery is hanging on. I'm fuming at the thought of Uncle Daniel impersonating me, but I expected nothing less. The worst part is, if he didn't realise I was married, he does now, and he knows my wife is on her way.

'It's updating the location,' my wife offers, breaking a short stretch of silence.

I feel a sudden spark of hope. 'Write it down for me, will you?'

'Okay. It's coming up.'

She reads it out. I repeat it three times in my head while flipping through the phone book, trying to find the number for the local police. 'Okay. Click on *Actions*, then I think it's *Lost Mode*.'

'It's asking for a phone number where people can reach you.'

I find the local police station's number and give it to her.

'It's asking for a message to be shown. It's optional.'

I try to think of some stupid threat, like: *I know where you are, I'm coming for you.* Probably best to say nothing, though.

'Just leave it blank.'

'Okay. Anything else?'

'No, that'll do.'

We talk for a little longer. We make a list of supplies Lucy can get before leaving, and I give her directions to the studio.

'Already got them on my phone. Just have a couple more things to sort out. I'll see you in about five hours.'

I end the call, dial the local police, ask for Gary. Wait on hold, listening to elevator music and an ad about helping the community.

The line clicks, the ad silenced. 'Henry? You're lucky to get me. I was called in today.'

'Shifts never end, huh?'

'Just the usual weekend stuff. I was about to call you. How did your meeting with Mrs Haynes go?'

'She wasn't willing to give me much.'

'She'll warm to you.'

'I bought her an ice-cream.'

'She'll definitely warm to you. Did you give her your number?'

'Yeah.' I cringe. 'Shit, someone might need to monitor her.'

'What do you mean?'

I don't hesitate to tell Gary everything about my uncle and his mates. If Uncle Daniel was willing to threaten and beat me, I don't feel guilty handing him over to the police. Gary tries to show concern in his voice, but I can tell he's excited. Abduction, intimidation, assault, stealing property. Then I mention the cottage's set-up with the white boxes and his voice pitches higher.

'Servers? Do you think it's some kind of PirateBay setup?'

'Could be. But I don't think my uncle and his mates are smart enough to run something like that.'

'Someone else could have set it up for them. They supply the location and maintenance, get paid to run it. Could have installed a few generators or solar panels, so they're not caught sucking power off the grid.'

'Well, I got my wife to use our *Find My iPhone* app. We got an address. I bet it matches where the cottage is.'

I give him the details. I can hear scratching on paper, like he's underlining everything three or four times.

'Your uncle and his mates have booked themselves in here just for what they did to you,' Gary says. 'We'll take our time with the questioning while we organise a team to search their cottage. The servers are a bonus. A promotion-worthy bonus.'

I agree. 'And Lynden, the Māori bloke who bashed me? I'm sure he's got a broken arm. Fingers crossed it's not a fractured skull, too, or some kind of broken back or shoulder. There's a good chance he's got a concussion, at the very least. Maybe check the doctors or the hospital?'

'I'll ask around if we don't find him with your uncle.'

'Do you think they'll charge me for what I did to him?'

'We'll go down the line of self-defence.' Gary clears his throat. 'I've got to say, you put in a remarkable effort to get out of a horrible situation. If teaching gets too much, would you consider applying to rejoin the force? We could do with someone decent down here. I mean, to add to our already stellar line-up, Leigh. Stop listening in!'

'I've already left teaching,' I finally admit, 'but I don't know what I want to do. I don't think I'm made for... A better officer wouldn't have let themselves get into such a situation.'

I thank Gary, ending the call before his rebuttal. I picture his team leaving for Uncle Daniel's cottage and almost fist-pump the air, but know better than to rejoice too early. It might take a while to arrest Uncle Daniel and Lynden. His mates may have scattered, too, or be looking for me.

I hope Gary follows through on sending someone to look after Leonie Haynes. She may have changed her mind and tried to contact me. Uncle Daniel wouldn't have hesitated to arrange a meeting under my name, since he'd already said he was going to talk to her. I consider driving back to Busselton Jetty, but the better part of my brain shuts that down. I'm not leaving my studio until I know I'm safe. Besides, if Uncle Daniel sets up a meeting with Leonie and then turns up, she's going to realise it's not the same person who bought her an ice-cream, and I doubt he's going to abduct an old lady. He's not that batshit crazy, is he?

Maybe I should call the rest of my family, warn them, just in case he is? Psychotic tendencies, batshit craziness... Although, I'm the one he seems to have a grudge against. And it started with the photograph, not years before. Maybe the rest of the family has dismissed him as a threat. Aunty Janice was yelling at him last night, she seems to have him under control. Besides, I don't have their phone numbers now to warn them, anyway.

I return the phone to Saul with a gracious thanks, then head back to my studio. My stomach's grumbling. I rustle whatever's leftover from yesterday and cook it up: mushrooms, scrambled eggs, toast. Not too shabby. Then I make myself the coffee my body's dying to drink.

I eat, drink, clean up. Try to think of what to do next.

I head over to the coffee table, look at all of Uncle Graham's items again. Find the notepad and start another list. This time, I separate the items into ones that are probably just my uncle's favourites, things to display around his coffin, and ones perhaps listed for a different reason; running with the theory that Uncle Graham was trying to send me a message.

The favourites include the Akubra hat, the flask of whiskey, the Indiana Jones mini-figure, the *Back to the Future* movie poster, the DVD of *The Castle*, the framed hundred-dollar bill, the shark tooth necklace, and the compass.

The items listed for a different reason could include the photo albums, the CDs, the books, and the letter C typebar.

I stare at the list. Group the items on the table accordingly, then stare some more until I admit I'm not satisfied. The letter C typebar could stand for Charlotte Harris, but it could also just reflect my uncle's love for repairing typewriters. Assuming I'd find the photograph, it could represent confirmation that the woman's name started with a C. Or it's just a coincidence. The photo albums could be for sentimental reasons, only. Then there's the movie poster, almost a metre in height. Why choose this instead of a postcard-sized version? Or the DVD version, as I'd thought earlier? Maybe Uncle Graham wanted me to notice the odd choice until I questioned it. Maybe he wanted me to go back to the future. Wait, the past. Right a wrong before I return to the future, which is the present. Not with a time machine, but through people who might know something about both eras. People like Leonie Haynes. Except I wouldn't have met Leonie if it wasn't for Gary.

I feel a headache creeping back.

Maybe I should just admit that everything is purely for the funeral, none of it related to my search for Lillian. I throw the notepad at the table. Everything scatters, one item pushing another until several drop to the floor, clattering against the timber. I bend to catch them, cursing, watching as the framed bill teeters over the edge. I miss it. The glass cracks, the frame falling apart. I curse, turn, kick the couch.

I leave the mess, storm outside, jump off the decking, stand on the dry grass. Count down from a hundred, trying everything within my willpower to calm myself. I try to let nature balance me, try to focus on the call of the birds, the chirp of the crickets, the rustle of the leaves in the mild wind. In the distance, I can see a family of kangaroos eating grass. I clench my eyes shut, open them, willing the mob to have disappeared. They're still there, though, ghosts haunting me by daylight.

'I'm sorry,' I whisper.

I hurry inside, set up the stereo and television, put on the DVD of *The Castle*. I sit on the bed, the television angled towards it. Let me just escape into this piece of Australiana cinema for an hour or two, pass the time until my wife arrives.

The DVD doesn't work, though, forcing me to watch the local news instead. There's nothing on there about Uncle Graham's death, nor lying and threatening members of my family. Just reports covering which diet we all need to try next, and which members of parliament are fighting amongst themselves.

I last half an hour before thoughts of my wife's arrival make me return to the coffee table. I can't leave this mess, it will be the first thing she sees. I put what I can on the table, back in two piles, then retrieve a broom from the kitchen cupboard. I pick up the shattered frame, trying my best to avoid the shards. It comes apart even more.

'Sorry, Uncle Graham,' I mutter, continuing my round of apologies. Maybe I can take out the hundred-dollar bill, put it in his burial suit? He didn't need the frame, did he? The sentiment's still there.

I sweep the glass into a dustpan. My uncle has mounted the bill on a piece of brown card. I ease it out, try to pry the bill off. It's held by tape. My fingers curl around the brown card, touch something else. I turn it over. There's a black object stuck to the surface. I rip it off. It's paper, the same kind I found in the Lillian typewriter. Something uncurls from the centre. I put the card down, the bill forgotten. I'm holding another square print, the word Kodak shining off one side's surface. Someone has ripped this print, too.

I turn it over.

It's a photograph of a man, seated at a table. His right arm is reaching out of the image. I can see a few curls of black hair near the rip, belonging to a woman out of frame. I know this because I've seen the woman, have sent her image to my family.

I don't need to send this second image to my family, don't need to ask them who is holding Charlotte Harris. Despite almost forgetting the way he sounded, the way he smelled, talked, and loved me, I can't forget his face.

I'm holding an image of my father.

CHAPTER TWENTY
THIS CHANGES EVERYTHING

Teaching often subjected me to the constant fads of my students—the latest game, toy, saying. Some of my peers took the authoritarian approach, banning as much as they could. I was a pick-and-choose teacher. Sometimes I went with it, sometimes I didn't. In my last year before long service, there was a popular saying from the *How to Train Your Dragon* TV series. The phrase went: *This changes everything.* I must admit, I often went along with this one. Got thirty per cent in the latest fractions test? *This changes everything.* Forgot your sneakers for sport? *This changes everything.* A raven went to town on the lunchbox you left outside? *This changes everything.*

I'm looking at the photograph now, the two halves together, and that phrase has crept back into my mind. My father, his arm around another woman.

This changes everything.

This time, the phrase isn't amusing.

I don't know how long I sit there, just staring. If I were still teaching, a student would have distracted me by now. But I'm alone, left to my thoughts; left to analyse every part of the image and create as many scenarios as I can.

My father looks the same age as he was before he died. I've seen that face in a few photos my mother didn't manage to hide from me. And although this image with Charlotte could have captured old school friends or clients having a catch-up coffee, such innocent scenarios seem more implausible than awful ones. People don't tear photographs of good memories.

It's time to face the truth. My father was having an affair. And he wasn't trying to hide it, was he? He'd posed for a photo with the 'other' woman. She's got an uncomfortable smile on her face, as though she's unsure about capturing the moment, but he's flashing his teeth in a wide grin as if he's having the time of his life.

How did my uncle find the photograph? What was his reaction?

Did my mother know? What was hers?

Did anyone else in my family know? If it was just Uncle Graham possessing both halves of a secret, then it's a terrible burden he took to his grave. Is that why he left it for me to find?

How did he expect me to react? Instead of freaking out, did he expect me to answer questions he never could? Does this all relate to Lillian? It has to, or else why get me involved?

Regardless of the truth screaming at me, I try to downplay what I'm seeing. Even if my father was having an affair, perhaps it was a brief one, a secret between two consenting adults, unbeknownst to people like Leonie Haynes and Uncle Graham until a chance discovery years later.

Wait. What if Leonie had known? Maybe her foster daughter confided the relationship to her. Maybe Uncle Graham had already approached Leonie about it. She'd said she'd seen him a couple of times. I need to buy her as many ice-creams as it takes to get the truth.

For now, maybe there are details I missed in Gary's notes. I leave the studio, head to my car, open it and wrench the driver's seat back along its rail, feel around until I find the file he'd given me. Returning to the studio, I sit on the outside chair, open the folder atop the wooden table. Reread the notes. Check a few key dates; attach them to other memories.

Make a connection.

My father and Charlotte shared more than just the relationship captured in the photograph. They both died in car accidents. Those accidents occurred in the same year, nineteen ninety-three. Six months apart.

CHAPTER TWENTY-ONE
SHOW ME HOW TO DANCE

I need to access my father's accident report. Someone had killed Charlotte during a hit and run, the other driver never found. Was my father in a similar accident? Were they connected, someone determined to end a relationship in the worst way imaginable?

I walk back to the front office. On my way, I notice there's a car parked beside the studio opposite me. I didn't hear them pull in. It's a car I don't recognise. An Audi. Just someone there for a perfectly innocent holiday.

Saul laughs as I step inside the office and ask for the phone.

'Maybe we should get them installed in each studio, like a hotel,' he says. 'Except you're supposed to be escaping from things like phone calls and work.'

'I know,' I say, taking the handset. 'Last calls for a while, I promise.'

I sit on the chair outside, dial Gary first.

'He's out,' I'm told by a gruff-voiced male. I picture the bear-like man who was hostile to me at the police station. I'm pretty sure it's him.

'Could you take a message? Please?'

'I'm not an answering service, try again later.'

'I'm pretty sure you're supposed to pass messages on. You got a review coming up? Maybe I can let him know about your service; or lack of.'

He growls. 'Fine. Name?'

'Henry Herbert. He knows me. I need him to find an old report. On a car accident.'

'You can do that yourself online. Apply for an abridged crash report. There are some details to fill in. There's also a small fee to process it.'

'Yes, but I need Gary to help. I don't have constant online access, and I can't come in to talk about it.'

An enormous sigh. 'Fine. I'll leave a message that Sir Henry Herbert called.'

'Thank you.' I say, ignoring the condescension.

'Anything else we can do for you, your Lordship?'

'I'd hate to trouble you. I—' The line's dead before I can finish.

The bear's either an arsehole or he's had an awful weekend. Hopefully, he's not part of the team arresting Uncle Daniel and his mates. He'd tell Uncle Daniel to put the handcuffs on himself, then complain as he ran away.

I grip the handset and stab the next set of numbers. I've already had one frustrating call, may as well go a second round while I'm in the zone.

My mother picks up on the third ring.

I almost hang up before I give away it's me. She has a handset that shows the caller's number. She might write it down, get someone to look it up.

'Hi, mum,' I say, deciding she wouldn't bother.

'Henry?' As if she has any other children.

'Just checking to see when you're coming down.'

'Tomorrow. I told you that, didn't I?'

'Yeah, I just… I wanted to make sure.' I fight every urge to ask about my father, about Charlotte Harris. 'Where are you staying?' I need to see her face. See the expression on it. If I ask her about my father now, she can rehearse, lie again.

'At Janice's. You arranged all this. Henry, where are you? Janice called me this morning, all flustered. You came to her house for dinner, but she said you just left.'

'Yeah, I think I had something off to eat. I felt weird.'

'Well, you shouldn't have left without saying your thanks and goodbyes.'

'I went to the toilet and then… I didn't know what I was doing.'

'Then you shouldn't have been driving!' There's panic in my mother's voice. She hates driving for obvious reasons, but Western Australia is so spaced out, it doesn't lend itself to walking everywhere.

'I'm okay, mum. Honest. So, what time do you think you'll get to Aunty Janice's?'

'Trent is picking me up, nine at the latest. He's dropping me at Voyager Estate for lunch with Janice. Then we're meeting with the funeral director.'

'Good to know. Can you call Aunty Janice, let her know I'm okay?'

'You need to call her yourself.'

'I'm calling from a public phone. I've lost my mobile.'

'What? What public phone? Where?'

'Aw, did you hear that? The credit's running out.'

'Henry?'

'See you tomorrow, mum.'

I end the call, watch the handset. It doesn't ring. Satisfied she's not trying to call back, I hand the phone to Saul with more thanks, return to the studio. My legs are aching by the time I step inside. I lock myself in, sit on the edge of the bed. I should go back to the clues, back to Charlotte's file, but I'm already exhausted. I turn the TV back on, try to laugh at the outdated jokes of an '80s comedy, and let my head sink into the pillow.

Something wakes me. Not the movie—that's finished, the TV plugging an ad for all-in-one gym equipment. Had the roof creaked again? No. It was a distinct sound. Birds?

I sit upright, turn the TV off. Hear the noise again: the squeal of a brake, the crunch of gravel. I leap off the bed, everything rushing into focus. It could be the people in the neighbouring studio, but…

A car door opens, slams shut. Gravel crunches in a *pat-pat* rhythm. It's sounds too close to be the neighbours. Which means I have a visitor.

The door's locked. The windows are closed but uncovered. I don't have long enough to pull their blinds down. I rush into the bathroom, a few steps from the bed. There's a white curtain between the spa and bi-fold French windows. I yank it closed, just as I hear the gate's latch open, then duck behind the spa. Footsteps clunk against the decking. I'm unseen in the bathroom, but the intruder can walk right up to the front glass door, look inside, tell someone's there. They can see my uncle's possessions spread out on the coffee table, guess what I'm doing.

There's a tap on the door. Soft. Would Uncle Daniel and his mates approach like that? No, they'd be smashing their way inside. Unless they're trying to trick me, trying to make sure I'm in, trapped before they advance.

I look to the bed. The cricket bat is under it. On the opposite side.

'Henry? You there?'

The voice swirls through my body, makes it shudder in relief. It's not Uncle Daniel or his mates. I jump up, throw back the curtains, wave my hands. My wife laughs from the other side of the glass, a day bag dangling in her hands.

'Caught you at a bad time?'

Her brown skin glows against the sunlight. She's wearing black shorts and a plain purple shirt and I know they're just casual, appropriate clothes for a long drive but dammit she looks amazing! I hurry to the door, unlock it, step outside, wrap her in the type of embrace we haven't shared for far too long. It's filled with every conceivable emotion I've battled through, and it's not till I hear a grunt that I realise I need to pull myself back. I stare down at the green irises of her eyes, losing myself in their swirling mystery. Why did we fight before I left? Do I even care any more?

'Thank you *so* much for coming here,' I whisper.

'Of *course* I'd come down, you big goof.'

She leans in, pushes up on her toes and kisses me lightly on the lips.

As we enter the studio, she makes a tutting sound, points at the coffee table. 'What are you up to?'

I lock the door, carry her day bag to the bed. 'Sorting through my uncle's things.'

'Why the different piles?'

'My OCD is flaring up.'

She laughs. A genuine laugh. God, I love that sound.

'Do you really want me to explain?' I say, hoping she says no, knowing it will kill the amusement.

'It was a long drive. I'm all stinky; I think I'll have a shower first. This place has a shower, right?'

'Oh. Yeah, it's a big one. No screen, just a curtain, so you can dance under the water without knocking into anything.'

'You've tried, haven't you?'

'Maybe. There's a spa, too.'

'I think I'd fall asleep in the spa.'

I nod as she walks over to the bed, removing fresh clothes from her bag. A few days apart and I feel like an awkward teenager again. Am I supposed to hug her, kiss her, say some corny line like, *You won't be needing any clothes* after *your shower*? No, she's driven for hours, she doesn't need someone jumping all over her.

Lucy heads to the bathroom. 'You want to go into town later?' she asks, turning on the water.

'No! I mean, you've been in a car long enough. You brought food, right?'

'It's in the car.'

She starts closing the door as steam curls its way out of the room, leaving it ajar enough to continue talking.

'We can just enjoy the studio,' I call out. 'The owners left a bottle of wine here as a welcome gift. We could try that.' If there's any left.

She doesn't respond.

'Or we've got lovely instant coffee if you need that.'

Still no response.

'Or fresh Margaret River water. Better than that city stuff.'

The shower is so hot it's fogging up some of the windows. My wife always has apocalyptically hot showers.

'Henry?' she calls out.

'Yeah?'

'Is there any shampoo?'

'I think there's a little bottle. Above the sink.'

'Can you get it for me?'

I ease open the door, navigate my way through the mist. I find the bottle and hover by the shower curtain. 'Here you go.'

The curtain rips open. Lucy has tied her shoulder-length hair back. Several black strands have escaped, though, framing her face. Soap-suds slide down her naked body. I follow their trail. Gulp a little too loud. She laughs again.

'I was wondering,' she says, 'could you show me how to dance under here. There's plenty of room for two.'

I wake in bed, in a tangle of sheets, my wife's arm draped over me. I try to shift without waking her, but the slightest movement causes her breath to catch, and she stirs.

'That was a delightful dance,' she mumbles.

'It's been a while.'

She sits upright, pulling at the sheet. 'Don't. I know it's been a while.'

I sink into the pillow. Why did I speak?

'We've got some things we need to talk about,' she says, 'and we'll do that soon. We'll get through it, and there'll be more showers since we've finally got time for each other.' She lowers her hand, trails fingers across my ribs, then my thigh. 'But first, we need to talk about these bruises. I know I didn't do that, and all that groaning wasn't just because of me. What the hell happened to you?'

'It's nothing.'

She rips the sheet away and slaps my knee, just missing the welt.

'Shit! Okay, I'll tell you.'

'Does it have something to do with your missing phone?'

'Yes.'

'And your uncle?'

'Yes. Well, sort of.'

I didn't hesitate to tell Gary about everything that's happened. I shouldn't hesitate to tell Lucy. Secrets could harm rather than protect her. Before I know it, we're out of bed, clothed, standing around the coffee table. I start with the list, my first encounter with Uncle Daniel and Lynden, the abduction, my escape. I mention Gary's help, about everything we've pieced together on Charlotte and Lillian. Lucy asks questions when she needs to—I can tell she'd love to ask a hundred more. When I've said enough, she stands there, touching a few items on the coffee table.

Finally, she asks, 'Are you going to keep looking for Lillian?'

'I think I have to.'

She nods, the two halves of the photograph in her hand. 'So, your father may have had an affair with this woman.'

'Charlotte.'

'With Charlotte.'

'Please, I don't want to—'

'You need to keep talking about it. Cause if this woman was pregnant, and your dad's the only one she was with... Well, you're not just finding a funeral guest.'

'I know. I might be finding my sister.'

CHAPTER TWENTY-TWO
KEEP DIGGING

My entire life, I've skirted around the truth about my father. When he'd died, I'd just accepted the story around the accident. I'd visited the crash site once, after getting my driver's licence. Touched the remnants of the tree he'd careened into. When I went through the academy, became an officer, I never used my powers to look at his incident report, never once folded to satisfy curiosity. Never questioned what time of day the crash was, how fast he'd travelled, whether he was intoxicated, whether he was alone.

The truth always finds its way out.

Now I need to deal with the likelihood that my father had an affair, that his family in Perth wasn't good enough for him, that he could've been starting a new one down south. The constant long drives for his landscaping business, to glorify a new home along Mandurah's canals, was the perfect front. Maybe he did some work down there, then some work with the other woman.

Producing a baby.

My half-sister.

'How long do you think he knew?' I ask my wife.

'Who? Your father?'

'Uncle Graham.'

'Maybe he wasn't sure. Maybe he needed to—'

'He knew.' I grip the edge of the couch. 'That's why he got me involved. He knew I'd connect things. Knew I'd keep digging.'

'He was dying. Why not just write you a letter revealing everything? Or tell you when he called?'

I shake my head. 'I don't know. He loved puzzles. Sudoku, cryptic crosswords. Maybe he wanted to give me a puzzle, too? Just to frustrate the hell out of me?'

'Or maybe he wanted to reignite your investigative skills? You said when he called, he went on about your police work.'

I can't help but give my wife a strange look. 'Did you talk to him about this?'

'I haven't talked to him at all.'

At least my wife isn't lying to me. She wants me to have more direction than an electronics salesman employs, something that challenges me, but she hasn't resorted to setting up some bizarre game with my uncle. Which means he took the reason for his secrecy to the grave.

'I think you need to talk to the ice-cream lady again,' Lucy says.

'I thought that, too. But I don't know if she'll trust me.'

'She's obviously protecting Lillian. But maybe if you explain your connection now, she'll be more willing to help.'

I let go of the couch, swivel to hug my wife. 'You're right. You know, just because my dad was a cheating arsehole, doesn't mean it's like father, like son.'

'I don't know,' she says, smiling, 'you haven't seen me in another ten years. Future me might be this fat.' She holds her arms out as wide as possible, chuckling.

'I'll love you, no matter what.'

'You say that now.'

I tickle under her arms, grab her, carry her to the bed. We're laughing, kissing, pulling at everything loose. Making up for lost time.

But something makes me stop.

'Did you hear that?'

We jump upright, adjust clothing, hurry to the front door. I crack it open. Outside, there's another squeal. Another crunch of gravel.

Another visitor.

I close the door, lock it.

'The blinds.'

We run to each window, tugging and twirling each thin plastic rod and wire to pull the slat blinds into place. The room darkens, portals of light covered. I look towards the bathroom. No time to close those curtains again. I hear the latch of the gate, listen to it smack against the frame. Hear the *thunk, thunk, thunk* of boots against floorboards.

We wait behind the blinds.

There's no knock. I creep over to the bed, reach underneath it until my hand clasps the cricket bat.

How did Uncle Daniel and his mates find me? Have they bugged me somehow? My car?

I leave the bat. It won't last much longer. I find Lucy, grab her arm and guide her into the tiny kitchen area. Somewhere in the darkness, there are knives and pans and glassware we can use to throw. The second the intruders break a window and allow light to filter back in, we'll grab as much as possible. We're not going down without a fight.

How many people are outside? Just Uncle Daniel, or all the inbred bastards from the cottage? Maybe he's rounded up a pub-full of mates.

Although, I only heard one distinct set of footsteps.

There's finally a knock on the glass door. One heavy knock.

Nothing more.

I edge my way to the door, maintaining silence.

There's a scrape outside. Is he going to throw the outdoor set through the glass?

I reach the blinds beside the door. I've heard nothing else, no additional cars or footsteps. I touch a slat, ease it upwards just enough to glance at what's out there. A figure is on one of the outdoor chairs, their back to me, peering at the distant field. They turn as if sensing my stare.

'It's okay,' I exhale. I find the door, open it. 'Hi, Gary.'

'Henry! I thought maybe you'd gone for a walk.'

I reassure Lucy we're okay, that the man out there in the police uniform is the Gary from my story. She appears beside me, eager to put a face to words.

Gary takes stock of her appearance, the closed blinds. 'Oh, I see.' A smile stretches across his face.

'She just arrived,' I explain, then realise I'm adding credence to the closed blinds. I cough, try to start again. 'Lucy, this is Gary. We went to high school together.'

'Oh, the stories I can tell you about this one,' Gary says, getting up, shaking my wife's hand.

'Oh, really,' Lucy says, playfulness in her voice.

'Like this one time, when he and Ben and Alistair were playing soccer at lunch, and they *accidentally* kicked the ball off the oval, and they crossed the road to go get it and just kept on walking away from school. Where did you end up the rest of the day, Henry? Alistair's house?'

'Yeah, she doesn't need to hear this,' I say.

'Or this one time, when he snuck out and went to Mrs Pasipio's Science room and changed all the labels on the beakers so the Year Tens made a stink bomb without realising it.'

'Yeah, you can stop!' I echo *la la la la* until Gary gets the message. He might have remembered things I once did at school, but I have no desire to talk about them again. Besides, I can't remember any stories featuring Gary. Things shouldn't be so one-sided.

My wife is laughing. Great, she'll ask me for more details later.

'We thought you were someone else,' I say, trying to refocus.

'Don't worry, I've spoken to Saul at reception, asked him to monitor the comings and goings. He knows the police don't want you for anything nefarious. I told him you're down from Perth to help in an investigation.'

'Well, you just made me sound like a criminal to my wife.'

'Petty stuff. We all grow up.'

'Really?' Lucy chuckles.

I wave Gary inside. 'You know, I've tried to get in touch with you about my dad.'

He sees the objects on the coffee table, frowns. 'Sorry, mate. It's another busy day today, thanks to your family. And Sunday is supposed to be an easy shift.'

'You know there's no such thing. You've been to Uncle Daniel's cottage?'

'That's why I'm here. This all from Graham?' Gary removes something from his pocket, a paper bag. 'Never mind that. We've got a problem.'

He holds out the bag, opens it. I think my phone's inside.

CHAPTER TWENTY-THREE
LIKE THE EXTRA CHANNELS

Gary shakes the bag. 'We found this at the cottage. Man, that place was a dump.'

I hold out my hand. 'Is it *my* phone?'

He holds onto the bag. 'It was on a table outside, kind of just left there for us to find. Or for you to find. Tell me, do you think your uncle expected you to go back to the cottage?'

'I wouldn't think so. Honestly, he probably just dumped it. Or forgot about it. Wait, why do we have a problem?'

Gary drops the bag in my hand. 'Can you get it out of Lost Mode?'

'Sure. Can I take it out of the bag?'

'We've lifted some prints, charged the phone. We're breaking all sorts of preservation protocols, but there's an urgency to this.'

'What do you mean?'

'Can you just… Can you unlock the phone? Our IT guys aren't down yet.'

I remove my phone from the bag. 'Did you bring the iPad?' I ask Lucy.

She grimaces. 'Sorry, I think I only brought my laptop.'

'Should be okay.'

I press the phone's Home button and go through the steps to unlock it. Since I know the password, I don't need a secondary device. We wait for a while for the signal to return. When it does, the mobile pings for a good ten seconds.

'Wow,' Lucy exclaims.

'I hope that's not work calling,' I joke.

Gary's face is quite serious. 'I need you to check for messages or calls from Leonie Haynes.'

'Why?' A heaviness ripples through my body. I know the answer, the problem Gary's alluding to. 'I asked you to watch over her!'

Gary holds out his hands, urging me to calm down. 'I made a call to our pals in Busselton. Two officers went to check up on her. She was supposed to be volunteering today, but she never clocked on.'

'Fuck!'

'I'm so sorry. I need to know if she contacted you.'

I open my messages. It's right there, a string of texts from an unknown number.

*I need to tell you more about
Lillian.*

That would be most lovely. When?

*I volunteer at ten. How about
nine thirty?*

Where?

Treat me to another ice cream.

Deal

I show the messages to Gary, my wife looking over our shoulders.

'Where did you buy her an ice-cream?' Gary asks.

'Just next to Busselton Jetty. Uncle Daniel knows I talked to her there. How can no one have seen her turn up?'

'Maybe something happened in the parking lot. Someone's looking through footage of the area, but that won't help us right now. Henry, we're playing catchup. If your uncle met her, where do you think he took her?'

Not why, but where. Gary will deal with the reason later. I slip my phone into my pocket, close my eyes, trying to think. The problem is, I have no idea. I don't know the land. He could have taken her anywhere.

'You can't trace his phone?'

'Ang is trying, back at the station.'

'What about Aunty Janice?' Lucy says. 'Could she get hold of him?'

I smile. Using one family member to get hold of another. 'It could work. He responds to her.' I neglect to mention their disagreement the other night.

'Or we could just use your phone?' Lucy adds.

'Better for Daniel to think we haven't found the phone yet,' Gary says. 'He hasn't called it himself, and it buys us some more time.'

'Are we going to call her on yours, then?' I ask.

'Let's ask her face to face, so I can get a read on the situation.'

I nod. 'Then Aunty Janice's it is.'

Gary rattles keys out of his pocket. 'Get whatever you need. I'll drive.'

It's the first time this week I haven't seen a line of cars parked outside Aunty Janice's house. There's just one vehicle. I think it's Uncle Roland's. The passenger door is open, a vacuum cleaner waiting beside it. The old wash-your-car-on-the-weekend Aussie tradition. Uncle Roland isn't around, though. We approach the front door, ring the bell. Knock. Wait.

Uncle Roland greets us with an ice pack pressed against his temple. I picture him taking a beating from Lynden, but after saying hello, he points to the pack and laughs.

'This? Oh, I almost knocked myself out. Was vacuuming the mats in the car, slipped and smacked my head against the dash. What kind of fool does that?'

I try to laugh with him. Lucy says hello, then introduces Gary.

Uncle Roland's gaze lingers on Gary's uniform. 'Everything okay, Henry? You left so abruptly last night. And have you seen my Langer bat? I can't for the life of me—'

'We need to speak to your brother and his associates, with some urgency,' Gary says, all business.

'My brother? He died years back.'

'He means Uncle Daniel,' I explain.

'Oh. He's an in-law. Came as a package with my wife, like the extra channels on Foxtel you don't want but have to pay for.'

Now I laugh for real, surprised at my uncle's take on the family. Uncle Roland sees the positive in everyone, turns negative situations into learning experiences. Maybe he's withheld a few honest opinions.

'Do you know where Daniel is?' Gary asks.

'Sure.'

It can't be this easy. 'Where?' I blurt before Gary.

'Janice went to meet him. She left about a half hour ago, at most. That's why I'm cleaning the car, not much else to do.'

'Uncle Roland, *where* is she meeting him?'

'The lighthouse.'

'Lighthouse?'

'Up at Cape Naturaliste. It's at least a forty, fifty-minute drive. Do you want me to call, see if they'll be staying around?'

'No!' my wife and I yell at the same time.

'We'd appreciate if you allow us to talk to Daniel without him expecting us,' Gary offers. 'It's a sensitive matter. We don't want to make it worse.'

'No problem.' My uncle steps towards me, pats me on the shoulder with his free hand. 'Terribly sorry if he's done something to you.'

'It's not your fault,' I say, though I wonder why he thinks Uncle Daniel has done something to me.

'What kind of car does your wife drive?' Gary asks.

'She's still got the Kluger. Comes in handy when we've got all the rellies over.'

'Colour?'

'Red, of course. Like her favourite wine.'

'Thank you, sir. You've been a big help,' Gary says, as if he wouldn't look up the license.

'No problem. Again.'

'And be careful with that vacuum.'

Uncle Roland chuckles, retreating into the house. He closes the door, obviously not intending to return to his car in a hurry. Maybe the cricket's starting. I hope he isn't ringing Aunty Janice. If it was me, though, and I knew the police were looking for my wife and her brother, I'd call. I'd warn her. I wouldn't be able to help it.

'Should we ring Busselton police?' I ask as we strap into Gary's car.

'Nah. The lighthouse's almost the same distance from them.'

'We're going for the glory, then?'

'Sounds about right. Maybe I can get a double-promotion.'

'Or piss off the Busselton crew.'

'That too.'

Gary swings the car around, tearing off. A cloud of red dust swirls in the air, heading for Uncle Roland's open car door. Something extra to keep him occupied.

Soon we're on Caves Road, beginning the long, winding journey along the coast, just far enough inland that it appears we're still in the middle of a forest. The drive is silent to start, leaving me with too many thoughts.

Lucy leans over from the back, squeezing my arm. For some reason, I sat at the front with Gary. I wish I could shuffle back there now, be with her. I hope she doesn't feel like the accessory we're treating her as. A few messages are pinging on her phone, keeping her occupied. If it's school, they should have a relief teacher to cover her class tomorrow. Too bad if they don't.

'When you found my phone,' I say, desperate to break the silence, 'was anyone at the cottage?'

Gary shakes his head. 'Empty.'

'Were the boxes still upstairs?'

'It looked like they'd tried to take a couple apart, then abandoned them.'

'Are they servers?'

'Whatever they are, they're beyond my limited technological knowledge. As I said, we've got some IT guys coming from Perth. They'll be here tomorrow, then it's out of my hands.'

'You have no idea what—'

'One of the younger lads reckons it could be a setup for a VPN hub or hosting or something like that. Some illegal online network. But I don't want to speculate.'

VPN or hosting? Illegal network? Something that seems way beyond the capability of my uncle and his mates; though I guess anyone could be a prodigy with technology.

'There's one thing we know,' Gary continues. 'The cottage itself, the property, is registered to David Herbert.'

'Daniel's brother?'

'He bought a struggling B&B a while back, closed it down. We'll have to wait for some other offices to open tomorrow. They'll give us a bigger picture of what's been going on. Sunday's the worst day for all this to happen.'

'I take it Uncle Daniel and his crew aren't at Uncle David's house?'

'*David* isn't at David's house. Your family's disappearing, Henry.'

Gary leaves it at that as the traffic thickens. We queue at a turnoff. I glance over at an old timber building that looks like a church in disguise. Its car park is full, people milling about with their families, all smiles and a happiness I can't fathom. We turn left onto Cape Naturaliste Road, wind our way around a changing landscape. Tall trees give way to coastal scrub, clay soil mixing with white sand to create every colour in-between. We pass a brewery. I almost ask Gary to turn at its entrance. God, I could do with a beer. But my family is on the lam, and an old woman's life could be at stake, so the reason I need a beer is the same reason I can't have one yet.

We're prompted onward by the signage, reach the car park for the lighthouse, follow the one-way traffic. There are a few spots free, but Gary wants to get closer, searching for a loading bay. We round a corner and he slams on the brake as a young child runs across the road, just missing the bonnet. A father chases after him, grabs his arm. He shrugs at us as if to say, *Well, what can you do?*

Watch your kid. Hold his hand. That's what you can do.

'Shit,' Gary mumbles.

'I know, right,' I reply.

'No.' He jabs a finger at something further ahead of us.

Lucy unclips her seatbelt and leans forward. 'Oh, please don't let that be for our thing.'

I can't respond, can only stare in disbelief.

An ambulance is pulled up on the footpath.

CHAPTER TWENTY-FOUR
IT'S JUST A PLAQUE

People are milling about the ambulance, having a look. Nobody of notable authority is near it.

'Should be someone here,' Gary mumbles.

A fence runs across the property, filtering visitors towards a small, whitewashed building. We enter, hurry across dark timber floorboards. Gary flashes his credentials to a man standing behind a counter and we're instantly waived through.

'Do you have a photo of your uncle?' Gary asks.

I shake my head.

'Let's just be on the lookout, then. If it's Leonie with the ambos, he might still be here.'

We rush along a path to another limestone-wash building, now a café. We round it, see more people gathering on a grassed area. They part enough to provide a glimpse of a stretcher, but I can't see who's on it. Gary uses a deeper-pitched voice to clear the way, reaching two ambulance officers. They've got a mask on their patient. It's a woman. Her eyes keep fluttering open, then closing.

She looks so much like Leonie, but it's not her.

'We're running some tests,' one officer tells Gary. 'Don't have the full story. People said she just collapsed.'

Gary helps clear a path, leading them to the awaiting ambulance.

Lucy leans in, hugs me. 'That means Leonie's still safe.'

'We don't know that.'

She sighs. 'It helps to believe it.' She nods towards the lighthouse. 'Should we go for a walk? Maybe they're with some more tourists.'

The lighthouse is in the distance, a white-walled tower complementing the smaller buildings. Several tourists are coming down its sloped path, turning to take photos. Posing, pretending to hold the lighthouse in the palm of their hand. Oblivious to a woman needing medical attention a hundred metres away. Would they pay attention if another woman was near them needing help?

'I don't understand this,' I say.

'What do you mean?'

'If you abduct someone, would you bring them to a public place like this? Somewhere where lots of people can remember you? Identify you? Somewhere the person you've abducted might call out for help?'

Lucy shrugs.

'He took me to a cottage hidden away in the forest. Why not somewhere else like that?'

Gary returns, panting. 'Too much time's gone. Call your aunt.'

'You sure?'

The ambulance lets off a series of shrill sirens, an attempt to move people out the way. Gary's right. That woman's receiving the help she needs, but Leonie might be out there, injured or worse, needing immediate attention.

I grab my phone, call Aunty Janice. She picks up on the second ring.

'Aunty Janice? It's Henry.'

I hear her let out a tremendous sigh. 'Oh, Henry, where have you been? I was so worried about you. You disappeared last night and...'

Her voice becomes fuzzy, my mind swimming. I put a finger to my free ear, block it, release it. On the line, I can hear an ambulance beginning its hurried siren. I rest the phone against my shoulder. There's the same sound near me. I listen to the call again.

'...and I hope Aunt Gertie's sausages didn't make you throw up. I told her not to keep leaving meat out on the bench all day, but—'

'Aunty Janice,' I snap, 'where are you?'

'Having a Devonshire tea at the lighthouse. Where are you?'

'Close by.'

I hang up the call. Start running.

There are tables outside the café. Aunty Janice isn't at any of them. I burst inside, my feet thumping against the old floorboards. A barista lets out a startled *Woah*. I check several small rooms on my right. Everyone's a stranger.

'Here?' Lucy yells.

There's a thin passageway on the other side, branching off the main area. We hurry down it, turn right and reach a large sitting room with a disused fireplace.

Aunty Janice is here.

She's not alone.

I fight to catch my breath, straighten my clothes, and saunter over as if I hadn't just run the most panic-stricken dash of my life.

Aunty Janice catches sight of us. 'Henry! You weren't kidding when you said you were close! And Lucy, how are you, dear?' She gets out of her chair, brushes past me and walks straight to my wife. She grabs Lucy by the arms, appraises her, then brings her in for a hug. 'It's been so long. Henry didn't tell me you were coming down today.'

'I moved things around,' Lucy says, trying her best to smile despite the situation. 'Who's your friend?'

Gary thumps into the room.

Aunty Janice stiffens, then turns to her table, waving us to some empty seats. 'Everyone, this is—'

'Leonie Haynes,' I interrupt.

'Oh, you've met each other?'

'We have.'

Leonie rises. She offers my wife a hand to shake. 'That young man bought me an ice-cream.'

I glance at the skin on her arms, her face, scanning for bruises, for any signs of a struggle or abuse. Her voice is a little slurred, but she might just be tired.

'How did you get here?' I ask, unable to fathom that Leonie's in front of us after the awful fates I'd imagined.

Leonie shakes Gary's hand instead of answering. 'You're a handsome young officer.'

Gary blushes. 'I'm Sergeant Winters, Mrs Haynes. We spoke the other day over the phone. I set up the ice-cream date.'

'Thank you for that. I love ice-cream.'

'Happy to help.'

We find seats. Sit.

I lock my gaze on Aunty Janice. 'How did she get here?'

Aunty Janice eyes Gary's uniform in the same way her husband did. She adjusts her hair, deciding what to say. 'You know what's happened. That's why you've brought the police with you.'

'Then where's Uncle Daniel?'

'He left.'

'Why did he do this?'

Aunty Janice closes her eyes for a long time. When she opens them, she's looking straight at Gary. 'There are so many families, good families, that have that one member, that one person who just messes up. And they keep messing up, no matter what the family does to help them.'

Gary nods, prompting Aunty Janice to keep talking.

'We try to help Daniel. David leant him one of his properties, out in the forest. Free of distractions, so he could get away from that dump he rents with his mates. But his mates followed, and he got more distracted. Now, Daniel can make his own choices, but they showed him another world he hasn't escaped.'

'What's this got to do with Leonie?' I ask, trying to cut the extended version.

'You need to understand, I think he's on the meth or something. I can't prove it, but...'

'What did my uncle do to you?' I ask Leonie, tired of my aunt's stalling.

'He picked me up where you wanted to meet again,' Leonie replies, 'bought me a cookies and cream ice-cream. Wasn't as nice as the one you got me. He said you were waiting in the car. I could see someone in the back, but I couldn't tell for sure, there was sunlight and shadows, and…' She stops, takes a sip from her tea, wipes her lips '…I got in. He locked the doors, started driving.'

'Leonie, you don't have to talk about this again,' Aunty Janice says.

Gary looks around, confirms there's nobody else in the room, then eases forward in his seat. 'Would you both like to come to the station, have a little chat there?'

Aunty Janice shakes her head.

'Then if you're comfortable to talk here, I suggest we get to the point.' He takes his phone out, checks it. Maybe he's recording the conversation?

'The man kept asking if Henry had shown me a photograph,' Leonie says. 'He wouldn't stop. He started swerving on the road. Cars were honking. Then he pulled over. He looked like he was going to… going to…' A tear rolls down Leonie's cheek. 'I had to say, "Henry asked me about Lillian". He perked up after that. Wanted to know everything about her. I told him only what I told Henry. Then I said, "Let me show you something", and I took this photo from my pocket.'

She takes a photograph out now, hands it to me.

'I said, "That's where Lillian is. I'll show it to Henry. Would that make you happy?". And he said it would, but he started crying.'

I look down at the photograph, and it takes a while to understand what I see, to comprehend the finality of it.

'He said he was sorry. So, so sorry. He drove me here, called Janice, left me the second she arrived.'

'You just sat with him?' I ask.

'He wasn't hurting me, but he could have. Best to stay on someone's good side. I've learned that through the families of some foster children.'

Gary and Lucy both look at the photograph in my shaking hand.

'The plaque in this photo,' I squeak out, 'where is it?'

'In Perth. Karrakatta Cemetery.' Leonie reaches over, taps the picture. 'You're wondering about the surname. It's what I told your uncle. It says Lillian Satler, but that's my Lillian. She married young, then changed her name to escape her bastard of a husband. Named herself after that scientist in Jurassic Park. She always wanted to be a palaeontologist. Wanted to dig up fossils.'

The air is becoming unbearably hot, the room swirling. 'So, you're saying Lillian's dead?'

'It's just a plaque. I reported her missing a few years back…' She stares at Gary. 'Surely you knew this? They never found her body. Never gave me closure. But she always said she wanted to be buried there, up in Perth. I honoured her the start of this year. I have a friend who works at Karrakatta.'

'But she might be alive?' I ask.

Leonie's grim face says enough, but she explains, 'When they reached eighteen, Lillian and Tiffany moved out together. My two foster girls, looking after each other. At least once a week, they would call. Then, when Lillian married, they would both write, at least once a month. Or call. Or come and see me. But Lillian just stopped one day. Tiffany still writes. She's travelling, you see.

But she doesn't know what happened, either. I think Lillian's husband… well, that man's in jail for other things, now. I've learned to let her go. Lillian's happy, resting in peace.'

'She disappeared. It doesn't mean she's dead.' I look to Lucy for support. Doesn't Leonie understand? The air's shifted, every breath difficult. I try to stare at Aunty Janice again. There's two of her now. 'What's your involvement in this?'

Aunty Janice fidgets with her teacup. 'I'm just righting Daniel's wrong. It's the meth. He sees a photograph and hears a name; he thinks it's connected to something he did in the past. He fixates on it. He assaulted someone once, you know. On the mines. One of the female workers. Got some jail time for it. Since then, he thinks everyone's out to get him, out to prove he's hurt other people.'

'Oh, boo-hoo,' I say, my aching body reminding me just how innocent Uncle Daniel is. 'Maybe he's freaking out because it's connected to something else he did?'

'No!'

'You sure about that?'

Aunty Janice sighs.

I look to Gary. He nods, typing something on his phone. I hand the photograph back to Leonie. 'Did you get a good look at the other person in the car? The one you thought was me?'

Leonie stares at Aunty Janice for a while. Is she doubtful of the woman's explanation, too? 'Yes. Not like you, once I saw him in the light. Little guy. Fat. Well, podgy.'

I glare at Aunty Janice. 'I know who she's talking about, but I don't know his name. How about you? Do you know Uncle Daniel's mates?'

She nods. 'Has to be Ian Campbell. Lives back in Margs.'

Gary produces a card, hands it to Aunty Janice. 'Call us or use this link to make your statement. Busselton Police are coming to get Mrs Haynes.'

'You want me to go?'

'Can you get your brother to come to the station?'

'It'll be hard to reach him for a while.'

'Then you've done all you can to help, and I appreciate it.'

Aunty Janice's face sours a little, then she stretches out a smile. 'No problem.' She rises from her chair. 'Talk to me soon about the funeral, Henry. When you're done with all of... this.'

As if the abduction of a woman is a mild inconvenience. As if her brother hasn't marked himself as someone who desperately needs to be detained. Someone who desperately needs help.

'She'll call him, won't she,' Lucy says the second Aunty Janice leaves the room.

We all nod.

'We should have taken her phone,' I say, 'pretended to be her and got Uncle Daniel to meet us somewhere.'

Gary points to his uniform. 'Got to think of more law-abiding ways, Henry. Don't worry, they'll find him soon.'

'Do you think they sell ice-creams here?' Leonie cuts in, reaching out and prying her photograph from my fingers.

'I'll see,' I offer.

As if ice-cream will make her forget everything that's just happened.

As if it were that easy.

CHAPTER TWENTY-FIVE
HIDDEN THINGS

With Mrs Haynes safe, escorted home by the two officers, Gary drives us back to Margaret River. Along the way, he fields call after call: a complaint from someone at the Busselton station, an alert for Uncle Daniel and Ian Campbell, the disappearance of a farmer who just up and left his young family. Gary deals with each call with an admiral professionalism. Until ending the last call and slamming his phone into a cup holder.

I lean against Lucy, enjoying our space on the back seat. 'Careful,' I say. 'One knock and you crack the screen. It's how they get you.'

Gary grunts something in response.

'Before you blame me for everything, remember I've barely seen this side of my family for fifteen years. Not my fault there's a psycho in the bunch.'

Lucy squeezes my hand.

'Besides,' I continue, 'I asked you to find out about Lillian and she's a missing person who could be dead. How did you not know that?'

Gary sighs. 'I'm sorry. I quickly found what I could on Charlotte Harris, based on her car crash. My focus was on her. Then I got a connection to Lillian. I didn't even know if it was the right Lillian, but I thought Mrs Haynes would tell you more, let you decide.'

'That's bullshit.'

'The one file I could access at the time was on Lillian's birth. It was a start. I was going to apply for more information, but I've been in the shit all weekend and I'm sorry but it's because of your fucking family!'

Gary honks at a driver ahead, who sees the police vehicle, slows to the speed limit. Gary keeps honking. The driver pulls to the siding, then we fly past.

'Tell me why you left the force, Henry. Be honest.'

'You think it's cause they found out I'm as crazy as the rest of my family?'

Gary shakes his head. 'I could look it up, though.'

'Oh, *that* you'll look up,' I snap.

'He didn't like the way a case panned out,' Lucy offers, before I make things worse.

'We've all been there,' Gary says.

'Plus, he saw the inside of a hospital twice in six months.'

'The first time, beaten after attending a domestic disturbance,' I add, since Lucy shouldn't have to tell this. 'The second time, a drug bust at a tattoo parlour that went south. A child was involved.'

Gary winces. 'I'm sorry.'

'Well, I shouldn't have been there. I acted of my own accord, and because of that they threw the case. So, I vowed to help people differently.'

'Is that what led you into teaching?' Gary asks.

'You could say that. But I quit because I wasn't making a difference there, either. You can help shape kids to reach for the stars, but lots of parents are great at squashing dreams. I'm in retail now.'

'You're helping people by selling them stuff?'

Lucy stares daggers at me. She'd said something similar the other day. Sure, selling electronics is a far less noble cause, but at least I'm alive, free from stress. Well, until this trip.

We travel in silence for a few minutes. Then Gary glances at my wife in the rear-view mirror, says, 'Did I ever tell you the time Henry thought he was Mr Hot Stuff, and he tried to ask Lauren McHale out while class was in the library, only he—'

'Stop right there!' I yell.

'He farted as he got close to her!'

'I said stop!'

'And he kept on walking, right behind a stack of books, except there was this other guy near her named Freddie, and he copped the blame. Cause of that, he forever became known as Farting Freddie.'

'Please have mercy!'

'I'm mean, it's perfect. Farting Freddie.'

'Did you ever ask this Lauren McHale out?' Lucy says.

'That's what you got from the story?' I ask. 'No, she didn't even know I existed.'

We all burst out laughing. Gary shares more stories and I let him, thankful he's trying to lighten the mood. Plus, he's unlocking more memories I'd repressed. I'm even starting to remember stories that involve him. Soon it becomes a back-and-forth of embarrassment, tales to block out the possible, forthcoming tragedy.

Before I know it, the sky has darkened, helped along by the increasing canopy size of the trees, and we're pulling up to the studio's entrance.

I shuffle forward. 'Why are we here?'

'I've tasked other officers with finding your uncle. They have his friend's details. They'll sort that out, too.'

'But I thought we were going to—'

'Get some rest, Henry. Enjoy some time with your lovely wife. I'll call you first thing tomorrow, give you an update. Unless you've got an update for me first.'

Lucy leads me out of the vehicle. I turn to wave goodbye, still stunned. I thought we were going to chase my uncle down, have the pleasure of arresting him. Without that, I feel robbed.

Gary drives away before I can object.

'Let's go inside,' my wife says, catching me eying our cars.

'We have to get him.'

'No, we don't. Trust the police.'

I almost say I don't, almost mention how my uncle has evaded them for over a day now. For *years*, with his operation in the cottage. But when I was an officer, there were times people didn't think they could trust me to protect them, to solve their case. They weren't afraid to tell me. It was awful. Lucy is right. I need to trust that they'll try their best.

Unfortunately, I don't leave my frustration at the studio door, and it doesn't take long to say something stupid, triggering memories of the fight Lucy and I had before I left.

'Don't spoil this place,' Lucy says, trying to resist.

'Spoil this place? I'm *hiding* here.'

'You've got *me* now.'

'Which is why I want to talk about our fight, or else it'll be hanging over us this whole trip. I want to get it over with, then see if you want another dance with me.'

My wife sighs, sinks back against the couch. 'Fine. Do we start with how you said I'm never around?'

I wince. Shit, I did say that.

'You know why I'm busy. You were a teacher, too. There are times of the year I'm consumed by planning and marking and report writing and the ten thousand other things a teacher needs to do. You of all people know we don't get to have the holidays everyone thinks we get.'

I nod.

'And?'

'I get it.'

'And?'

'I appreciate the time you are around. And I guess...' I sit beside her. 'I guess I feel guilty, because that was the both of us, and it didn't matter as much, and now it's just you. You're overworked and I can see it more clearly, and—'

'I've never blamed you for quitting your job. You've got to stop thinking I do. Most teachers don't even last five years. You gave it ten.'

'Almost ten. But the cash flow…'

'I don't know why we argue about that. We're fine for money. Two incomes, no kids. We're not exactly broke.' Lucy reaches over, grabs my hand. 'I just wish you were doing something you wanted to do. Something you're passionate about. Every job you've taken, it's helping other people. And I love that, but you need to let other people help you, too. Most of all, me.'

'Have we finally cracked the secret of marriage?'

'Fifteen years? We've made something work.' Lucy smiles. 'You know, watching you work with Gary today… It focused you.' I start to object, but she adds, 'Maybe we can talk about all this stuff on the table, see if it means anything?'

I glance at the stereo. 'How about that dance first?'

'An actual dance?'

'An actual dance.'

We get up, and I lead her over to the stereo unit. I put my uncle's CD back on. A slow melody wafts through the studio, mumbles of a whiskey river. We dance in a waltz-like pattern, taking turns to lead each other, stumbling around the room in no real rhythm. Enjoying the moment, the heat of our conversation dissipating.

'This isn't the most romantic song,' she whispers.

'I don't know what it is.'

She lets me go, wanders over to her phone, asks the virtual assistant to tell us what we're listening to. I'm about to say it won't work, the internet's lousy, when a robotic voice answers: *Willie Nelson, Whiskey River.*

She walks back over, waving her phone. 'I think the guy's drowning memories of someone in whiskey. You going to do that for me?'

'Depends. Are we finished fighting?'

My wife nods. 'We're just sorting issues out. Round One. You've got to stop thinking it means I don't love you. Or want you. Now, did your uncle like whiskey?'

'Are you kidding me? He loved the stuff. It's an item on the table over there. The distillery's just down the road.'

'Should we go there, get some for ourselves? For research?'

'I wouldn't appreciate the complexities.'

'You'd miss the subtle aromas?'

'It'd just burn my throat.'

The next song comes on. A country tune. I don't know how to move my body to its backbeat. Lucy starts to boot scoot, her limbs exaggerating every movement, then stops with a wide grin that morphs into a look of concern.

'Is this what your uncle listened to?'

'I have no idea.'

'What's next?'

We skip to a reggae-style beat, a completely different song compared to the last two. They're singing about police and thieves. Does that mean anything? My wife's already looking up the artist.

I have an idea. I fetch my notepad and pen, write the search results, our dancing forgotten. After about thirty-five patient minutes, we have the tracklist for my uncle's CD:

Whiskey River - Willie Nelson
Are You Sure Hank Done It This Way - Waylon Jennings
Police & Thieves - Junior Murvin
Something On Your Mind - Karen Dalton
Have You Seen Her - The Chi-Lites
Poncho and Lefty - Townes Van Zandt
A Song For You - Donny Hathaway
Jealousy - Queen
The Payback - James Brown
The Kiss - Judee Sill
Famous Blue Raincoat - Leonard Cohen
Wild Horses - The Rolling Stones
When the Levee Breaks - Led Zeppelin
Born to Run - Bruce Springsteen
Dreams - Fleetwood Mac
Baby's On Fire - Brian Eno
Into the Mystic - Van Morrison
Darkness On The Edge Of Town - Bruce Springsteen

'Interesting choices,' my wife says. 'They can't be for his wake, can they? Wouldn't it be cool if they were all part of a message?'

'I thought the same thing.'

'And?'

'The typewriter had one half of a photo taped in it,' I say, 'and a framed bill had the other half behind it.'

'So, your uncle's definitely hidden things within other items?'

'But these songs make no sense. They're so different. I can't put it together.'

Lucy's already looking over at the coffee table. 'Then maybe we should both try.'

'Found something!' Lucy jumps from the couch, waving the Robotham book. 'Page one hundred and ninety-nine. Near the bottom. Someone's written the word *mammoth*. Is it your uncle's handwriting?'

'Could be.'

'Does the page number mean anything to you?'

'We've never had a house with that number. My badge number was nowhere near that. Maybe it's related to some high-scoring sport like bowling?'

'Is it related to your uncle, or your mum, or your dad, or—'

'Wait. Turn to page three.'

I drop beside my wife, peering at the book. Page three is full of the story, nothing more. I grab the photo albums, turn to the third page of each one. No extra wording, no clues in the photographs. I look at the tracklist for my uncle's CD. Mammoth police and thieves? No, can't be right.

'Why three?' Lucy asks.

'I just thought, in line with everything else... If you put it together with one nine-nine...' I grab the other book, the one about ghosts, flick through the pages '...you get nineteen ninety-three. The year Michael Jordan's Bulls won their first three-peat championship.'

'Basketball?'

'And the year my dad died. Charlotte, too.'

'Oh.'

'And the year Lillian was born.'

'Your uncle knew you'd make a connection?'

'I think he expected me to, yeah.'

I hold the ghost book to my wife. The story on page three is about *The Cave Dweller of Jenolan*.

'Jenolan?' Lucy says. 'That's not in WA, is it?'

'No, says here New South Wales. So, the opposite side of the country. But notice how someone's underlined the word *cave*?'

My wife gasps. 'Mammoth Cave.'

'Big tourist cave, and it's about fifteen minutes away!'

My wife squeals in delight. 'Hidden things…'

'Caves'll be closed now, though. So… keep dancing?'

Lucy looks to the bed. 'Yeah. Keep dancing.'

CHAPTER TWENTY-SIX
A FINAL FUCK YOU

Lucy's car is the second to enter the cave's gravel-lined parking area. The morning air is crisp, slivers of sunlight trying to find their way through skyscraper-sized trees. As we exit the car, rays fall on my wife's head, highlighting the blend of shades in her hair. Black, brown, red. She catches me smiling at the sight.

'What?'

'Nothing.' I lock the car. Maybe it's the break from the routine of our city life, the lingering effect of resolving part of our argument, or the spark of excitement at discovering my uncle's clues—whatever the reason, it's reignited a spark we've let the pressures of life smoulder. 'You hear that?'

I'd expected a symphony of sounds: bird calls, insect chirps, distant traffic. But it's almost silent, the thick forest a buffer to everything.

'Ominous,' Lucy says, taking my hand.

We follow signs to a dark timber boardwalk overhanging scrub. A woman in khaki clothing is putting a noticeboard up.

She sees us and smiles, welcomes us, then says the tours don't start for another forty minutes. She leads us to a kiosk, offers a self-guided tour if we're interested.

'Self-guided?'

The woman points to a rack of headphones and black boxes. 'You put the station on, it'll tell you to stop at certain points and give you all you need to know.'

We pay for the right to be led by a recording, fix the equipment around ourselves, and continue along the boardwalk. At the mouth of the cave, stalactites hang onto an arcing limestone wall, creating the outline of a shark's gaping jaw. Maybe they should have called it Megalodon Cave.

I leave the headphones hanging around my neck, ready to focus on what Uncle Graham may have seen and heard. Lucy disappears into the mouth, the darkness shifting as I follow. We reach a wall of metal bars, step through an open gap, and enter the chamber. I instantly remember why this cave earned its namesake and not something else. It's enormous. The illuminated pathway arcs around the remains of a bed of water, the ceiling extending as far as the eye can see. Stalactites hang like chandeliers, lighting drawing our gaze. Further within the cave are rocks the size of houses.

Presenting one enormous area to explore.

And I don't really know what I'm looking for. Would Uncle Graham have scrawled a clue on a rock wall, painted something on a stalagmite? A message, or arrows pointing the way to our next discovery? There are already so many places that disappear from public view. Gaps in fallen rocks, tunnels and crevices leading into darkness. We can't look in any of these, the boardwalk restricting our exploration.

'Let's try up here,' Lucy calls out, reaching the first of multiple landings on a staircase that climbs the rock floor.

On a landing, there's a pedestal with a salt crystal atop, pulsing orange. It's fixed in, no messages around it. Down another platform, there's a glass cabinet housing remnants of megafauna discovered in the cave. All designed to lure a tourist's eye. Not where Uncle Graham would have left something for my eyes only.

'Keep going,' I urge.

We continue through the cave, taking its winding, wooden path. We walk at least two city-sized blocks, then the scenery changes. The path turns to concrete, the air dropping at least five degrees in temperature. On each side of the pathway, the cave floor is black. Ashen remains of a dry riverbed. We slide around a large rock jutting onto the path, then it's a short walk and the light changes to an external source. Sunlight. We've reached the end.

That can't be it.

'Are you coming out?' Lucy calls, starting up another set of stairs. So many stairs, so many knife-like stabs into my muscles.

The cave floor has strips of moss here, sunlight providing life. I join my wife up the staircase and hear more life. A loud buzz I first mistake to be cars. Lucy points to long black hives hanging off high cliff walls. Bees. Native ones, the kind that don't sting.

'I don't get it,' I call out as we reach the top, come to a black gate. 'We found the clues, we put them together, and it led us to nothing.'

We open the gate, pass through it, then hurry across a major road, re-entering a forest trail.

'There's two tracks to take,' Lucy says. 'Should we look down these?'

'No. We're done here. Maybe something else was highlighted in those books. Maybe we only saw part of the message and jumped on it straight away.' I shake my head. 'We wasted our time.'

'We had to try.'

Not for the first time, I wonder if Uncle Graham crafted all of this to torment me, a final *fuck you* for seeing him so little; a game designed to have me running round in circles for weeks, months, years, causing hurt and confusion while he's resting in his grave.

That's not Uncle Graham, though. He wouldn't have written a different list for me if it wasn't for a purpose. He wouldn't have phoned before he died if he didn't want to pique my curiosity.

We travel in silence for a while, exit the forest trail near the tourist kiosk. A bus has pulled up, several families exiting, excitement plastered across their faces, cameras at the ready. We go back to the kiosk, return our devices. Then I return to the car, sit behind the steering wheel, slump against its surface.

What do we do now? Go back to the studio, look through all the list items again, rearrange them until the real message magically appears?

'We can always come back,' Lucy says, 'when we know what's going on.'

'If we ever know.'

'Well, who might tell us?'

'I think everyone knows more than they're saying.'

'Can we access any old newspapers that might've reported on Lillian or Charlotte?'

'I wouldn't know where to start.'

'I'm sure you do. You don't have any dates?'

'Gary gave me a file.' I thump the dash. 'I left it back in the studio.'

My phone starts ringing. It's Gary. I answer it, turn on the speaker function.

'I literally just mentioned you,' I say.

There's a lot of background noise on the line. A long rustle.

'You there, Henry?'

'I'm here. I was just telling Lucy about the file you gave me.'

'Ah. Sorry, where are you?'

'Mammoth Cave.'

'We've got a situation.'

I look at Lucy. Her eyes widen. 'Go on.'

'I can't officially involve you. Yet. Can you wait at the station?'

'What about the studio? We're in Lucy's car now, but I don't want to risk being seen. My uncle and his mates—'

'You don't need to worry about that.'

'What do you mean?'

'This concerns your uncle. We've found him. And the friend, Ian Campbell.'

We can hear someone shouting for Gary. There's another rustle over the line, voices smothered. I'm as wide-eyed as my wife now. I sense how this conversation's playing out, can all but predict the next line to leave Gary's lips. When he returns to the call, his voice echoes through the car.

'Someone has beaten them, Henry. Real bad.'

CHAPTER TWENTY-SEVEN
BRIEF BUT IMPRESSIVE

I can't help but let the phrase, *This changes everything*, creep into my mind again. I do everything to hold off blurting it. Instead, I say, 'Meet us at the café near your station. Wasabi-coloured walls.'

'Yep, I know the place. Give me twenty.'

Gary ends the call. Lucy and I stare at each other. She needs to speak first because I don't know what I'll say. Part of me shudders at the thought of someone having beaten my uncle and his friend. The other part wants to shake their hand.

We drive to the café. Lucy allows me my silence, waiting for carefully chosen words to emerge. I manage to jag a parking spot just up from the building. We wait outside for a moment, head in when it's clear Gary's still on the way. Last time I came here, I broke down outside. I can't say my mindset's improved. Thankfully, the breakfast rush has passed, just a few people sipping coffee. We're greeted by the same woman who'd served me the other day. She flashes a spark of recognition but says nothing. I almost turn back, eager to suggest we try elsewhere.

I just wanted to avoid the police station, hoping Gary will tell me more than he officially should, hoping he doesn't get in trouble for talking to me, at all.

'You just want a coffee?' Lucy asks, grabbing a seat.

'I guess so.'

She goes to the counter, orders for us. 'I got us a muffin, too,' she says, returning with a numbered wooden spoon. 'Got to have something to nibble on while we wait.'

She puts the spoon in a blue tin full of knives and forks, waits for me to respond.

'I don't know how to feel about all this,' I admit.

Lucy holds my hand, doesn't reply until after the coffees arrive. 'I don't think it's a positive. Your Uncle Daniel was a potential link to everything, and now someone's silenced him. I've read enough Jack Reacher novels to know that's usually a bad thing.'

'I know, but... He had me beaten. He abducted me and an old lady. Whatever happened, it was comeuppance.'

Lucy takes her cup, turns it in her hands, staring at the liquid within. 'Who do you think did it, then?'

I shrug. 'No idea. He's half the size of his mates, but he bosses them all around.'

'Maybe one of them had enough?'

'Lynden? The one I introduced to a cricket bat.'

'Won't he turn up in hospital?'

'He's like the Hulk. The Hulk doesn't need a hospital.'

'Even the Hulk's human sometimes.'

My wife, full of wit, knowing just what to say. We hold hands again, smiling despite the news. We keep holding hands, sipping coffee, until Gary turns up. He looks like he's had about three hours of sleep. Maximum. He waves us to the tables outside, ordering another round of drinks.

'Had to make a few calls,' Gary says, 'then fill up the car. Lot of driving in the last few days. Not great when petrol prices are skyrocketing.'

We sit on hard metal chairs, the sole group outside.

'Will my uncle make it?' I ask, straight to business.

'Not for me to say. It's up to the medical staff now.'

'But what do you think?'

'It's not good.'

'Does anyone else in the family know?'

'You're the first. But someone will be phoning listed contacts.'

'How was he beaten?'

'Again, too soon to say for sure. Some kind of blunt weapon. Worked the body all over.'

'Where were they?'

'Vacant lot in a housing estate, near Ian Campbell's house. A dog walker discovered them.' Gary sighs. 'This entire case... Look, I filed a report on what your uncle and his mates did to you. Someone might conjure a connection, make you a suspect. That's why I wanted to see you first. Don't worry, if I thought you did it, I wouldn't have given you all this information.'

Gary did suggest meeting at the station, though. Maybe he has his doubts. I would, too.

I sigh, figuring it out. 'They'll make a connection because of the blunt weapon. It was something like a bat, wasn't it?'

Gary nods.

Our new round of coffee is brought out. I can't hold mine up to my lips, my arms trembling. 'Did you find Lynden?'

'Not yet,' Gary says. 'No check-ins to any local medical centres.'

'And Reg?'

'We don't have enough to warrant a search for him, too.'

'My mother's meeting Aunty Janice for lunch at Voyager Estate today, around noonish. Maybe they'll think I'll make an appearance, too.'

'I'll make a note of it.'

'Did anyone find Uncle David yet?'

'Still hasn't returned home. We have an officer watching there, more watching and working at the cottage. As I've said before, your family's keeping us busy.'

'And the tech at the cottage? Any more on that?'

'Haven't heard from the team. Give them time.'

'But what if it's related? Like, my uncle was doing something illegal for someone and the police started shutting things down, so they were pissed. Beat someone to death kind of pissed.'

'Makes sense,' Lucy says.

Gary nods. 'I'll make a call, check it's a priority to trace who owns the gear.'

I manage to sip some coffee. 'Are you going to get in trouble for talking to me?'

Gary shrugs.

'Then why are you doing this? Just because we went to high school together?'

'Hey, we've got to look out for survivors.'

'Seriously?'

Gary chuckles. 'I got round to looking up your record. The longer version. Still brief, but impressive.'

'Brief but impressive.' I wink at Lucy. 'Story of my life.'

Lucy rolls her eyes.

'I doubt everything was glowing,' I say.

Gary shakes his head. 'Seems you drifted off duty a couple of times to continue pursuing leads.'

'I followed my instinct, made two major drug busts. Would have made a third.'

'Punching above your rank, disobeying your superiors.'

'And you want me on your team?'

'You'd fit right in.'

'Or you'd fire me within a week.'

We stare at each other for a while, a silent showdown, until Gary flutters a smile.

'Do you think they'll come for me?' I ask. 'Whoever got my uncle.'

'Depends what the angle is. If it's because of the cottage tech… Maybe, since you alerted us to it.'

'Great.' Lucy matches my frown. 'Maybe we should head back to the studio, keep safe? Or go back to Perth?'

I shrug. 'If it's not about the cottage, then it's about the photo. Maybe someone else is asking about it?'

'That doesn't seem as likely,' Gary says.

'Could we contact Busselton Police again, get them to watch Mrs Haynes? Just in case.'

'They're not so hot about me at the moment.'

I dig my phone out. 'Well, I could call her. I have the texts she sent when my uncle pretended to be me.'

I bring up the text chain.

I need to tell you more about
Lillian.

'Shit.'

I'm an idiot.

'What is it?' Lucy asks.

'We were so worried about Uncle Daniel doing something to Leonie, we glossed over her initial message.'

I show them my screen.

'Maybe she'd planned to show you the picture from the cemetery?' Lucy tries.

I type a new message:

> *Hi, Mrs Haynes, I would really like to hear about Lillian. I'd like to know about the person she was. Call me on this number, please.*

We wait, finishing our coffee. Gary answers some one-sided calls. As he walks a few metres away to fan another fire, my mobile pings.

> *What ice-cream did you buy me?*

I smile. It's good to see Leonie's being cautious.

> *Mint chocolate chip. In a cup.*

Ten seconds later, my phone rings.

'I've got a couple of days off,' Leonie says. 'Doctor's made me take stress leave. I tried to explain I'm a volunteer. They said I should volunteer to have some time off. They can try to stop me.'

I offer an apology for what my uncle did to her, which she dismisses, saying that we can't pick our family. I try to ask why she messaged me before, what she wanted to tell me about Lillian, when she says something odd.

'Your aunt, Janice, she was a lot nicer this time around.'

'Excuse me?'

'I mean, it was a long time ago.'

Gary sits back down as I ask, 'You've met her before?'

'Oh yes, took a while to remember. My brain's not a hundred per cent these days. She didn't mention it, either.'

My hand is shaking so much I put the phone on the table, turn on its speaker function. 'How long ago did you meet Aunty Janice?' I say, looking from Lucy to Gary.

'About six months after Lillian was born. She tried to offer me money to look after the baby.'

'For you to look after it, or for her to take it off your hands?'

'She wasn't clear. She said she was a relative. Relatives aren't supposed to have access unless approved, but it can happen. Sometimes, they piece a few details together. In a place this size, I guess it was pretty easy, even though Lillian's birth was shielded from the media.'

'What did you do?'

'Turned her away. If a child didn't end up with family, there's a good reason. And I wasn't a foster mother for the money. Boy, she was angry. But I asked her if she had a family of her own. She said she was trying, so I said, save the money for your own baby. Never heard from her again, after that.'

'How much money did she offer you?'

'I know it was a lot, but I could be getting it wrong.'

'A rough amount?'

'Twenty, thirty thousand.'

Gary whistles, pulls out his mobile.

'Do you think she remembered you yesterday?' I ask.

'If she did, she hid it well. She was more concerned about her brother.'

I'm too stunned to process what Leonie is telling me. I almost hang up, then remember to ask her why she'd messaged earlier.

'I'm going to make it down for Graham's funeral tomorrow,' she says. 'Perhaps we can talk then?'

'Definitely.'

I thank her for her time, wish her a relaxing recovery, and end the call.

Gary is already standing, swinging a set of car keys around his index finger. 'Your aunt's house?' Before I even nod, he adds, 'If you get a parking fine, I'll waive it. I'm driving.'

CHAPTER TWENTY-EIGHT
RETRO CLASSIC

This time, there's a complete absence of cars outside Aunty Janice's house. It doesn't mean nobody's home—Uncle Roland's car could be parked in the garage—but it might mean Aunty Janice has already left for lunch with my mother.

'You don't have to be with us,' I tell Gary.

'Well, your aunt never provided any more details about the lighthouse incident,' he says, 'so I thought I'd come make a follow-up call.'

'Right.' It's a nice manipulation of his duties, but at least it won't get him in trouble. Unless someone mentions he was with me.

Gary parks the car. The unmistakable sound of heavy metal music shudders out of the house. 'At least someone's home.'

We hurry to the door, knock with a loud thump. It takes a while for someone to answer, the music paused. It's Trent, the son with big city dreams.

'Shit,' he mumbles. 'Hello, officer, how can I, um… How can I help you?'

'Where's your mum, Trent?' I ask.

'Oh. Hi, Uncle Henry.' Trent blinks as if seeing me for the first time, Gary's uniform distracting him. I can already smell a somewhat distinct aroma wafting through the doorway which would explain his red eyes and demeanour.

'Where's Aunty Janice?' I ask again.

'She said she's going to lunch. With your mum.'

'Trent, weren't you supposed to drive my mum down from Perth?'

'Oh, yeah.' He chuckles. 'Someone else volunteered.'

'Is your father home?' Gary asks, before I get into an argument.

'I don't know. He was in his shed before, but I think he stepped out.'

'We need to come in, have a look,' I offer.

'Are you sure?'

'No problem at all, Trent,' Gary says. 'Thanks for offering.' He pushes through the doorway, making Trent step aside.

Trent talks fast, offering us a drink, a snack, asking us to wait in the garden out the back cause the patio's remodelled and it's nice, with a koi pond and everything except there isn't any koi yet just the water.

We're halfway through the house when we hear a sound upstairs. Could be Uncle Roland or Uncle David. We don't waste time, stomping up the staircase, Trent trailing. Lucy's behind us, too, giggling, enjoying Trent's erratic behaviour. He hasn't even asked who she is, and I doubt he'd remember her. We reach the top landing and enter the attic-like room. There's a guy slumped on one of the beanbags, a video game controller in one hand, a smoke in the other. The television's on but muted, a retro classic pulsing against the light. The guy isn't one of my uncles. I've never seen him before. He's as young as Trent, with thin arms and legs covered in tattoos, his black singlet and tight footy shorts leaving room to show off as many designs as possible. As his gaze lifts from the screen, he sees us, tries to smile.

'Oh, hey. Pizza time!'

'It's not the pizza guy, it's the fuzz!' Trent calls out.

'Oh. Oh, shit!' Tattoo guy grinds whatever he was smoking against a metallic ashtray. He brushes his singlet, then runs a hand through his hair.

'Nice tats,' I try. They're not. They're all flash art, no real meaning.

'Cheers,' tattoo guy says.

Trent starts cleaning the room, as if we haven't seen everything.

'Is this part of your degree, Trent?' I ask. 'The effects of drugs on food taste and consumption?'

Trent's face reddens an extra shade. 'I think we should talk outside, on the patio. Please?'

I look at Gary, who nods. 'Sure.'

We wander outside, leaving tattoo guy to continue his game. I wonder what Uncle Ronald would say if he walked into the house, drew in the scent of marijuana. It could be an everyday thing. Maybe Uncle Roland joins in. Or perhaps he just grins and bears it, the way he does to his wife's wine-drinking habits. Since Aunty Janice was so quick to blame her brother's faults on drugs, I'm sure her reaction would far less blasé, unless she's in denial.

'Are you here to arrest me about the… you know…' Trent says, his voice scattered.

'About what?' I say.

'The Mary Jane.'

'No,' Gary answers. 'Not today.'

'Oh, thank God.'

'Where's your dad, Trent?' I ask.

'I thought I already told you.'

'Show us the shed, just in case.'

Trent points to a paved garden path, starts leading us along it.

'Have you heard from Uncle David?' I try.

'Uncle D? No, but I can call him.'

'Will you?'

Trent pauses on the path, tries to work his mobile phone. He unlocks it, then locks it, repeating a weird pattern of button mashing until he finds his contacts. I'm grateful he's baked; he hasn't even asked why we want to talk to his father or Uncle David.

'No one's picking up,' Trent says. 'Ah, it's going to voicemail.'

'Hang up,' Gary says.

We keep wandering along the path.

Trent leans closer to me, whispers, 'Are you sure he's not gonna arrest Logan and me?'

'Logan?'

'My mate up there. He needs the smoke, you know. Keeps him calm. Shit's rough back at his house, his old man's farm's seen better days.'

'Just take us to the shed,' I say, 'then disappear.'

'No problem.'

Gary's mobile pings a few times. He checks it, dropping a few steps behind us. The path turns to a dirt trail, narrowed by overgrown bushes and interspersed trees. We head deeper into the property. I wonder how enormous this place is, how much of the land I've yet to see. As if in response, the path widens into a clearing. Gigantic trees with ghost-white trunks form a ring around a brick shed. I'm pretty sure they're Karri trees. I'm not sure it's a shed, though. It's the size of a granny flat. A home away from home.

Trent points to its open red door. 'If he's not in there, I don't know what else to tell you. The old man doesn't keep me on his calendar lately.'

I thank Trent. He hurries back to the house before Gary can stop him.

I enter the shed first.

'Uncle Roland?'

Nobody answers. I wave Lucy and Gary in. The shed looks like the dream of every testosterone-fuelled Aussie male, a self-made man-cave. A place for Uncle Roland's cricket memorabilia. It smells like oil and wood and sweat combined in calculated quantities. White patches are painted on the brick walls, other areas left exposed. There's a wooden rack to the right of the door, fixed on the wall. Hanging off its hooks are an assortment of hats. There's even an old army helmet, caked in mud. One of the longest walls has windows set at head height, letting minimal sunlight in. I spy a pinball table in one corner of the room, covered in books and rags. There are shelves full of plastic tubs, steel tins and paint palettes. The other long wall has a few framed images: sports scenes, movie posters, a Playboy pinup from an era where modesty was an afterthought. One of the movie posters is for *Back to the Future*. It's not quite the same as Uncle Graham's. It's for the second movie. I don't have time to wonder about the coincidence of two brothers having posters for the same movie trilogy. Lucy's drawing our attention to a large table at the far end.

'Just have a look,' she's saying.

The table's covered in thick cream-coloured paper, paintbrushes, and several tubes of watercolours. I don't understand what I'm supposed to be seeing. Uncle Roland likes to paint in his spare time? Makes him even more normal than the rest of my crazy family.

My wife leads me closer, points at the wall above the table. There's a wire running between two shelves. Photographs and small pieces of card are clipped to the wire. The pieces of card have famous paintings my uncle has tried to copy using various mediums. The photographs are assorted images of different family members.

Lucy taps an image.

It's of Uncle Roland and Aunty Janice. Looking much younger. Sitting at a restaurant. There's a plate of food on the table before them, a waitperson visible in the background.

'Look familiar to you?' Lucy asks.

I stare at the photograph, but I don't understand what she means. It's my aunt and uncle, of course they look familiar. I lean in, examine the surrounding details. Red and green decorations on the background wall, a candle in a vase. On the very edge of the picture, beside Aunty Janice, black curly hair sticks out, belonging to an unknown person sharing the table.

The details hit me at once.

'They knew.' I pull the photograph from the wire. 'Uncle Roland and Aunty Janice both lied to me. They knew about the baby cause they knew about the affair. All this time they've said they didn't know Charlotte, and they'd had dinner with her.'

CHAPTER TWENTY-NINE
I'M A FUCKING IDIOT

'What do we do with this information?' Lucy asks Gary.

He's about to answer when his phone rings. He excuses himself, walks outside the shed.

Lucy asks me the same question. I put a finger to my lips. Gary's saying something about a car accident.

He says *Okay* a lot. Doesn't sound happy.

Lucy takes the photograph from me, snaps a copy on her mobile phone, then puts it back on the wire. 'Can't let your uncle know we've been in here.'

I nod. Lucy's a better teacher than I could ever be, and she'd put more effort into making a better officer. We wait until Gary pops his head in, motioning for us to join him outside.

'Daniel's in an induced coma, from the damage to his head. Ian's faring better. His partner's given us Reg's details, and some officers are out looking for him and the Māori bloke. I've told them to try Voyager Estate.'

'Should we wait here for Uncle Roland, then?'

Gary shakes his head. 'Henry, at the moment, everything I'm allowed to pursue ties to your Uncle Daniel. Now he's in hospital, I'm going to have to dedicate time to other cases. I want to keep running around for you, but my job's on the line if someone reveals what I've been up to.'

'So, unless you find more of my family beaten, this case is paused?'

Gary holds out his hands in mock surrender. 'I know what you're getting at. But I've still got officers out there dotting I's and crossing T's.'

I stare at Gary, waiting for him to say he's joking. He avoids my eye contact, though, and I know he's serious. I shouldn't complain. He's done more than he should have for me. The rest of Margaret River hasn't paused while I've sorted my family shit out. He should get back to looking after locals. Still, I can't help the bitterness rise into my voice. 'Fine, we'll just sort it out ourselves.'

'Your uncle's funeral is in one day, Henry. Just stay safe until then.'

'What about Charlotte and Lillian?'

'I don't have enough to open a case.'

'Sure you do. For a start, my family's lied about knowing them.'

'Families lie, Henry.'

'Lillian's disappeared! Someone allowed Leonie to install a plaque for her at Karrakatta.'

'I'll look deeper into her file when I get a chance.' Gary takes a deep breath, shakes his head again.

'What is it?' I ask.

'Carla just relayed some notes about your father's crash.'

'Maybe now's not the best time,' Lucy says.

'Now's a perfect time,' I snap.

Gary rubs his hands together, considering what to say. 'What did your mother tell you about the accident?'

'That dad overworked himself. He fell asleep at the wheel, drove off the road.'

'He drove off the road, that's for sure. No evidence of foul play, no sign of skid marks or impact from another vehicle. But he wasn't just tired, he was plastered. The coroner identified a BAC of at least point-o-eight. It compromised his tracking, among other things, so when the road changed, started to bend, he didn't adjust.'

'You're saying he had a big day at work, hit the sauce and crashed?'

'I can't confirm what he did before the crash. That's all they gave me, but there'll be a report waiting when I return. If there's anything else, I'll let you know.'

I look to Lucy, Gary, the trees. My vision's blurring, a terrible weight dragging me towards the soil. I resist as much as I can, try to keep upright. 'Why would mum lie to me?' I squeak out.

Lucy squeezes my arm. 'You know why. A crash is a crash. He was already dead, he didn't need his faults.'

Gary points towards the house. 'We can talk in the car if you like. I'll drop you back in town.'

'What about Uncle Roland?'

'He might be gone all day,' Lucy says.

I nod. No point waiting around.

'If you need to speak, you know, to a counsellor...' Gary nudges a rock along the dirt '...I can arrange one.'

I shrug. 'Let's get this trip over with first.'

'Look, I shouldn't have said anything about your father. With the cottage and the funeral… I'll come back later to speak to your aunt and uncle, see if they can help shed more light on Charlotte and everything else.'

I reach out, pat Gary on the shoulder. 'It's okay, mate. Don't bother.'

'It's no bother. I wouldn't have driven you here if I wasn't interested in what the hell is going on with your family. And if you feel like you need protection from them, I can arrange something.'

A smile cracks on my face. A genuine, unforced smile. Given what's just happened, my wife is certain to think I've gone mad. I explain, 'We need to talk to so many people in my family, right? But you need your team to devote time to other cases. So, why run around looking for them today when we already know a time and place they'll be together?'

Lucy slaps her forehead, already understanding. 'The funeral!'

'If you don't arrest them, Uncle David will be there, plus Aunty Janice and Uncle Roland. Maybe even Reg and Lynden, on Uncle Daniel's behalf.'

'All in the one room,' Gary says.

'All in the one room. Thinking I'm on the defensive. Thinking I won't say anything. So, let's plan how we'll take advantage of that on the drive back to town.'

I'm standing outside the IGA supermarket on Bussell Highway, just like I'd done days before. Lucy's gone back inside to buy a bottle of sparkling water she'd forgotten, leaving me with a few bags of shopping in one hand, an iced coffee in the other. I put the shopping down, uncap the coffee and gulp its contents. Enjoying the ability to do so without the lingering threat of Uncle Daniel and his mates rolling up to grab me.

It's like I've pressed the reset button on my trip down south. Sure, I haven't finished writing my uncle's eulogy, haven't solved the mystery of his list, I'm yet to involve myself in his funeral preparations, and I've just heard a bombshell about my father. It's just that it's so fucking nice to down a chilled bottle of extra-milky coffee and become lost in the sounds of life getting on with itself.

Until a black four-wheel-drive nears me. Squeaks to a halt.

The drink bottle slips from my frozen fingers, clatters away. I don't try to get it. I can't move. Why was I content?

The passenger-side window starts to roll down. I picture a hand reaching out to grab me. Imagine being thrown into the rear seat; the car screeching away to whisk me to another cottage; my wife walking out of IGA with her bottled water and thinking I've left her, the shopping bags on the sidewalk the only reminder I existed.

A voice calls out, 'Hey there. Hello?'

If I don't move, will they see me? That worked when I was a kid.

'Excuse me, mate.'

I'm a fucking idiot. Why did I return to the scene of my abduction? It's the first place anyone would look. History repeating.

'Can you come here a second?'

I'm an idiot for thinking my uncle's mates were no longer a threat.

'Just need some help. You know where Brauhaus is?'

It takes a while for the words to register. I allow myself to blink, my limbs able to function once my brain realises I'm not in danger. I'm a fucking idiot for jumping to conclusions. Here with my shopping bags, I must look like a local to another tourist.

I point the way to the brewery. The guy's almost there, anyway. He thanks me, says he'll buy me a beer if he sees me down there. I nod. I might need it. He drives off as Lucy steps out of the supermarket.

'Everything okay?' she asks.

No need to tell her about my panic attack. No need to say that every time I see a black four-wheel-drive, I think I might lose my mind. Maybe I will need that counsellor Gary suggested. At some point.

I pick up the shopping bags. 'Everything's great.'

My wife smacks my arm. 'Liar. Are we heading back to the studio?'

We *could* stay there for the rest of the day. Eat, work on the eulogy, test the shower again. But my reaction to the four-wheel-drive leaves something lingering.

I don't want to seal myself away. Again. And I don't want to be traumatised every time I see a black four-wheel drive, cricket bat, kangaroo, or anything else symbolic of this trip. I need to explore a few more angles to Lillian's case before I settle back in that studio.

'We need to go for a drive, first,' I respond. 'I want to show you where Uncle Graham lived.'

If Uncle Roland's property is so large that it contains at least one Karri-concealed shed, then maybe Uncle Graham's property is the same. I explain this to Lucy on the way, confess that I only looked in two visible buildings. Maybe my uncle hid more clues elsewhere, hoping I'd explore the area.

We enter his property, begin the nerve-racking drive over the rock bridge. My wife doesn't see my anxiety; she's pointing outside, commenting on the beautiful water catchment.

'We could go skinny-dipping there,' she says.

I accelerate over the bridge. We round the path to the house, the large shed visible in the distance. Its door is open.

'I think I lost my desire to go skinny-dipping,' I sigh, pointing towards the shed. Towards the car parked outside it.

'Who's here?' Lucy asks. 'Wait, is that your...'

She knows the answer. We've seen the same car for the last eight years, since the day my mother bought it.

'I thought she was with Aunty Janice,' Lucy says.

I park Lucy's car, ease-out, look around. 'Yeah, me too.'

I don't have to say it, I can tell from my wife's expression she's thinking the same thing: *What the hell is going on?*

I dig around in my pocket, remove the photograph of my father and Charlotte. No need to wait until the funeral. I'm getting some answers now.

CHAPTER THIRTY
COVERED WITH BITING ANTS

My mother is inside the shed, her hand running across a typewriter. She sighs when she sees me. Not the most welcoming response.

'What are you doing here?' she snaps.

'What are *you* doing here?'

We stand in silence for a while, a couple of metres apart.

'Is there a kettle in the house?' Lucy says. 'I'll go check if there's a kettle in the house, get some tea.'

I fish a set of keys out of my pocket. 'Here, I forgot to put these back in the planter.'

My wife exits the shed, leaving me alone with my mother. Lucy means well—she doesn't want it to seem like the two of us are ganging up—but I'd rather she stays by my side. My mother responds to Lucy more. She tells her stories she's never disclosed to me, treats her like the daughter she always wanted, not the son that death left her with.

'You didn't even say hello to Lucy,' I comment, since that's as odd as her appearance here.

My mother's body shudders. I take her in, all five feet-four of her. She hasn't aged well. She's sixty-five but she could pass as my grandmother, thinning grey hair and a wrinkled face helping her blend with other seniors. Unlike Aunty Janice, she looks so fragile. I fight the urge to lean over and give her a hug. We rarely hug anyway, and we've lost the moment, but it looks like she needs one now.

I return the photograph to my pocket. 'Are you okay?'

She just stands there.

'How did you get here?'

She clears her throat.

'I've seen Graham's typewriters once, you know,' she says. 'Just once. A lot of people have told me about them, about how his business had taken off. He'd started with two machines in this shed. Now look at them all.'

'They're really something.'

'And he names them after townsfolk. Did you know that? He got to know so many people at the markets. There's going to be a big turnout tomorrow.'

'I thought you were going to lunch with Aunty Janice,' I try.

My mother runs a hand along another typewriter. 'She's with the funeral director. I couldn't go. We're meeting up for lunch a bit later.'

'Was I supposed to go? Didn't some of the stuff on Uncle Graham's list need to be buried with him?'

'I don't know. It doesn't matter.'

'It does if he asked for it to be buried—'

'He's dead, Henry. He won't haunt you for forgetting.'

I step closer to my mother, hesitate. 'Mum, please tell me how you got here. Who drove you?'

'I drove myself.'

'But Trent said you'd arranged a lift with someone else.'

'I'm safer driving myself than letting some young hoon take me.'

I think about Trent at his parents' house, in a haze. Mum's right, but she shouldn't have driven so far.

'You hate driving. You hated knowing *I'd* driven here.'

'If I crash, I crash.'

I sigh. This is how Uncle Graham's death has affected her.

'Have you looked in the house?' I ask.

'Not yet. Just the shed.'

'Do you want to go inside?'

'I'm not sure.'

'Aunty Janice cleaned it. Except some back rooms.' And a passageway, thanks to me.

'Okay.'

My mother edges around me, still avoids a hug or kiss. She stands by the shed door, looking into the sunlight.

'Janice messaged me a photograph,' she says, 'said you've asked about the woman. Why did you have to do that?'

'Because Uncle Graham wanted me to.'

My mother grunts and hurries outside, towards the reservoir. I have to jog to catch up. She passes a row of bushes loaded with mulberries and stops by the water's edge. It looks like she's about to jump in, but instead, she plonks down on a rock, staring at the water.

I catch up, sit beside her. She's wiping tears from her face.

'I lied to you, too,' she says. 'I'm sorry.'

'About lying?'

'About everything. I thought the truth would die with Graham, but he got you involved.'

'What truth?'

My mother turns to me. 'You father loved me, Henry.'

'That's not quite what I've been finding—'

'He was leaving her.'

I gulp for air. '*What*?'

'I knew about Charlotte.'

For a moment, I can't respond. This isn't where I expected the conversation to go. At least, not straightaway. My mother doesn't continue. She wiggles against the rock as if it's covered with biting ants. Then she stands, heads back towards the shed.

I find my voice. 'Mum! I need to hear this!'

I hurry after her. It's easier this time, though. She's trudging to the shed, her mind racing in so many tangents it looks like she's having trouble coordinating her legs. She reaches the shed door and all but stumbles into it.

'Mum?'

I reach out, grab her arm. It's shaking. I prop her up, ease her into the shade of the shed. Find a rusty stool and sit her down.

Wait.

She's gazing from typewriter to typewriter. Her breathing is slow but unlaboured, her body still twitching. I'm sure nothing's wrong with her heart, she's just upset herself. She's carried this deception for over twenty years, keeping me in the dark since my teens. She's deciding how much to give me, how much I can handle.

'Your lovely wife,' mum finally says, 'she was making some tea, wasn't she?'

She stands again, energy returned. She heads outside.

'Mum!' I scream.

She turns. 'He told her he couldn't be with her, that he wanted to stay with me.' She keeps moving towards the house. 'It didn't go down well. Stupid cow thought he was going to leave me and spend a new life with her.' Her voice jumps with her stride as she veers towards the house. 'He met up with Roland after it was done. They were just supposed to have one drink. But your father could never have just one drink.'

We reach the house. As she grasps the door handle, I place my hand over hers. 'Mum. Let's stay out here, talk about it some more. Just the two of us.'

'It should have always been the three of us, Henry. Just the three of us. That cow robbed me of... of...'

I let go of her hand. 'She didn't make dad drink and drive.'

My mother stares at me with a soured face that says I won't ever understand. She shakes her head and opens the door, stepping inside. I follow. There are no lights on, but there's plenty of natural light streaming through the curtains.

'Lucy, dear,' mum calls out, 'I could do with that tea now.'

Lucy doesn't reply. She's sitting on the edge of Uncle Graham's couch, rubbing a tea towel between her fingers. Beside her is Uncle David. Dishevelled; his eyes wide and wild, darting from person to person as if daring us to continuing speaking. As if the next loud sound will make the gun in his hand go off. The gun that's pointed at my wife.

CHAPTER THIRTY-ONE
I KNEW ABOUT CHARLOTTE

The first thing Uncle David says is, 'Shut the door.'

I quickly comply.

He follows with, 'Move over there, next to her.'

But all I can do is ask, 'Did you hurt Uncle Daniel?'

He shakes his head. 'Damned if I'm going to be next, though. Now, anyone else here?'

'No.'

'Then move it, next to her.'

My mother has said nothing. I don't want to escalate the situation, so we ease across the room, around the coffee table, and stand beside Lucy.

Uncle David is like the bulldog of the siblings. Shorter than everyone except Daniel, stockier, built like a rugby player. You'd think he'd be the one to avoid if things got rough. But to me, Uncle David has always seemed a pacifist, the peacekeeper who'd rather play a song on his guitar, share a drink or crack a joke than let conflict escalate. Which makes it hard to understand why I'm seeing him point a gun at my wife.

Well, a rifle. I'm pretty sure it's the same type of firearm Uncle Daniel forced me to use near his cottage. If there's any advantage to this, it's that such a weapon's not designed for close combat. I could try sidestepping in an arc towards my uncle, force him to track me, close in before he can lock on a target. But his wild eyes and shaking arms tell me that if I try to move now, he might just shoot Lucy. And at that range, no matter the gun, he won't miss.

I need to wait this out, exploit an opportunity. Be smart, for once.

'Have you been here long?' I ask, trying to cut the tension. He looks like he's slept in the same crinkled clothes for at least a day, his hair plastered to one side.

'Long enough,' Uncle David mutters.

This wasn't the man I'd seen when I'd first come to Aunty Janice's house. The man who'd hugged me hello, who'd wandered off with Trent, in high spirits, to work his way through Uncle Roland's scotch.

'Why are you doing this?' I ask.

First his brother, now him.

'I don't have a choice.'

'Of course you do.'

'No!' Uncle David stands, wobbles, then points the rifle at me.

I change tack. 'Why are you hiding, then?'

'You know why.'

'The cottage?'

Uncle David nods.

'Who's after you, then?'

He coughs, shakes his head. 'Daniel's an absolute idiot. You didn't even know about the cottage, did you? You were just trying to find out about the woman in the photo.'

'Charlotte.'

'Yeah, Charlotte. Then Daniel says he's gonna scare you real good, stop you asking questions, except he gets too wannabe gangster and fucks it up, and you escape and alert the cops; then a decade's worth of planning just crumbles.'

'What's in the cottage? Illegal tech?'

'See, you barely know. We're getting the shit beaten out of us for it, and you barely even know.'

There's a muffled *beep-beep*. Uncle David steps back, away from the couch. He slides a hand into his pocket, the other hand still propping the rifle towards me. He fumbles around for something, presumably his phone, the rifle dipping. This is my chance. What can I remember about disarming someone with a firearm? I'd learned it in the academy, never used it in real life. Some basic Krav Maga training. We'd all laughed when we did it, acting like we were Jackie Chan. Reach in, some kind of sloth grip, hand over theirs, push the gun out of its line of fire, twist and redirect. I can do it. I'm fifty per cent sure I can do it. All I need to do is burst forward, snap my hand out.

Uncle David retrieves his phone, reads the text. He's still looking down. I can't move, though, can't bring myself to try.

'I messaged them when it was just your wife in here,' he says. 'They're on their way.' Uncle David's gaze lingers on my mother. 'I'm sorry, Helen. When you arrived, I prayed you'd just have a look around outside. You should have taken off. Things've become complicated, now.'

My mother doesn't respond.

'How long do we have?' I ask. Not, *"Who's on their way"*, just a question about the time I have before my life's endangered again.

He slides the phone into his pocket. 'Not long.'

He's not kidding. I can hear the squeal of a brake outside. My mother takes a step towards the front window.

'Stay there!' Uncle David cries. 'In fact, you two women, go over there, into the kitchen. Stay in the kitchen. Act natural. Actually, don't make a sound. It's better if we just involve me and Henry.'

My wife opens her mouth to object, stops as she sees me shake my head. I stare at her for as long as possible, take every feature in. I try to smile, reassure her. She turns towards the kitchen; when she glances back, I can already see the cogs turning in her exceptional brain. She stands, takes my mother's hand, leads her into the tiled area.

'Henry,' Uncle David says, 'you're going to open the door.' He creeps to the other side of the room, near the passageway, hiding in a patch of darkness. I can't see the rifle but assume he'll be pointing it at my back.

There's a louder squeal of brakes. The shudder of an engine powering down. The creak and slam of a car door. Then a pause. I wait, wondering who I'm about to see, wondering if they'll have a gun in their hand, too.

There's a knock on the door.

'Go on, open it,' Uncle David whispers. As if I have a choice.

'They'll hurt you, too,' I try.

'Just open the fucking door!'

I start turning the handle. Best not to do this the slow way. I wrench the door open. The person on the other side jumps back, startled. They take off their hat, rotate it in both hands.

There's no gun.

It's Kevin. Uncle Graham's business partner from the markets.

He looks me up and down, then asks if he can come inside.

Kevin can't be the person who's out to get my family. This old man makes leather-bound notebooks to sell at markets. He can't be the ruthless owner of a cottage-full of illegal technology.

I try to join him outside, but my uncle calls out, 'Kev! Come in, mate.'

I have to step back, let Kevin inside. He shakes my hand, enters. Says nothing about the lack of artificial light. Maybe he lets the windows do all the work in his own home. Does he have a home? Kevin looks like the guy who'd be comfortable living in something more nomadic.

I shake my head. I'm trying to avoid what's happening, my brain telling me Kevin's about to be introduced to the rifle. Uncle David emerges from the darkness, stepping towards Kevin, hand outstretched. There's nothing in his hand, though. I look to the far wall, where he'd waited. The rifle's either concealed in the darkness or he slipped it down the passageway, out of sight.

A stupid error.

I close the door.

'Nice to see you, David,' Kevin says, shaking my uncle's hand. 'Didn't expect you here. Had problems sleeping, have you, mate?' He points to Uncle David's hair.

'You could say that.' Uncle David flicks a look at me, dares me to interject. 'What are you doing here?'

Kevin drops the handshake, fumbles for something in his pocket. He's between Uncle David and me. I'd hate to hurt the guy, but he presents an opportunity for a distraction. I could push him into my uncle, run to the passageway and look for the rifle.

Kevin quickly changes that, though. He turns to me, holding something in his hand. 'Brought this over for you, Henry. Came through the post for me but I opened it up, and it's a note for you.'

'Is it really?' Uncle David asks, scepticism in his voice.

'I remembered you said you were staying at Graham's,' Kevin continues. 'Thought I'd just bring it, rather than call. The drive's good for me. I haven't been getting out enough. Well, besides the pub. Missed me markets on the weekend, you know.'

Kevin pushes a slip of paper into my hand. I slide it into my pocket.

'What's on it, Henry?' Uncle David asks.

Kevin turns back to face him. 'It's just a playlist. Figure it's for the songs Graham wanted at his funeral. Remembered Henry's collecting things for it, figured he might have the music already.'

'Figuring out a lot,' Uncle David mumbles.

'Thanks, Kevin, I've got the CD,' I say, able to see Uncle David's face over Kevin's shoulder, knowing he's trying to piece it all together.

Now. Last chance to push Kevin. If he's not involved in hurting Uncle Daniel and myself, someone else is on their way. I need to gain control of this situation before that happens. I tense my leg muscles, ready to push off. Uncle David looks back towards the passageway as if thinking the same thing, ready to regain control.

Then there's a blur out the corner of my left eye, followed by a *thunk*.

Uncle David's head swivels on its neck. He lets out a mighty groan, grasping the sides of his head as if he's trying to keep everything intact.

Multiple blurs crash into my uncle's arm, chest, leg. Something else misses, hits the far wall. Shatters at a high pitch. Porcelain. I recognise the sound, many a coffee mug dropped in my day.

My wife's beside the couch with an armful of mugs. I want to keep watching, take delight in her ninja-like throwing skills, but her moment's paved the way for mine. I run around Kevin, right beside my uncle. A coffee mug hits my swinging arm. It hurts like hell, but I keep going. I reach the passageway before my uncle knows what's happening, find the rifle on the carpet. I pick it up, check that it's loaded, hurry back. Aim it at Uncle David, just like he'd done to us.

'Thanks, honey,' I call out.

'Stay in the kitchen,' she yells. 'As if it's a perfect, natural place for a woman. Everyone in your family's a backwards arsehole.'

'I remember why we haven't seen them in so long.' I keep the rifle aimed at Uncle David. He's rubbing his entire body, stemming the pain from the mugs, but he has enough of my attention to see the weapon. 'Sit on the couch.'

'What's going on?' Kevin asks. He's stepped back to the front door, stuck between whether to run or see what's playing out. I wish he'd run, leave my family behind, go back to the simple life of selling notebooks.

'Sorry, Kevin,' I say, 'I've tried to look for that Lillian woman I told you about; seems I've uncovered some criminal enterprise my uncles were part of.'

'Oh,' Kevin replies as if I've explained everything. 'Graham too?'

'No.'

'Thank God.' He waves at my wife, with a little hesitation. 'I'm Kevin.'

'Lucy.'

'My wife,' I say, as if that's the part that needs explaining. 'Maybe you should go?'

'I think I'll stay. I can help you.'

Uncle David returns to the couch, glaring at me. 'You're making a big mistake.'

Lucy walks to my side, mugs in hand. 'We should all go.'

'I need some answers first.' I lower the rifle. If Uncle David tries to grab it, there are enough of us to overpower him. 'What's in the cottage that's worth all this?'

He scoffs. 'You think we're all backwards hicks or something. Like, we live in wine country so that's what we must do, either make wine or work on a winery. Or surf, or ride our BMX bikes, or be some kind of hippy on drugs. Bet that's all you see of us on your *Perth news*.'

'But you're just a bunch of friendly people who threaten their own relatives, huh?' I turn the rifle, almost daring my uncle to lunge for me, eager to smash the stock against his face.

'The police are going to stop what we had going. We've lost a lot of money.'

'You can buy the tech again, start somewhere else. Tech is cheap. I know, I sell it.'

'The police'll be watching us now. They know what we're doing.'

'Which is what?'

'I don't have to tell you.'

'This all started when I asked about Charlotte. Is this about Charlotte?'

'Who?'

'The girl in the photo.'

'Oh. Her.'

'The one you said you didn't recognise.'

'Of course I recognised her. We just don't talk about her anymore.'

'Why not?'

'No point talking about the dead.'

'Why not?'

'You can't un-kill someone.'

'What did you say?'

'Henry?' Lucy grabs my arm, pulls on it. I'd raised it in the air, ready to swing the rifle down.

I shudder. 'Did you kill Charlotte?' I ask, allowing Lucy to lower my arm.

'I don't have to tell you,' Uncle David says, miming zipping his lips shut.

'Charlotte?' a voice calls out. 'I knew about Charlotte.'

We all look over to the kitchen. My mother's sitting on a barstool, sipping a cup of what I presume is tea. I'd love to say I'd worried about her safety, that I'd rushed to check she was okay after being threatened with a rifle. How awful is it that I didn't?

The person who gave birth to me, reduced to being part of the furniture. And she was okay with it, making and drinking a tea while a power struggle was taking place, while my wife took action and rounded up items from the kitchen to use as weapons.

'What else can you say about Charlotte?' I call out.

My mother just sips her tea, though. I'm not going to get anything else from her or Uncle David.

'It's time to leave, Helen,' Lucy says, reading my mind. 'Let's go for a drive.'

My mother puts her teacup down. 'Sure.'

'We're just going to call someone first.' Lucy looks at me, says, 'Call Gary, sort this out.'

'I will.'

'Then we can go back to our secluded paradise. Let the police deal with this, new leads and all.'

I nod. Sounds like a fantastic plan.

I look at Kevin. He's got the door open, but he's still hovering inside the house. 'Thanks for the letter, Kevin,' I offer. 'Sorry about all this.'

He tries to laugh. 'Family, huh? Sometimes makes me glad I just have me sister.'

We glance back at Uncle David. His body echoes defeat now, slumped against the couch cushions.

'Yeah,' I reply, 'family...'

The roar of a motor interrupts my thoughts. I look out the doorway, push myself past Kevin, take two steps out of the house. The sunlight is strong, forcing me to squint. Still, I can make out the blurred shape of a car beyond the rock bridge. It roars again, then stops at the start of the slippery stretch. Blocking any chance of an exit.

'Back inside!' I yell at myself. At everyone.

It's a black four-wheel-drive. The car of my nightmares.

Two people are stepping out of it.

CHAPTER THIRTY-TWO
LINE UP THE TARGET

I'd told myself to run back into the house, but I ignore instinct, make a split-second decision that will baffle me for years. I close the front door. Remain outside. Alone. I run to the closest parked car, Kevin's. Duck against it. The metal burns my skin, but I've got bigger problems. I risk a peek up and through the vehicle's windows. Catch sight of the two people who'd exited the four-wheel-drive. Swear. Watch them start walking over the rock bridge. Swear some more.

I can hear my wife shout at me from inside the house. I know I should join them, but something's stopping me. There's a weight in my hand. I look down. The rifle. Had I realised I was still carrying it? I edge to the bonnet of the car, round it a little, glance over. They're still crossing the bridge on foot, trying not to slip. I lift the rifle, stretch out over the bonnet. Look through the scope. Take a deep breath.

I could have hit that kangaroo when I was with my uncle. Back when I'd practised at the Swanbourne Rifle Range, I'd made a bit of a name for myself. I was reasonably accurate to at least three hundred yards, striking at least the eight ring, more often than not the nine or ten. But I'd stopped practising weekly, then altogether. So, I could have hit the kangaroo, but luck would have played a big part in it. Now, I need luck on my side. I *must* take this shot.

I try to remember the drill. Slow your breathing. Still your body, drop into an almost-comatose state, reduce human error. Line up the target then adjust for distance, the curve of the earth, the wind swaying the trees.

Except my breath is rapid, refusing to slow; and my arms are shaking, adrenaline and nerves combining to make the rifle jitter against the bonnet's metallic surface.

Maybe it's because of who I see down the end of the scope. Taking up half the bridge with his gigantic frame, bandages visible beneath a hat on his head, a sling wrapped around one arm. Lynden. The other person is behind him, gripping onto the Māori's shirt to keep their footing. They're tall and thin, wearing a balaclava, black tracksuit pants and a hooded jacket. Ignoring the heat of the day to hide their features.

The frame's a giveaway, though. Reg. Has to be. Tall and thin. He's turned from a redneck Aussie to an '80s thug.

'Stop right there!' I yell, squinting, the sunlight decreasing my ability to shoot with any accuracy.

Lynden keeps walking across the bridge.

I take a deep breath, aim low, for the ground in front of them. To scare them back. Or hit their shins. To maim them, at worst.

I squeeze the trigger. Misjudge the recoil. The bullet hits high— the windscreen of the four-wheel-drive. A hole explodes in the glass right where the passenger's head would have been. Both men spin round, look at it, spin back to the house. Lynden's face flashes a look of disbelief, then survival instinct kicks in. He retreats along the rock bridge, to the four-wheel-drive, pushing the other person ahead of him. He jumps in the driver's side, the other person falling onto the passenger seat, the door still open. The car reverses, increasing the distance between us. Making my next shot harder.

I slow my breathing. Try with every ounce of muscle to stop my arms from shaking. I wait. The car is still reversing. Maybe they're leaving? Perhaps they'll come back later for a second attempt? In that case, no need to shoot. We'll be gone by then. I stand, look back at the house. I can't hear anyone inside. Maybe I should join them now?

There's a loud rumble. The four-wheel-drive has stopped reversing, its engine revving. I crouch against the bonnet again, line up the next shot. The car springs to life, accelerating towards the rock bridge, dust swirling behind it. It hits the hard surface and the tyres seem to lock. The vehicle drifts over without fishtailing. I pull the trigger. Hit part of the car. The grill, I think. It does nothing. The four-wheel-drive crosses the bridge, hurtling towards me. It's too late to take another shot.

I glance back at the house. Too late to think of how much safer it is inside. Or how we could have escaped out the back, pretending no one was home.

Too late for regrets. I leap out the way as the black beast slams into Kevin's car, picking up the vehicle and throwing it down again. I scurry across the ground, praying nothing flies towards me. I've dropped the rifle, but I don't care. I don't stop until I'm at least ten metres from the crash, behind my mother's car. Safe enough to risk a look.

I spy balaclava-face inside the four-wheel-drive, slumped against an airbag. Succeeding in hurting himself. The cars are a giant tangle of steel, but they haven't struck the house. I almost let out a whoop of joy. Then I hear a creak, a crunch. Lynden is still conscious. Of course he's fucking conscious! He thumps his way out of the driver's side. Rounds the rear of the vehicle. I'm the one watching in disbelief, now. Blood trickles down Lynden's forehead, dripping off his nose. He doesn't care. He looks around Kevin's car, searches for me. Glances at the house, then down the path towards the shed. Locks onto my gaze. Smiles.

Lynden wrenches the boot open, reaches in and grabs something. Draws it out. A cricket bat. He twirls it in his hand. Grins even harder. He's saved this for me. Probably bought it for the occasion.

I turn to the shed. Run.

I pray his bulky, crash-riddled frame is hobbling towards me as slow as possible, but as I reach the shed door, I turn to see a bull charging. I hurry inside, pulling the door shut. I search for something to lock it, then groan. The door opens outwards, there's no way to hold it closed. I turn, scan the room for something to help me, anything to prolong my life. I try to remember what I saw in the shed last time. There's no quad to escape on. What about the pitchforks and shovels hanging on the wall? One handheld weapon to counteract another. I run to their rack and take one of each down. There's a short-handled shovel that feels good in my hands. I slide the pitchfork further into the room. It can be reached later. What about the typewriters on the benches? Would a typewriter make a suitable weapon? Some of them are heavy.

The shed door opens. I'm a few feet away. I haven't hidden. I'm exposed. There must be something I can say to stop Lynden, a plea for everything to end. But Lynden's still charging, pure rage puffing from his reddened face. He winds the cricket bat behind his right shoulder and swings. I twist my body in sheer panic. He misses, the breeze slicing across my face. Before I can retaliate with the shovel, Lynden swings from the left. I don't have time to evade the blow. The bat slams into the right side of my neck. Pain ripples to the back of my head, to my ears. I'm lucky, though—the swing had less momentum, the blow more like the weak jabs I'd tried on him. I slide to the left, fighting the pain, and bring the shovel up. Lynden swings again, fury guiding him. I slam the shovel into his arm. Stop the blow. Swipe the shovel's blade in a high arc. Lynden twitches his head back, the blade missing it by millimetres. He kicks out, connects with my upper thigh, right on the welt, buckling my leg. As I go down, he swings again. I hold the shovel near my face, a pseudo-shield. The bat clangs off the surface. I spider-crawl backwards, the shovel tumbling out of my hand.

Lynden watches me, gives me a bit of distance. Before I can wonder why, he raises the cricket bat above his head, charges; grunts and growls and swings the bat with all his might. I push off as the bat nears. It strikes the ground, at the ghost of my crotch. There's an explosive, vibrating *thunk* to emphasise what could have happened.

Lynden's bent over, panting, energy temporarily gone. I seize the moment. Skitter backwards, pick myself up. I look for the pitchfork. It's out of reach. I lunge for the bench, grab a typewriter. I hate to do this, to destroy my uncle's hard work, but no one's going to finish restoring them, anyway. May as well put them to good use. I throw the first typewriter. Low. Lynden looks up, flings his free hand downward to deflect it, drops the bat. I've already grabbed another, a cherry-red model with a steel handle.

I swing it at Lynden's unprotected head. The typewriter clunks off the bandages, gives off a satisfying ping. Lynden stares at me for a brief second, then the lights go out. He falls, face first, onto the ground.

I drop the typewriter. Ease my body down. Gasp for breath. Try to ignore the excruciating pain in my neck. When it ebbs enough to make movement possible, I stand, wobble, then edge around Lynden's body. I should leave the shed, lock it from the outside to keep the colossal beast at bay. Assuming he's still out cold. Assuming he's not going to shoot a hand at my ankle.

I reach the shed door, search for something to lock it with. Then I hear the whoop of a police siren, look back towards the house and see a vehicle cross the rock bridge. Lucy must have called someone. I wave my arms, trying to draw their attention, point to the four-wheel-drive. As I do that, though, it's clear something is wrong.

The four-wheel-drive is empty. Balaclava-face is no longer slumped against the airbag.

My first instinct is to check the house, hoping the hostage situation hasn't restarted. As I near the police vehicle, Gary steps out, along with two officers.

'Can't you let me get some other work done?' he says with a smirk, which falters as I point to the shed.

'That huge Māori's in there. Lynden. Cricket bat guy. Out cold for now.'

Gary gives some instructions, sends the other officers to claim their prize.

'There's another one. Wearing a balaclava. He's missing.' I urge Gary to follow. 'We need to check the house.'

As I reach the door, I stop. Look back at the car wreck. Remember that as I scrambled towards the shed, I dropped the rifle. I can't see it on the ground anywhere. 'Wait!' I pull us away from the door, explain. Gary rounds the vehicles, searching. I hang beside the door, praying someone isn't in there with the rifle trained to shoot the first intruder.

'Got it!' Gary yells.

The relief is almost euphoric. I knock on the door, call out for my wife. Lucy opens it, drags me inside. Kevin's by the windows, Uncle David's still on the couch, and my mother is in the kitchen again. I swear she's getting another tea.

Lucy wraps me in an embrace I wish could last for days. When this is all over, I'm going to do that—cancel everything, raise the middle finger to responsibilities and just embrace my wife for hours on end. Like we used to do when we were first dating.

'You're crazy for staying out there,' she whispers.

'I know.' I pull back. 'Someone was wearing a balaclava. They didn't come in here?'

'Nobody's come in here,' Kevin says.

Gary enters, points to the couch. 'Is that David Herbert?'

I nod. Gary goes through the motions, drags my uncle's defeated body off the cushions, brings out the handcuffs. I lead my wife outside and we look at the car wreck. Kevin joins us, lets out a strangled sob.

'I'm so sorry, Kevin.'

'Had that beauty for twenty years. She was my girl. Never thought she'd leave me. I'm gonna be needing a few drinks, now.' He pulls at his shirt for a while, then straightens up, forces a smile. 'Oh well, guess insurance will get me a new one. Sunshine after the storm, and all that.'

'That's the spirit.'

'Maybe they'll give me a van? That'll help move me stuff between markets.'

'Couldn't hurt to try.'

'I'll probably be needing a lift home, though.'

'We'd love to give you one.'

I'm going through the motions with Kevin, because what I'm really doing is scanning my uncle's property, trying to figure out where balaclava-face would have hidden. Not in the car wreck, or my mother's car, their interiors visible or inaccessible. Not in the reservoir—they would have surfaced by now. Or the shed, I would have seen them. The garage? No, everyone inside the house would have heard it open. It's doubtful they went back over the rock bridge, too, since Gary and his team would have spotted someone leaving. What escape routes remain, then?

I break away from my wife and Kevin, tell them I'll be back, wander to the house's far side. Round it. There's a clear path of red pebbles, then an open area, then thickening forest. Some of the pebbles have been kicked around. I take the path. The open area is brick paved. There are roses in pots at its perimeter, some deck chairs, a tiny table with an ashtray. Further along the back of the house, there's a Hills Hoist awaiting laundry. It's the equivalent of a city folk's backyard, only there's no fence or gate, just trees marking a boundary.

Nobody is hiding around this paved area, and nothing else looks disturbed.

I can hear movement behind me, my wife and Kevin talking. But I can also hear something in the distance, amongst the trees. The swish of leaves, the crack of a branch. It could be a kangaroo. Or it could be balaclava-face, making a getaway.

I hurry towards the sound.

There's a dirt track starting at a break between the potted roses. I take it. I glance back, consider calling out for my wife, for Gary, but that would give my chase away.

The track narrows. I push my way through, grabbing at branches and swinging them away, making the same swish and crack noises I'd heard. Any subtle approach is gone. I stop. Listen. Hear nothing besides a soft hum of insects. Would balaclava-face have taken the same path, or would they have ventured into thicker undergrowth? I take what's left of the path. Quicken the pace. It twists and turns around tree trunks. The shrubs by my side reach my waist, shoulders, head. I glance back, can no longer tell where the house is. I'm lost, trying to find someone.

I reach a small clearing.

There's an old wooden shack at its centre. A man-cave, perhaps, just like Uncle Roland's. This structure seems a hundred years older, though. Its wood is grey and rotten, a cousin of the cottage: *The Shack in the Woods*.

Dark-trunked trees surround the shack, gaps filled with dense bush, the track ceasing to exist. Almost the same as at Uncle Roland's. If balaclava-face has kept running, they've entered the depths of the wilderness, lost amongst the growth. Otherwise, they've hidden in the shack. I know I should wait, should go get Gary this time, but I find myself approaching the structure.

I reach the door. Doubt someone has gone inside. A small mound of soil has built up against the door, stopping it from swinging outwards—nature's doorstop. I scrape the soil aside with my shoe, pull the door until it budges. It carves a line in the earth. No lines were there before. Pretty clear no one's entered, but still worth a shot. I'd wanted to find a shed like this, anyway. It's the reason I'd brought Lucy to the property. Even with balaclava-face lurking somewhere, I need to look inside now.

This shack is far from the man-cave Uncle Roland had created for himself. It's a building designed to hold things long forgotten. More evidence of hoarding, pile after pile of scrap. When will Aunty Janice get to this and box it into neat piles? Probably quicker just to burn it down. I can't get inside more than a few feet. Old fluorescent tubes hang out of boxes, threatening to trip me, thick cobwebs keeping them suspended mid-air. There's a stack of plastic chairs covered in brown dust, an old boot on top. I can see the slats of an old bed frame, a crate filled with rusted gardening equipment, framed paintings of work by unrecognisable artists.

I wait by the door. Balaclava-face doesn't return, doesn't ambush me. I'm about to leave when something catches my eye. It's the boot. Sitting there, alone, yet free from the thick dust of the surrounding items. Placed later. Designed to draw my gaze. Which moves past it, past the chairs, onto the wall beyond. There's a poster on it. For *Back to the Future*.

I kick the fluorescent tubing to the side, shuffle my way inside. Glass crunches against my shoes as I reach the chairs. I drag them back, creating the slightest of gaps to reach through. My fingers grasp the top edge of the poster. I yank it. The poster doesn't rip, just slides off the wooden surface as if held on by nothing more than static. Something thumps onto the floor, though, behind the chairs. I squat, reach beneath the legs. My hand slides into one cobweb, then another. Silk sticks to my fingertips. I try not to think about what else I'm touching, hope the web is long abandoned. My fingers reach a heftier object on the floor, wrap around it, pull it out. Web covers my hand, along with the remains of a black beetle. But I'm also holding an envelope.

I look at the movie poster. It's an alternate design I've never seen before. It's got Marty McFly's parents in black and white, stuck in nineteen fifty-five, with the main character tumbling into their world through a rip in the page, bringing with him the glorious colour of the '80s.

Heavy.

Uncle Graham left false breadcrumbs. He knew Aunty Janice would find one movie poster, blatantly left on a wall in his house. This was the poster he wanted me to find, though. With another clue slotted behind it.

I leave the poster, exit the shed. Pull back the envelope's flap, remove what's inside.

My hands shake, my pursuit of balaclava-face long forgotten.

I'm finally piecing the story together.

CHAPTER THIRTY-THREE
ALMOST READS LIKE A STORY

I peer in the shed one last time, make sure nothing else stands out, then head back to the house. Lucy and Kevin meet me halfway along the track. I tuck the envelope into the waistband of my pants, adjusting my shirt over it before Kevin can see.

'Why did you run off?' Lucy asks, working hard to hide the panic in her voice.

'Thought I heard someone.'

'And?'

I wave an arm at the surrounding forest. 'They disappeared.'

'And after I said you were crazy for staying outside!' Lucy glares at me for a while longer, knowing there's something I'm not telling her. I avoid her gaze, keep heading towards the house.

'Do you want to keep looking?' Kevin says.

I don't even know what this property's boundaries connect to. More properties? Forest? 'They're too far gone. But we'll tell Gary.'

We reach the house, hear grumbles and curses from two of the officers. They're trying to shove Lynden into the back of their vehicle, an ambulance forgone. They've got everything but a leg in. One officer is complaining about his back, the other's telling him to shut up and help. Gary's standing on the opposite side of the vehicle. He sees me and points downwards. Uncle David's already inside, his face hung low on a limp neck.

'Where'd you go?' Gary calls out.

'Thought I heard the missing person amongst the trees,' I explain.

'And?'

'No luck. Heard something, saw nothing.'

'Did you get a look at them before that?' he asks, wandering over.

'They were wearing a balaclava, remember? And a hoodie.'

'In this weather?'

'Didn't want to be seen, obviously.'

The other officers succeed in getting Lynden in, close the door and whoop with joy. 'Idiots,' Gary mumbles. 'Now wait there until the ambos arrive to clear him,' he yells. 'Like you should have already! And start photographing the wreck and the shed.' He shakes his head, turns back to me. 'The offer stands to join the force down here.'

'Pending a talk with others at your station?' I add. 'Since I just attacked a man with a typewriter, and my relatives are holding a reunion behind bars?'

'You mean you didn't knock that beast down with your fists?' Gary winks at Lucy, trying to lighten the mood.

'The cricket bat incident made him a little fragile,' I say.

'He's got the type of face that attracts hard objects, I guess. Get it, *typeface*, cause you hit him with a *typewriter*.' Gary holds a hand up as we all groan. 'Sorry, had to give it a go. Should be compassionate, and all that, but the guy's a bruiser-for-hire.'

We wait around as the scene is processed. An ambulance arrives and the two officers are made to help carry the enormous man again, much to Gary's delight. Tow trucks come to make sense of the wreckage. Gary gets one officer to go with the ambulance, the other to herd Uncle David to the station. He stays, arranging for a lift so he can question us some more. We agree to take Kevin home, too. Lucy offers to drop my mother back at Aunty Janice's, but she refuses help. Which means she won't continue the conversation she'd started inside the house, either. The old woman's insistent she can drive herself, that she has a lunch date she'd like to attend. Ignoring everything we've just gone through. Continuing to downplay her fear of driving.

Lucy's car is the last to leave the property. As we near the gate, I look at the reflection in the rear-view mirror. For a second time, I wonder whether I will ever see this place again. I've avoided it for so long, yet it's becoming familiar to me.

Kevin gives us directions, which Gary translates into landmarks and turns. Soon, we near what I think is the opposite side of the Education Campus, its buildings visible in the distance. We enter a tourist park. It's scattered with tents and caravans, some hitched to small verandahs as if they'll never move again. A mix of permanent residents and temporary tourists. Kevin takes us around a one-way loop between a stretch of demountable-style vans, then tells us to park by a tan-coloured one.

'This is me,' he says.

I guess I was kind of right about his nomadic lifestyle. It's a caravan that would have looked majestic when first purchased, a holiday on wheels. It's fixed to the ground now. There's weathering on the paint, a sagging canopy off its side. It doesn't look too liberating.

Kevin gets out, says goodbye, tells me he'll be at the funeral tomorrow. I ask if he needs a lift and Kevin says he's fine, some of the other locals are walking with him.

'They've listed me as a pallbearer, you know,' he says.

I didn't know.

I watch him disappear into the caravan, hope we can get Uncle Graham's property into his hands. Unless, of course, he likes the park life.

Gary guides me back to the central part of town. In the few minutes it takes, he asks me to retell what happened at my uncle's property. I see him writing some notes. As I finish, we reach the station. He tells me he'll call if there are any updates. I remind him to make sure he has a team ready at the funeral. He nods. He's exceptionally trusting of me, and I'm nothing but appreciative. Most officers would have at least thought about detaining me, since I was involved in most of their weekend workload. His intuition has told him he can trust me. I'll prove him right tomorrow.

Lucy and I arrive back at the studio. A symphony of bird calls greets us, guiding us to the entrance. We step into a dark world, the blinds drawn. I don't remember putting them down, but Lucy thinks she did. I pull each blind up, looking out at the distant field.

No kangaroos lurking nearby, they've heard about my reputation. I walk around the studio, trying to remember how things were when we left. Everything appears untouched. If one of my uncle's mates broke in, I'd expect them to leave the place trashed.

I lock the front door. Lucy slumps on the couch, grabbing the crime book and retreating to its pages. She glances at me with the same expression as in the forest. Silent daggers. It's okay, I get it. I put myself in a dangerous situation twice, *after* having a rifle pointed at me. I'm not sure I could forgive myself for being that stupid.

At least it rewarded me. I lift my shirt, remove the envelope, place it on the coffee table. Stare at it a while, then fumble around in my pocket for a slip of paper. I find the note Kevin gave me, the reason he'd turned up at Uncle Graham's. I unfold it. It reads:

> *Note for Henry*
> *Final tracklist. Play in this order, please. It sounds best.*
>
> *4, 10, 5, 18, 8, 9*

Simple instructions. But with everything else that's happened, I'm going to take it as a coded message. A backup piece of information Uncle Graham sent in case I hadn't figured everything out. He trusted his business partner enough to post the note to him, knew the man would seek me out in time. Thank heavens the postal system came through. Just.

I find my notepad. Open it to the list of music on Uncle Graham's CD. Originally eighteen songs to decipher. I'd figured at least one of them had to have lyrics that told me about Charlotte or Lillian. Time to see if the note clarifies that.

I match the numbers to titles, write them in the stated order. Stare at the resulting list:

Something On Your Mind
The Kiss
Have You Seen Her
Darkness On The Edge of Town
Jealousy
The Payback

It almost reads like a story. The only problem is, I'm not sure who it's about.

'What are you doing?' Lucy asks, curiosity overpowering anger.

I show her.

'It could be the plot of this guy's next bestseller,' she says, waving the book in her hand.

'That's what I thought, too.'

I pick the envelope off the table, lean back into the couch cushions, and remove the contents once more. It's a bundle of photographs. I'd wager that these are the actual photographs missing from album number four. So maybe this is the real album number four?

Uncle Graham had an alternate *Back to the Future* poster, an alternate set of photographs. A tracklist within a tracklist. A photo inside a typewriter, another behind a framed bill. Secret words within books. Subterfuge to make sure that someone like myself, once given a push, would find the truth he'd uncovered.

The first photograph is another shot from the red-and-green-restaurant. This time, there's no hiding the connection. It's a wider frame, showing Uncle Roland, Aunty Janice, my father, and Charlotte Harris all seated at the same table. In front of them are scattered plates, wine bottles to the side. They have their arms around each other's shoulders. Charlotte is giving an awkward peace sign.

I show it to Lucy. She grimaces.

The second photograph changes things. It's almost the exact same image, except Uncle Graham replaces my father. Charlotte is no longer giving the peace sign; her hand is resting on top of my uncle's.

Has my uncle misdirected me? I'd thought a staff member had come past, taken the photographs for my father and Charlotte. The photographer was likely Uncle Graham, though. Now here he is, on the other side of the camera.

I show it to Lucy. She puts her book down, shuffles forward on the couch. Studies the picture.

The third photograph is a closeup of Uncle Graham and Charlotte at the same table. They're looking at each other, smiling. I wonder if my father ever had a copy of this photograph; if he'd ripped it in half like Uncle Graham did to its twin. Had Uncle Graham even ripped the first photograph in half? Maybe he'd just found the pieces. If so, why leave the halves for me to find? Why not leave this photo instead, make it clearer from the start?

Lucy snatches the photograph out of my hand. 'Which man was Charlotte with?'

'I don't know.'

From what my mother said, my father was definitely having an affair. But was Uncle Graham seeing Charlotte, too?

I take the fourth picture. This time, it's of my family on my father's side. At a beach. I'm there. I'm young again, looking like

I've just entered the realm of double-digits. My mother is behind me, squeezing my shoulders. My father is beside her. In a row, there's Uncle Daniel, Uncle David with his arm around a woman I can't remember, Aunty Janice embraced by Uncle Roland, and Uncle Graham. Standing in front of Uncle Graham, less than a metre from me, is Charlotte.

I can't remember this moment in time. It looks like I'm old enough to have remembered it. I know I blocked a lot of my memories when my father passed away. Regardless, it means I met Charlotte at some stage of my life. Everyone in my family met her. For one day, at the very least.

There are more photographs, ten in all, of our family playing on the beach. Charlotte looks like she fitted right in. Uncle Graham is always smiling beside her, splashing water at her, holding her arms as she swings a bat in beach cricket.

I recognise Uncle's Graham's gaze. He was madly in love with Charlotte.

I look at my notepad, at the remixed list of songs. I could construct the story I need to out of the titles now, stretch the truth to make everything fall into place. There was a rift between my father and Uncle Graham, two brothers fighting over a woman. Some kind of confrontation, a tragedy. Hardly unique, but a secret my family has kept from me for almost thirty years.

If I'd found these photos days ago, I would have talked to everyone differently, confronted them with actual evidence, forced the truth to emerge. I'd known my family was lying. Now I can prove it.

I hand the stack of images to Lucy. 'I wonder how long he thought I'd take to find these.'

'What do you mean?' Lucy asks, flicking through them.

'Well, he scattered smaller clues. How did he know I'd find the ripped photograph first, and not this bunch? It's like he predicted every step I'd take.'

'The ripped photos were in things that were visible, right near each other. This was much more hidden.'

'Why is he leaving them for me at all? To fuck up everything I knew about my family?'

'So, they covered an affair. You know, when my grandfather, God rest his soul, met my grandmother, he was already engaged. He—'

'It's not just an affair, though, is it. There were deaths and a resulting love-child. And I think something's happened to Lillian, too. Why didn't Uncle Graham just take this to the police? Surely that's what he wants me to do?'

'We can't know.'

'Not yet. And I guess I've got the police involved, in my own way. He would have predicted that.'

Lucy nods, holds up the photographs. 'What do you want to do with these?'

'What *can* I do?'

She grins. 'Your uncle's funeral will have a photo montage, right?'

'It should do. That's what the instructions say.'

'Then I think we need to add some of these photos, tie it in with your eulogy.'

I match her smile. 'You think I can force a confession?'

'While you have everyone there? It's worth a try.' Lucy rubs her finger along the whole-family beach scene. 'I haven't seen many photos of you as a kid, you know that?'

'Mum boxed them up. I always thought it was because they reminded her of dad.'

'Which version?'

'Ouch.'

Lucy's eyes narrow, the grin disappearing. 'Drinking then driving, your father chose to put himself in danger. Today, running out to confront thugs with a gun like you're—'

'James Bond?'

'*You are not James Bond!*' Lucy thumps the photographs on the coffee table. 'I admire what you did. It was brave. But you chose to put yourself in danger. I don't want to lose you for doing something stupid.'

'Then you won't want me to be a cop again.'

'There's a difference between calculated risks and sheer stupidity. Besides, there are other avenues of law enforcement, aren't there?'

'Like what?'

'I don't know. Private Investigator?'

'Sounds pretty stupid, but if that's what you want from your man...'

Lucy lunges for me, smacks me hard. 'You are so frustrating!' She grabs my shirt. 'Yet somehow sexy.'

She pulls me off the couch, all but drags me to the bed. I go along with it, of course, subjected to a strange mix of frustration and desire.

'I've got a eulogy to write,' I mumble at some point.

Lucy tells me to shut up as she jumps on top of me, and I keep going along with it. Because I'm not always an idiot.

Afterwards, we lay together until dehydration overwhelms me. I slip Lucy's arm off my chest, hobble over to the fridge, get a drink of water. Sip it, thinking.

'Hey, Lucy,' I call out, walking back to the bed. 'Do you think this thing at the funeral will help find Lillian, or is it all about Charlotte now?'

Lucy doesn't reply, though. She's asleep.

Leaving me with a lingering thought before I return to bed and drift off myself: *If my father* and *Uncle Graham were both seeing Charlotte, whose baby did she have?*

CHAPTER THIRTY-FOUR
PEOPLE MAKE PLANS

It's Tuesday morning. Today's the day—Uncle Graham's funeral. I start showering, trying to wash off a sleepiness that won't disappear. In just over an hour, we'll leave for the funeral director's, aiming to get there ahead of the time Aunty Janice gave us. The thought of what that might accomplish, of what I have the potential to reveal today, is exciting. But I can't shake the sense of despair lurking deep within.

I've failed. I haven't found Lillian. I've discovered awful things about my family. I've put my life in jeopardy. For what, though?

Lucy and I woke late last evening. I spent a good chunk of the night writing a new version of my uncle's eulogy. Finishing it, rehearsing. Lucy continued reading the Robotham novel, checking in on me now and then. If I've done my job right, I might tug at enough heartstrings to force a confession from at least Aunty Janice, Uncle Roland, or my mother. But there's a higher chance it will be a confession about Charlotte. I don't know if it will lead to revelations about Lillian, too.

I want to believe she's alive. Hiding, but alive.

Not just a plaque at a cemetery.

Maybe Lillian will be at the funeral. I won't even know. For all the talk about her, for all my efforts to find out where she might be, I can only guess what she looks like. I don't have her photograph. She could have walked past me a dozen times in town and I wouldn't have known.

Leonie had promised to talk to me after the funeral. Perhaps then she'll show me Lillian's photograph. Then I'll see who the woman resembles the most. I pray it's her mother.

I get out of the shower, stare at my reflection. I could do with a shave. And my eyes have bags under their bags. My hair's a ragged mess, all sense of style lost. Patches of skin are covered in bruises, a swirling mix of purple, green and blue; my neck the latest area to add to the pattern. I look like I competed in a lightweight boxing title and ended up in the gutter.

While Lucy is showering, I fix myself as best I can. I dress in a black suit, black shirt, tie. Most people will be in brighter colours, a new trend at funerals, but I'll stick to tradition. I box up Uncle Graham's possessions as Lucy changes, putting them in the boot of my car to save time. When I see Lucy next, she's wearing a simple white dress with a pattern of black vines swirling down one side. I want to say she's stunning, beautiful, amazing, but is that the look anyone's going for at a funeral?

I try to push away a pang of guilt. I don't seek enough opportunities to dress up, to go out to dinner or events as a couple. We don't even have kids, so we can't use them as an excuse. When this is all done, we're going out more. A weekly date night at the very least. I need this relationship to survive. After today, I might not have much left.

It's not long before we're in the car, heading out of the studio grounds. The funeral director isn't close. Uncle Graham chose one all the way in Busselton. I don't know why. It takes around forty minutes to get there. It's right across from the beach. Sun, surf, and dead people. We're close to the jetty—did he work in another hidden meaning with the location? Maybe we could pick Leonie up, take her to the funeral? But she doesn't live there, she'd be at her home getting ready. Wherever that is. I mumble all these thoughts and Lucy lets me, squeezing my hand. As we step out of the car, I take in the funeral director's property. It's like a large house, nothing too imposing except for a wall of tinted glass. It's impossible to see inside, grief hidden.

We enter. An elderly man greets us straightaway. Average height, rake thin, wearing a black suit a few sizes too big for his frame. He strokes a trimmed snowy beard, shakes hands as we reveal our names. He doesn't give us his, but his name badge reads *Lewis*.

'You're here for Graham Herbert?' Lewis asks.

'Yes. My uncle.'

'The visitation's not until ten, though.' He smiles, waiting for us to understand he's in charge.

There's a clock ticking on a white wall close by. It's nine thirty-five.

'We have some things,' I try. 'For a display?'

'Oh. Well, can you wait here a moment? Don't worry, your uncle's not going anywhere.' Lewis chuckles as if still amused by a joke he's used a million times.

He rushes off before I can stop him, his body rocking back and forth in a near-perfect mimic of a penguin. I glance at Lucy, shrug. We wait, the clock ticking away. He returns with a woman in her mid-twenties. She's dressed in white, her hair dyed jet-black to match her fingernails and the mascara around her eyes.

'June,' Lewis says, 'help Henry here with his uncle's things.'

She nods, follows me outside.

'You don't have to, you know,' I call out. 'It's only a box.'

'Gives me something to do,' she replies.

'You worked here long?' I ask, trying to make conversation as I reach my car.

'A few months.'

I open the boot. 'Done many of these? Visitations, I mean.'

'A fair few.'

'In a few months?'

'Only a handful of funeral companies around here, so business is steady.'

'People gotta die, I guess.'

'People gotta die.'

I lock the car, accompany June back inside. Lucy is sitting on a grey couch, scrolling through her phone. The old man is nowhere in sight.

'What have you got in here?' June says, rattling the box. 'It's heavy.'

'There's a typewriter, amongst other things.'

'Really?'

'My uncle restored them.'

She flutters a smile. 'Cool. I'll put it in my car.'

'So, nothing's going in the coffin?'

'I read through Mr Herbert's instructions,' June replies. 'He wants the items placed beside his coffin in the church itself. I'm driving there soon to set up a few things, so I can get it ready for you. It's no big deal.'

'Sure.' I take an envelope out of my jacket pocket. 'There's one other thing, though.'

'Oh?'

'He has a photo montage, right?'

'Sure. Your aunt arranged most of that.'

'Do you run it?'

'I've made it already. I just press play at the church.'

'So, do you think you'd have time to make another one? For when I'm giving the eulogy?'

'You're kidding, right?'

'It's just a few photos. No need for music or fancy transitions. I'll signal to you when I want each one up.'

June sighs, holds out her hand for the envelope. 'You're lucky your uncle's instructions said, *Help Henry in any way possible.*'

'They actually said that?'

'Yeah. He paid, we deliver. Don't forget that if you give us a review.' June leaves the room with the box and envelope, disappearing down a corridor.

'He had instructions?' I say as Lucy reaches out for a hug. I pull her close. 'First, he has a list, now instructions?'

'He knew he was dying, Henry. People make plans.'

I close my eyes, take a deep breath. 'Well, he's in here somewhere. Let's go find him.'

I can't remove my gaze from Uncle Graham's coffin. The lid is closed. I know it's stupid, but I'm thinking, *What if he's not in there? What if it's empty? What if there's never a body inside? What if the funeral home just chucks the body somewhere else, then parades the box in front of family and friends, so they think they're saying goodbye? But they're saying goodbye to nothing more than memories.*

'Why is the coffin closed?' I mumble.

'Pardon?' Lewis is beside me, having showed us inside.

'The coffin. Why's the lid closed? Isn't this a visitation?'

Lewis rubs his arm, the suit bouncing against his limbs. 'Um, well, your aunt decided it would be best.'

'Why?'

'I mean, I've worked wonders with makeup, so you don't notice the laceration on his forehead. If you wanted to, I could open it. Just give me—'

'*What* was on his forehead?' The world suddenly lurches, then static rushes through my head. As if I'm underwater. I take a deep breath, try to focus, keep upright.

'You didn't...' Lewis says, his voice barely audible. 'I mean, I don't mind discussing it, but I think this conversation's best had with your family.'

My wife says something, but it blends with the static. I take another deep breath. The coffin is three, four metres away, on a stand. I can't bring myself to move closer. Can't move at all. Is Lewis referring to the tumour in my uncle's head? It wasn't visible, right? Nor would it have caused a laceration.

Lucy is tugging my arm. As I realise it, sound returns, my head resurfacing. 'They're here,' she's saying.

I will my limbs to move, point at the coffin. 'Open it.'

'I'll see what I can do.' Lewis penguin-waddles to the front of the room.

'They're here,' Lucy insists, the echo disappearing.

I turn, look down the corridor. There's Trent. Dark blue shirt, black jeans, head down, kicking the carpet. My mother is beside him, a hand on his shoulder. Showing the type of affection she hasn't thrown my way in forever. Aunty Janice and Uncle Roland edge around them, leading the way. We lock eyes. They say something to each other, but they're too far to hear. I watch them approach, two peas in a pod. Same rigid movement. Tall and thin, almost identical in height and build.

When they near, another feature is noticeable straight away. They both have bruises on their face. Uncle Roland has a dark one on his forehead. Aunty Janice has one winding its way down her cheek. She's tried to conceal it with lots of makeup, but it's still noticeable. I've seen bruises covered up before, as both an officer and a teacher.

Tall and thin. Bruises on the face.

I turn to look at the coffin once more. I need Uncle Graham to be inside it. To jump out and say it's all a joke. To say he knows all about Charlotte. About Lillian. And identify the person who wore the balaclava.

But he doesn't jump out, of course. He's at peace, leaving me to my wild theories.

CHAPTER THIRTY-FIVE
THE DOWNFALL

After making sure Lucy gets a huge dose of attention, Aunty Janice wraps me in an inescapable hug. She says how sorry she is. She knows how much Uncle Graham meant to me. She wishes she could get him back. Playing the all-accommodating host in front of the funeral director, winning hearts. Hiding the fact that yesterday, she may have worn a balaclava, eager to hurt me.

Aunty Janice pulls away to make room for my mother, who stands still for a moment, looking at my face, chest, hands, unsure what to do. Eventually, she reaches out, takes my left hand from beneath, puts her other hand on top. Pats it. I grimace. I've received more affection from a person possibly arranging my demise.

Aunty Janice notices Lewis hovering by the coffin, turning one of the windup keys on the lid. 'No, we don't want it open!' She pushes past us, hurrying to stop the old man. My mother lets go of me, grabs Lucy by the arm and shuffles towards her.

Uncle Roland chuckles, trying to hide the awkwardness. 'Henry.' He reaches over, shakes my hand, then draws me in for a hug of his own. He tells me he's here for me, that we'll get through the funeral then consume copious amounts of booze. The bruise on his forehead looks worse up close, a rainbow of colours. Uncle Roland notices me looking at it, pulls away.

'The ice didn't work the other day,' he says.

He waits for me to remember what he's referencing. He'd smacked his head against his car—the dash, I think—while vacuuming it. Before he'd pointed us to the lighthouse and the bizarre scene at its café. He'd had ice pressed against his forehead, but I hadn't seen a bruise then. Was it a ruse for an attack he knew would happen soon? Is Uncle Roland far from the person I thought he was? Or am I reading way too much into this? I had attached the tall, thin frame of balaclava-face to Reg, Lynden's mate. He should still be the prime candidate.

'Let's have a seat,' Uncle Roland says, pointing to a row of chairs close to the coffin.

I don't want to sit, but everyone else is moving forward. Uncle Roland has his hand on my shoulder, guiding me. Aunty Janice has sandwiched Lucy between herself and my mother, the two of them separating us. I glance back at the doorway. Trent is there, head down. His parents aren't making him join them. Why does he get to stay over there?

We reach the front row of chairs, sit down. From here, I can see the honey-coloured grain on the coffin's surface, the petals on the white roses atop it.

It's just empty. There's nobody in there.

'Please take as long as you need,' Lewis says beside the coffin. 'We will drive you to the funeral when you are ready.'

I'm pretty sure there's a time limit, but it's nice of Lewis to pretend he cares. He bows theatrically and leaves the room, the coffin remaining closed.

My head's swimming. Uncle Roland and Aunty Janice are either side of me. If Reg wasn't balaclava-face, there's a fifty-fifty chance one of them was. A fifty-fifty chance I'm sitting next to someone who has a part in controlling a group of wannabe thugs. Someone who could have turned an out-of-the-way cottage into a hub for an illegal online network. Someone who's silenced Uncle Daniel and threatened Uncle David, hurting their own family to protect themselves.

Who could have easily done the same to a woman who'd pulled the heartstrings of one brother, had a baby with the other. To bury secrets. To protect themselves.

Uncle Roland shakes my arm. 'Okay, buddy?'

I take a deep breath, draw in as much air as possible, exhale. I want to shake my head, scream out, *No, I'm not okay*, but I focus on the breathing, try not to enter the dark world of unconsciousness.

'Why don't you want the casket open?' I whisper.

'What's that?'

'The casket.' I turn to Aunty Janice. 'Why do you want it closed?'

She doesn't respond.

'What happened to his head?'

Aunty Janice sighs. 'He had a fall, Henry.'

'I know. Off the ladder.'

'No. When he died. He must have got up in the middle of the night to go to the toilet. I found him in the bathroom that morning. Doctor said he'd had some kind of seizure, or brain snap. He fell down, cracked his head open on the porcelain. But it wouldn't have hurt. His brain had already shut down.'

'Why didn't you tell me?'

'I told you he'd died. No need for the details.'

'Why does everyone in this family hide the real reason we die?' I stand, wavering on jelly legs.

'What are you doing?'

'I need to see him.'

'It won't change anything.'

'I need. To see.'

Aunty Janice reaches out, grabs my arm, tightens a talon-like grip. 'Sit down, Henry. It's just a husk in there, nothing more. You had fifteen years to see him. You can't change things now.'

I drop to my seat. Aunty Janice releases her grip. Lucy's trying to say something. The booming noise returns though, filtering out her voice. A warm rush curls through my body. I lower my head to my knees, breathe deep calming breaths.

Aunty Janice is a spiteful bitch, but she's right. I had fifteen years to see Uncle Graham. I stayed away from him, though. Stayed in my nice bubble of a life in Perth. Everyone who sees me today is going to be thinking what she is: I never saw Uncle Graham, yet I have the nerve to do his eulogy?

I stare at the carpet until my body calms, sound returning.

Aunty Janice has moved on. She's talking about Uncle Graham to Lucy and my mother. 'Graham liked to keep to himself for a while, there. His typewriters were a sign he was getting back out in the community.'

I look up, gaze at the coffin as she continues recalling some of the funnier stories about Uncle Graham and the people of Margaret River. Revealing moments I've never heard, things I wasn't there for, using the others as a filter, her tone and temperament switching lightning-fast. She's talking about Uncle Graham with such love, she has me doubting my suspicions. She has, after all, lost a second brother now. With another in the hospital. And another arrested. This can't be easy for her.

Or maybe that's what she wants me to think.

I can't ignore the bruise. When the black four-wheel-drive crashed into Kevin's car, the airbag deployment would have left a mark. If not, a stiff neck, back, something. I try to remember how Aunty Janice had entered the room. She'd hurried in to stop Lewis. Was she masking the pain?

Uncle Roland nudges me. 'Come on, Henry. Graham wouldn't want you to be sad.'

'Why not?' I mumble.

I can hear Uncle Roland trying to form a reply, his mouth gasping for air like a fish. Trent saves him by knocking on the door, drawing our attention.

'Limo's here.'

Lewis appears. He asks if we want more time alone with the deceased. I almost say, *No, cause he's not really in there,* but hold my tongue. Lewis runs through the upcoming schedule, vocalising our movements so he doesn't forget them. The gist of it is, we're going to leave our own vehicles, get in a chauffeured car, head to a church back in Margaret River for the funeral. The old man will be ahead of us, driving the hearse.

We're led outside to the limousine before I realise I should have said goodbye or touched the coffin or something. A young man named Marshall introduces himself as the driver. Before I can ask to go back inside, he directs the six of us into the vehicle. Trent slides onto a row of seats on the far side, stretches out as if he's going to sleep. His mother slaps his leg, pushing her way down next to him. I make sure Lucy can sit beside me this time. My mother edges her way next to her.

'You can sit over there, Roland,' Aunty Janice says, pointing to a set of empty seats. 'Those were for David and Daniel. Won't be needing them, now.' She purses her lips, stares at me with such intensity I have to look away.

It's going to be a long drive.

Why do we have limousines for funerals? Is it to keep a large family together, to be one in the grieving process? I don't want to be with my family. Besides, limousines are supposed to be for celebrities and high school balls. I don't think Uncle Graham had ridden a limo more than once in his life, so why do we have to travel in such luxury today?

Aunty Janice has found her way into the liquor cabinet. She's poured herself a botanical gin, neat, sipping it while humming a tune I don't recognise. Everyone else is looking out the windows, taking in the scenery, avoiding eye contact and thus any conversation. Proving why families don't need to be together on the way to a funeral.

I should have made excuses. Should have just driven Lucy and myself from the funeral director's, met everyone at the church.

The whole car arrangement seems strange. Like, how do we get back home? But it's all about keeping up appearances. Just for a couple of hours.

'Did you finish writing the eulogy?'

I hear the voice but take a while to register where it's coming from. My mother. I think it's the first thing she's said to me today.

'Yes, mother.'

'Good.'

'I wrote a backup in case,' Aunty Janice chips in.

'Should I read mine to you all now, for feedback?' I ask.

'It's fine,' they chorus.

Lucy grips my hand, squeezes it hard.

'You want a drink, Henry?' Aunty Janice says.

'I'm right, thanks.'

'You sure? Could loosen you up, a little.'

'It's not a festive occasion.'

'Graham wouldn't want us to mope.'

'You guys keep saying that.'

'Well…'

'Maybe we should bury him first.'

Aunty Janice stares at me for five long seconds before raising her glass to her lips, downing the remaining liquid within. We return to sitting in silence. The ride lasts far longer than it should.

I look to the heavens in thanks as we reach landmarks I recognise: the bridge leading into the main town strip, the stretch of shops, the campus. We turn after the campus, round it, turn off somewhere close to Kevin's caravan park. It doesn't take long for the church to appear. It's framed by cleared surrounding land; red dirt covered by patches of green. Its roof pitches skyward,

Colorbond steel held up by glass panels. There's a rammed-earth tower out the front, holding a cross and bell for all to see and hear. Fancy, but down to earth. I can see why Uncle Graham chose it.

A handful of people are waiting outside. I see them chatting away until they spot our limousine. As we pass, they stare in silence, plastering as much sorrow as they can muster on their faces. The second our car edges away, their chatter resumes.

'Fuck it,' I call out. 'Pour me a drink.'

'Henry?' Lucy whispers.

'Too late,' Uncle Roland says. 'We're here.'

Aunty Janice had poured herself another drink as we'd crossed the bridge into town. As the car rolls to a stop, I scooch across the limousine and rip the glass from her, downing the remaining liquid in one gulp.

'That's more like it,' Aunty Janice chortles, unfazed by my action. 'But you'll have to wait for more later. I've pre-paid for a package at Brauhaus.'

'I know. I'll be taking advantage of that.'

'We'll take it easy today,' Lucy corrects me.

Aunty Janice leans over and dismissively waves at my wife. 'Honey, if ever there was a day when you're allowed to consume an excessive amount of alcohol, this is it.'

She looks at me, winks.

I try to smile back. Aunty Janice is right, but she doesn't know the real reason. I'll be needing alcohol to take the sting away. After I cause the downfall of my family.

Gary's waiting for me outside, in a dark suit. Lucy distracts the rest of my family while I hurry over to meet him. He lets me know he's got officers covering the church's exit points. All in suits, too. Like some kind of Secret Service, hidden to my uncle's associates. Unless they know the local cops, like Uncle Daniel did.

Gary starts telling me about the servers at my uncle's cottage, but I point to my family, to the church, remind him proceedings are about to start.

'I'll just be a minute,' he says. 'First, I didn't get to tell you. Two officers picked up one Reginald Thurston yesterday afternoon, still skulking around Voyager.'

'Reg?' I picture him awaiting instructions while everyone was being arrested or chased away.

'Yep. So, we've got everyone on your uncle's team?'

'If it was his team to start with.' Which I don't think it was. And if Reg was at Voyager, or being arrested, it means it wasn't him at Uncle Graham's. 'Who are you hoping to catch here today, then?'

'If anyone asks, we're paying our respect. But, well, you're going to want to see this.' Gary takes out a photograph, hands it to me. 'The tech team from Perth, they love what you found. Definitely some kind of VPN setup.'

'After the funeral, Gary.'

'Just… There's more. Some drives are full of content we'll need much longer to understand. Like an archive of videos and photographs putting lots of people in compromising positions. One of the latest videos features you, and it looks like you're shooting a roo. Woah, don't worry, I'll give you a chance to explain later. Anyway, the team went right back in the system. This photo you're holding was the oldest file they could source.'

'What am I looking at? It's just a car.'

'A car that was once licensed to your uncle, Roland Stevenson. Burgundy Mercedes Benz. Ninety-one model. Wagon.'

'It's pretty banged up. The bumper…'

'Looks like it struck something? Like, another car?'

'You don't mean…' I hand the photograph back.

'You have your family in the one room. Do you think you could—'

'Force a confession?'

'Emotions will be running high.'

'You want me to bring up a hit-and-run during my uncle's funeral?'

'It'd save hours of interviews and paperwork for something we can't prove or coerce.'

I can't help but grin. 'I'd already planned something similar. Take that photo to June. She's inside, part of the funeral director's team. Ask her to add it to the end of my eulogy photos. And say I'm sorry for the extra work.'

'Yes, sir.' Gary gives a mock salute, then hurries inside.

I look back at my family. They're waiting, talking to a few relatives who've appeared out of nowhere. Lewis is trying to urge everyone inside. Aunty Janice sees me, winks again.

I'm still grinning. For the first time all week, I can't wait to give the eulogy.

CHAPTER THIRTY-SIX
DROP THE HAMMER

I can't remember my father's funeral, the memories buried with the man I hardly knew. I don't remember being in a church, having everyone's eyes track you as you enter. Or looking to the front and seeing the coffin magically appear from the funeral director's room, even though common sense tells me we followed it the whole way. I don't remember the awful feeling rippling through my body as I see that coffin, knowing this is my last moment to say goodbye.

Knowing I'm going to ruin that moment.

Lewis directs us to a cleared pew at the front of the church. Before us, the front wall features a stacked pattern of dark stones and a large timber cross holding a ceramic, crucified Jesus. On the ground before the cross is a white-cloth-covered-tabernacle. To its side, Uncle Graham's coffin on its stand, a large arrangement of flowers atop.

'Wow, look at all that,' Lucy whispers. 'June did a marvellous job.'

Beside the coffin, there's an arrangement of my uncle's possessions on and around a small cloth-covered table; the movie poster next to it, taped to a painter's easel. Behind the display, hanging before the stone wall, is a large screen. Uncle Graham's younger face smiles from it, immortalised for the audience.

Anyone who approaches the coffin will see all this, will recall their own stories about Uncle Graham's life. I'm happy I found as much as I did, even if Aunty Janice sourced most of it. I know my uncle would have appreciated it.

Except I didn't find Lillian.

I force myself to scan the crowd. The church is full. There are at least three wooden rows of pews, then row upon row of plastic chairs, all separated by an aisle through the middle. Every seat seems occupied. Some latecomers are standing near the back. Everyone's staring at us.

Lucy leans against my arm. 'It's okay,' she whispers. 'You'll get through this.'

I nod. My mother's seated beside me. She clasps my right hand. I look at her, wondering what has brought on the sudden gesture, and see a face full of tears.

'Mum?'

She doesn't speak, just raises a handkerchief to her face, dabs her cheeks.

A song's soft melody winds down. The funeral begins. It looks like it's going to be run in tandem by a priest and the funeral director, something else my uncle must have arranged. Another song starts, an unseen choir making everyone else's mumbles seem fantastic. I stand, sit, follow the motions. Try to focus on what's important, locking my gaze onto Uncle Graham's coffin.

You'd better be inside that thing.

Everyone's voice is like the incomprehensible hum of adults in a Charlie Brown cartoon. At some point, there's a sharp tug on my arm. My wife, reminding me it's my turn to speak. Already? I get up, shift my gaze from the coffin to a lectern. Lewis is beside it, gesturing for me to join him.

I make my way to the lectern. When I reach it, I turn, take in the crowd once more. There are many familiar faces: Kevin, Jock, Leonie. Aunties and uncles I'd forgotten until the dinners at Aunty Janice's. Gary and the bear-like officer, standing by the main entrance. I take a deep breath, lock eyes with Gary. He nods. Then I shift my attention to the front row. To my wife, mother, Aunty Janice, Uncle Roland, Trent. To the gaps either side of them, reserved room for my uncles.

I tap the microphone hanging over the lectern. It echoes back at me. There's a cough from deep in the crowd. People fidget on their plastic chairs. I take out my notes, spread them over the lectern. Find June to the side of me. Nod. Look at the big screen, see another photograph of my uncle smiling at everyone. Take another deep breath.

I can't do this. Can I do this? I *have* to do this. Everything's led to this moment. It's the one chance I might have to catch my family out, before they disappear back into their own lives, no longer wishing to see me. I can't let the truth die with Uncle Graham.

I exhale.

'My name is Henry Herbert,' I begin, 'and Graham was my uncle. He rang me just before he passed away and asked me to give this eulogy. I was reluctant to, but you can't refuse a dying man's request, so here I am. I was reluctant because I haven't seen my uncle in the last fifteen years. You all here today, you know him far more than I did. Fifteen years is too long. People change, get new interests, live in new places, meet new people.' I glance towards Uncle Graham's coffin, to the small display beside it. 'Like, he restored typewriters? I can't believe he did something like that. A dying art he kept alive. I wonder, how many of you have a typewriter named after you? Uncle Graham left me one, but it wasn't in my name. He called it Lillian.'

I stare at my family on the front pew. No reaction.

I stick to my notes, recount Uncle Graham's childhood, where he grew up, what interested him when he was young, his first jobs. Anything I've been told, can remember, have researched. Then I share a few stories about the life he and I shared. Stories such as the time Uncle Graham showed up at my under-twelves basketball final, wearing a jersey he'd just bought, thinking I'd love it, saying it would motivate me. But it was the jersey of one of the NBA's most polarising players, Charles Barkley. It riled me. I couldn't stop thinking, *How did he not know I love Michael Jordan?* It made me so mad, I carried it onto the court, played aggressively, scored more than I ever had before. My team won by nine points. My uncle winked at me after the game, lifted the Barkley jersey to reveal a Jordan one beneath. Already hiding one thing within another.

I tell another story about how, after my father died, Uncle Graham gave me a book called *The Prophet*, a book about spirituality. We'd discussed death, our thoughts on the afterlife, and I remember telling him I thought you got to choose. That when you died, you went to a place where you could either elect to be reincarnated or pass through to some eternal resting place. My uncle said that sounded nice. He never shared which version he'd choose.

I close my eyes, take a deep breath. Trying to halt forthcoming tears.

'Then again,' I continue, opening my eyes, 'things may have never happened that way. I might be remembering the past the way I want. Because there are some moments in my life I can't remember at all. They happened, though. I've got photos to prove I was there.'

I nod at June again. On the large screen, the photograph of my uncle disappears, replaced by one of the beach scenes. 'This looks like a big get together, a family day on the beach. I recognise most people, but not the one in front of Uncle Graham.' I nod to June. Next photo. 'Uncle Graham sure looks smitten with her, though. See them playing beach cricket? A pretty memorable day, right? But when I asked my family if they knew the woman, they all denied it.' Next photo. 'There she is with my father, Aunty Janice and Uncle Roland, all having dinner. Hey Aunty Janice, Uncle Roland, how come you said you didn't know her?'

There's the slightest reaction from Uncle Roland, his vision dipping, eye contact avoided.

'I know why. Cause Uncle Graham loved her, yet my father had an affair with her.'

'Stop!' my mother snaps, standing.

'Her name was Charlotte Harris,' I continue. 'I bet a few long-time locals remember her. She died in a horrible car crash.'

I nod. Next photo. I glance at the screen, make sure it's the one Gary had shown me outside.

'Except someone else caused the crash,' I say. 'It was a hit and run.'

'Stop, Henry!'

'The car in that photo looks like it's just had an accident, don't you think? Who did that car belong to, Uncle Roland?'

Aunty Janice jumps up, joining my mother. 'This eulogy's supposed to be about Graham's life, Henry. *The wonderful memories!*'

The congregation murmurs, catching on to what they're witnessing, realising this isn't just a generic biographical spiel on the deceased. I scan my notes. I'd deviated from them a while back, letting the photographs guide me. The funeral director is trying to calm Aunty Janice and my mother, urging them to sit down. He scowls at me, a silent warning.

'Charlotte was pregnant,' I continue. 'Did everyone know that? Could have been Uncle Graham's child. Could have been my father's. I think someone killed Charlotte because of that, desperate to keep the baby from being born.'

'He was going to leave her!' my mother screeches.

I look at everyone on the front row. There's no turning back. Uncle Graham wanted this to happen, I'm sure. Why else would he leave his cryptic trail of clues? Why else would he choose me to speak at this moment, someone so distanced from their extended family that they wouldn't hesitate to accuse them of unspeakable things? He was so close to solving this mystery himself. He just left me to put two and two together at the right time. Exposing my family's lies in the most public way possible.

Either that, or he was fucking with me, and I'm about to continue making the worst decision of my life.

I catch Lucy's gaze. She's beaming with pride. Giving me the confidence to continue. Trent's laughing, enjoying the stress I'm creating. Too self-absorbed to understand the implications, not even alive when everything happened.

Fuck it.

Time to drop the hammer.

I point at the coffin. 'Uncle Graham loved Charlotte. Why did you kill her, Uncle Roland?'

CHAPTER THIRTY-SEVEN
THE NEW 007

The hammer dropped, I expect someone to call out, break down, scream their confession. My words do nothing but echo around the church. Aunty Janice and my mother stand there in silence. Uncle Roland refuses to meet my gaze. The congregation sits there, stunned.

The hammer has bounced unnoticed into the shadows.

I don't think Uncle Roland caused Charlotte's crash. I know it was naïve to think Uncle Daniel wouldn't hurt me because he was my relative. I was stupid, trusting my heart instead of the data they pushed through at the police academy, the insanely high number of murders involving people that know each other. The splendour of reuniting with family members—all hugs, conversation and booze—suckered me in until that choice almost killed me. But Uncle Roland's kindness has always seemed genuine. He's the smooth, level-headed counterpart to Aunty Janice. Instinct tells me he wasn't directly involved. Data tells me it was his wife.

Uncle Daniel has already proven himself psychotic, why not his sister?

I've accused the husband, though, to test the wife's reaction. So far, nothing.

'Okay,' I continue, noticing the funeral director and priest closing in, ready to whisk me from the lectern. 'So, it seems Uncle Roland doesn't want to talk. Yet. I'll keep painting the picture. My father died in a different car crash. When I was younger, I was told he'd worked a long day, had driven tired, crashed. Recently, I've found out that he'd left work earlier to confront Charlotte.'

'He was leaving her,' mum repeats.

'See, I don't think he was. Kevin made it clearer when he lost his car. He said it was his girl, that he never thought she'd leave him, that he'd need a few drinks because of it.'

'Too bloody right,' Kevin calls out, getting a few titters from the audience.

'Why would dad drink so excessively if he'd ended the relationship? No, I think it was Charlotte who ended things. Dad couldn't take it, he drank, he drove. Sorry, mum, dad was a cheating arsehole who couldn't be happy enough with us.'

'That's a lie!' my mother roars.

'Okay, time to stop,' the funeral director pleads, tugging at my jacket.

I look to Lucy for help. She mimes singing into a microphone. Am I supposed to serenade the crowd? No, idiot, the tracklist. I flip through my notes, find what I need.

'You knew about the affair, didn't you, mum? Aunty Janice and Uncle Roland had hidden it from you, but you found out. You were jealous. You asked where Charlotte was and found her one night, on the edge of town. You wanted payback for what had happened, so you and Roland ran her off the road.'

I wait. I've worked in each song title Uncle Graham left me in his final tracklist, voiced a version of events that *could* be true. My creativity at its peak. Although, I hadn't planned on throwing my mother into the mix. I'd written Aunty Janice in my notes, yet my subconscious substituted names. Shit. I've just accused the woman who raised me of conspiring to murder, haven't I? In a church full of people?

Wrong or right, I'm fucked either way, now.

Aunty Janice wraps an arm around my mother's shoulder. 'Time to stop, Henry,' she calls out. 'You got the story down pretty well, but it was Daniel who killed her.'

'Daniel? You're blaming the guy who's not here?'

'I blame the drugs.'

'The drugs?'

Aunty Janice nods, nothing more.

'Why didn't you tell anyone if you knew all along?'

She shrugs as if that's enough.

'What were his reasons for killing Charlotte, then?'

'I don't know his reasons.'

'Did he kill Lillian, too?'

'Who?'

'Please,' the priest whispers, pushing against me, 'stop talking about death.'

'All you ever talk about in here is death,' I snap back.

The priest jerks away, hurt etched across his face. If there's a hell, I've taken another step towards going there.

'Look,' I say to the crowd, 'Uncle Graham wanted me to find Charlotte's child. He was piecing all this information together, too.

He was so close, but death was closer.' I stare at the table beside Uncle Graham's coffin. 'All the items over there summarise my uncle, but he also chose them to help me find out what happened. The last piece of the puzzle is something to do with Mammoth Cave. So, over the next couple of days, I'll get onto that, and my uncle can rest in peace knowing I've unlocked the cave's secrets.'

There's an echoing grunt. A thump. I look back at the front pew to see Uncle Roland standing.

'Toilet. I need the toilet,' he says, veering to the side of the church.

'Something wrong, Uncle Roland?'

'Just... nature calls.'

Someone stands to offer directions. Uncle Roland pushes them out the way.

'Was it something I said?' I ask into the microphone.

Uncle Roland lurches into a sprint. He eyes someone stepping over to block the side door, changes direction, heads for the main entrance. The bear-like officer waits for him.

'I think he knows about Mammoth Cave.'

A screech rips through the church. Aunty Janice charges towards me. I freeze at the absurdity of such a sight. She reaches the lectern, lunges. Slams against me. For a split-second, we're airborne, then we're crashing against Uncle Graham's display.

Aunty Janice hovers her face over mine, pure rage contorting every feature. 'I did *everything* to stop Graham! The truth was supposed to die with him!'

I try to move. A sharp pain tears across my back.

'You'll regret this! Every day will be soured by what you've done, you dull, useless city-boy piece of shit!'

Aunty Janice starts pounding my chest, spittle flying from her lips. I try to hold up my arms, defend myself, but my limbs won't work. Aunty Janice pummels my body. Nobody stops her. Why isn't anybody stopping her?

'Fuck it!' Aunty Janice stops hitting me, reaches out and grabs the typewriter from the remnants of the display. She holds it high above my head, then swings it downward. Before she connects, a blur crashes into her, throws her off me. She screeches once more, then whimpers.

Silence.

A switch flicks inside me, my limbs springing to life. I shuffle away, cough the air back into my lungs; prop myself up, stand. Everyone in the church is standing, too, craning their necks for a better view. I follow their gaze to see my wife pinning Aunty Janice to the ground. Seconds later, Gary arrives, taking over. I help Lucy up, see the smile on her face. I know what she's going to say before the words come out.

'Just like James Bond.'

'The new 007.' I manage a smile, rub the pain in my back.

The funeral director has seized the lectern, tapping on the microphone. 'Mr Herbert, you need to follow the police outside so we can continue with the scheduled proceedings. Remaining attendees, we have some lovely readings that will help us restore today's focus, then a better montage reflecting Graham's life. If you could just give us a moment to tidy things…'

The priest is pointing to the side door. I get it. I've hijacked my uncle's funeral at a price. I don't get to mourn him in the traditional sense, now.

But then, I never expected to.

Lucy and I step outside. In the distance, the suit-wearing officers are already putting my aunty and uncle in a wagon. Gary's near them, but he isn't worried about me, yet. If I find my mother, we can all go to the station, wait for the truth to be pieced together. I spin around, wondering if she's still in the church. Trent's standing so close to us, I almost yelp.

'Uncle Henry?'

The way he's staring makes me all sorts of uncomfortable. Is he going to lunge at me in a blind rage, too, after what I've done to his parents? Lucy lets go of my arm, giving me space, as if she's thought the same thing. Wanting me to be ready.

'Trent, I'm so sorry.'

'Did my parents… Did they…'

'We're not sure. The police will sort it out.'

'Are they… Did someone arrest them?'

I'm not sure they will be arrested; detained at best, since all Gary has to go on is a photograph and their insane behaviour. Once they're given a lawyer, everything will be circumstantial. 'They're just helping answer some questions. Why don't you head back to the funeral?'

Trent's fingers are flexing along with his jaw, as if his body is fighting his brain.

'Will they find something in Mammoth Cave?' he asks.

'I don't know. It's an enormous place. It could take a long time.'

Trent scoffs. 'Enormous place.'

'Why did you say it like that?'

'It's an inside joke. When my parents found it, they named it after the tourist spot.'

I glance at Lucy. What's going on?

'Where did your parents find Mammoth Cave?' Lucy asks.

'On their property. Right at the back.'

I try to place a reassuring hand on Trent's shoulder, but it's shaking too hard. 'Can you show me where the cave is?'

'Sure. After the—'

'Now.' Before your parents lawyer up and make everything disappear.

'But we'll miss—'

'This is what Uncle Graham wanted us to do.' Trent could re-enter the church, but I can't, and I need him. How can I sweeten the deal? 'I promise we'll turn up for the wake. There'll be lots of good whiskey. And beer. It's at the brewery. Your mother's already paid for it. Deal?'

Trent almost cracks a smile. 'Deal.'

CHAPTER THIRTY-EIGHT
CONNECT 4

I lead us to the car park, then remember we didn't arrive in my car. I look around, spot June smoking a cigarette, staring down the street. I call out for her. She stubs out the cigarette, walks over.

'Smoking outside a church,' I say, 'you sinner.'

'I needed a smoke after your show. And, well, they drink wine *inside* the church, so… just saying.'

I gesture at Lucy, Trent and myself. 'Can you drive us to Trent's house?'

'When?'

'Right now.'

'I have to start the photo montage soon.'

'Can't your boss do it?'

June sighs. 'He's horrible with tech.'

'Didn't my uncle instruct you to help me in any way possible?'

'Why did I tell you that?'

'Maybe I could just borrow your car, drive myself?'

'No way!' June calls Marshall the limousine driver over, gives him some instructions on how to operate the laptop and projector inside the church.

'You need to tell Gary what we're doing,' Lucy says while we wait.

'No,' I say. 'I need to see this for myself.'

'We're talking about a possible burial site, aren't we?'

'We don't know that. It could just lead to another clue.'

'Come on. You know that—'

'I just need to see it first.'

'What's happening? Why're we rushing off?' My mother's voice makes me jump more than Trent's. She'd followed us in silence, too. I start telling her to stay behind, to see the end of Uncle Graham's funeral, but she shakes her head. 'I have to tell you something, Henry.'

'Later, mum.'

'But those things you said in there…' She trails off, eyes swelling with tears again.

'Look, come with us, then. You can tell me whatever it is in the car.' Then she can tell it to Gary.

June returns her attention to us. 'All sorted.'

'You sure you want to help?' I ask, giving her an out after roping her in. 'I don't think a limousine driver's supposed to be used in that way.'

'Are you kidding? If what you're about to do is as crazy as what you just did in there, I want to be part of it. Besides, Marshall is Lewis's grandson, so he does whatever you ask him.'

'We're going into a cave,' Trent says.

'Are we?' June looks Trent up and down, flashes a cheeky grin. 'If it's dark, you might need to hold my hand.'

I can feel my eyes rolling. I redirect everyone's focus and hurry them towards the cars. 'Where did you park?' I ask June.

'My car? No way, it's tiny. We'll take the limo. I've got the extension on my licence.'

Gary's still busy with Aunty Janice and Uncle Roland. There will be a few people who want me charged for my behaviour, especially Lewis and the priest, but Gary had encouraged the confession, and he's not made it a point to see me now. He knows I'll turn up at the station. Eventually. Hopefully, with some closure.

June floors it out of the car park.

'You don't have to speed,' I call out from the back.

'I'm just excited.'

'Did my uncle pay a lot for this service?'

'I don't get told about that sort of stuff. I just follow instructions.'

'You always do things like this, though?'

'Anything to break the monotony.'

We take the back roads, winding our way to Aunty Janice's house, Trent directing June from the front passenger seat. It's wrong, travelling somewhere in luxury to uncover a potential crime scene. Maybe not as wrong as being kicked out of my uncle's funeral, but still conflicting. I'm thankful the trip is brief. June parks the limousine and joins us. My mother doesn't even ask why we're here. Maybe she thinks the wake's had a change of venue? We didn't talk on the journey, my mind too occupied with what's about to happen. I know in my heart that Lucy is right. We're going to find a burial site in that cave.

I'm about to complete Uncle Graham's list in the worst way imaginable.

Trent walks us through the house, pointing out a few things to June—the electric guitars, some surfboards, a liquor cabinet—enjoying the attention. My mother starts heading elsewhere, maybe to her guest room to fetch something, but I redirect her. We hurry outside, down the path, past the gazebo, out to the shed. Before we reach it, Trent steps into the thick growth and grabs a bush. He pulls it and the entire plant seems to rip from the ground.

'This plant is a plant,' he chuckles, throwing it to the side.

Trent grabs another bush and does the same, then steps onto a once-concealed track. A vine-like weed covers the ground, but the area's quite flat. Trampled. We head along it.

'You know,' Trent adds, 'I was never allowed to go down here. Like, my entire childhood. We have a frickin' mini cave on our property, our own tourist attraction. Mum hosts so many fancy soirées, you'd think she'd make it a key point of her night. One more thing to boast about.'

'I think there's a reason she kept everyone away,' I offer.

Lucy is several metres behind us, walking arm-in-arm with my mother. As the ground dips, I call out, warn her.

'Thanks, dear.'

The ground cover stops as the track starts widening. The vegetation spaces out, too, making way for thin trees that twist from the ground like skeletal fingers. Trent edges ahead with June, pointing out various flora I've never learned the names of. The track dips at a steeper angle, winding around a hidden hillside. The soil turns to gravel, gains a limestone-white colour. It takes about five minutes to navigate the next stretch. Once again, I'm in awe of how big Aunty Janice's property is. I could walk around my backyard at least twenty times in five minutes, but we're yet to see the perimeter of this place. Maybe that's the appeal of living down south; truly owning a piece of land. Your own slice of the world rather than just a sliver.

No. I can't be in awe now. Not the right time.

'Do you think Uncle Graham'll want us to scatter his ashes someplace like this?' Trent calls out.

I shrug. I don't know about those sorts of arrangements. Is he getting cremated? Are we scattering the ashes, or burying them? I should know that. The next family funeral, I'll plan the hell out of it.

'Shut up,' I urge myself, maybe a little too loud. I look around. Nobody appears to have heard. 'Let's just focus on the cave,' I say a little louder.

'Should we ring Gary now?' Lucy calls out. 'In case we lose reception?'

I shrug again. If it's a crime scene, we'll be contaminating it the second we step inside. I need to know, though. Need to make the discovery my uncle never could.

If it's the right place at all.

'Just one look,' I say. 'Then I'll make the call.'

We reach the cave's entrance, a hole in the hillside two metres high and three metres wide. I know it's the right place just by looking at it. It feels... laced with sadness.

'At least we don't need a rope to climb into it,' Trent says. 'The cave's pretty much flat from the entrance, the size of something like a Kmart. It's got the occasional stalagmite and a dried-up waterbed. Nothing too fancy, though.'

'I thought you weren't supposed to go in there,' Lucy says, nearing us with my mother.

Trent grins. 'As if I always do what my parents say.' He winks at June, thinking the line has impressed her. I don't have the heart to say it's creepy.

'When was the last time you were down here?' I ask.

'Oh, well, at least five, six years ago. But it can't have changed much. It's a cave.'

We head through the mouth. Gravel gives way to a harder rock floor. I take my phone out, use its flashlight function. Trent leads the way, pointing out a few things: a dry waterbed, some interesting formations of stalagmites that look like people if you squint hard enough. I feel Lucy by my side. I can't see my mother. Maybe she's waiting outside. I don't care at this point. I'm too busy sweeping the beam across the ground, looking for anything out of the ordinary.

As usual, Trent has understated the magnificence of his parent's property. We've walked for a couple of minutes, until the entrance has shrunken into a distant pinhole, and we're yet to see the cave's end. I stop as the ground beneath my feet changes to soft soil. It must be the dried-up waterbed.

I hear a sound. Swing the beam to my side. Keep walking forwards. Nothing. Maybe Trent and June's footsteps echoing around me? Or Lucy's? Where's Lucy? I swing the beam back, but too late. The ground gives way. I stumble, holding out my arms to absorb the fall. I thump against the floor anyway, my phone flying from my hand. Rock dust bursts around me. I cough, lungs on fire. Lucy calls out, asks if I'm okay. I don't know where she is. I fumble for my phone, find it, swing the beam around. I'm in a small hole. It's roughly a foot deep, three feet round.

'I think I'm okay,' I call out.

I pick myself up, focus on the area before me. There are more holes. An array of them, like a giant game of Connect 4 etched into the ground. I call out for Trent. He takes a while to find me. When he does, I sweep the beam over the array. 'When you were down here last, did you see these holes?'

'Not at all.'

'Who's been digging them?' June asks.

'Uncle Graham did this,' I answer. 'He was looking…'

'For Lillian?'

I can't vocalise an answer.

'Call the police,' Lucy says, 'they can organise a search.'

She's right again, and I need to listen to her. All I wanted was proof we'd found the right Mammoth Cave. If there's something buried here, I can't keep digging around, can't destroy any evidence pointing to a potential killer. If my uncle hasn't done that already.

We ease our way towards the pinpoint of sunlight at the cave's mouth, burst into the intense Australian sun. I blink spots from my eyes, ready to rush up the hill for a better phone signal, when I catch sight of my mother. She's on a downed tree trunk close to the cave's entrance. At first, I think she's just been sitting there, waiting. Then I notice the tears shining off her skin. Coating her cheeks. She has a handkerchief in her hand, but she's given up on wiping everything away.

'Mum?'

She looks at me with glazed eyes. 'What did you find?'

'I think Uncle Graham's done some digging.'

She nods. 'He'd never given up, you know. I could never tell him the truth. I was forced into silence, and it's eaten away at me.'

I stand beside my mother, catch a look from Lucy. We're both thinking the same thing: *Where's this going?*

'In the church,' my mother continues, 'all those things you said… He found a way to help you figure it out, didn't he?'

'He left me clues.'

'So, he knew already.' My mother sniffs. 'I have to tell you something, Henry. I'm afraid you'll never look at me the same again.'

'After I accused you of murder back in the church?'

My mother stares at me, sorrow stretched across her face. Waiting for me to catch up.

'I was right?' I gasp.

My mother nods. 'We all did it.' She shudders, dabs at her tears. 'We all killed Charlotte, and I'm afraid the same thing may have happened to her daughter.'

CHAPTER THIRTY-NINE
I GET MY WISH

'What do you mean, you *all* killed Charlotte?'

My legs wobble, drop my body onto the limestone gravel so I end up sitting cross-legged in front of my mother. Like I'm awaiting a bedtime story. About a family of murderers.

Lucy sits beside my mother, wraps an arm around her. My mother keeps dabbing away at her tears. Debating what to say, whether to continue at all. I can't let her stop, can't let her shut herself down and escape to the inward realm she regularly inhabits.

'You've said it now, mum. You'll have to tell this to the police. May as well practice with me first.'

'Henry, honey,' Lucy murmurs. 'You don't need to hear this. Gary can talk to her about it.'

I used to do this, I almost cry. *Let me do it now.*

'I need to hear it,' I say instead.

Lucy looks over at Trent, gets his attention. 'Can you take June back to the front of your house and wait for the police?

We're going to call them now. We need you to show them the way down here.'

Trent raises his eyebrows. 'With June? Sure.'

They hurry away. He doesn't even want to stay to hear mum's confession, one that's sure to involve his own parents. Was I ever that overzealous with Lucy, and did she ever notice?

When they're out of view, I will my legs to stand. I brush some dirt off my pants, take a seat on the other side of my mother.

'Okay, Helen,' Lucy says, her voice as calm as possible, 'you choose how much you want to tell us. Does it start with Henry's father, is that why it's hard to say more?'

My mother shakes her head. 'This happened after William died.'

'What happened?' Lucy asks before I can. 'Tell us what you remember.'

'Family,' my mother chuckles, 'you think you know them. The short of it is, you don't.' My mother glances at Lucy instead of me, as if she'll understand. 'When Henry's father died, he left me a widow with a son in his teens, a boy who didn't want a mother-figure telling him what to do. Graham came and lived with us to fill the void, but it didn't last too long.'

'Why not?' Lucy asks.

My mother shakes her head. 'It doesn't matter. What we're talking about now happened a few months after William died. Janice and Roland were up from Boranup. They'd been renovating their property for a year or so, driving back and forth from Margaret River to Perth.'

'Wait. They'd always planned to live down here?' I ask.

My mother nods. 'Roland bought that property for a steal so long ago. You remember visiting when you were little, don't you?

They lived there a while, then rented it out and stayed in Perth. Then Roland's company started getting lots of work in Mandurah, developing fancy, new estuary accommodation. They were down there so much, they decided to live back in Boranup. He helped your father get the Mandurah job, you know. There were going to be lots more houses to landscape.'

So, it wasn't my father's death that made them leave Perth. It just hastened their departure.

'What happened after William died?' Lucy asks, trying to focus the conversation.

'Everyone was over at our house in Perth,' my mother continues, 'Janice brought too much wine with her; it loosened our tongues. We talked about the problem that was the knocked-up mistress.'

'What did Uncle Graham have to say about that?' I ask.

'He wasn't there. He was out. Getting pizzas, I think. Hawaiian, Portofino. That's the one with mushroom, isn't it?'

'Mum, the murder?'

'Yes, well, that woman had already broken Graham's heart, then she'd latched onto William. She'd robbed me of the chance to have the perfect family—husband, wife and child.'

'I was never perfect enough,' I mumble.

My mother pretends she doesn't hear. 'I admitted it would be easier if there wasn't a mistress to talk about, no illegitimate child to consider. Janice said we should pay her to disappear. Daniel said he'd take care of it in his own way. I said no, anger was making me suggest silly things. Anger and wine. And I thought that was the end of it.'

'Obviously, it wasn't.'

'Your father's family all completed their move down south, except for Graham. Returning to their roots, they said. Keeping away, I felt. We went to visit them while they were settling in. Do you remember this?'

'No.'

'It's no surprise. This was about six months after your father had passed. Your head was in another place for a long time. Anyway, while Roland was cooking dinner, Daniel said he'd take Janice and me for a drive, go get some more wine. David wanted to come along, too. You stayed with Graham, who said he'd take over the cooking, put some actual flavour in it. We always made fun of Roland's cooking. He took it to heart, and it's why he's so good now. But Roland had a huff at the time, said he'd need more wine, too, so he tagged along. Well, we got more wine, but Daniel kept driving. Suddenly, we're at a stranger's house, and Daniel's banging on their door, telling them to come outside. Only, it's not a stranger, it's Charlotte who answers.

'Daniel's taken my anger to heart. "Come and get her, Helen," he's saying. I didn't notice it straight away, but he's got a tyre iron in his hand. Charlotte sees it. She ducks inside, slams the door shut. Daniel bangs on the door. David joins him. Janice gets out, stomps on the woman's flowerbeds, says she'll crush her like she's crushing the flowers, something stupid like that. It's like one shark fuelling the predatory instinct of another. Everyone getting into a frenzy. Roland and I are in the car watching it all. We don't know what to do. I bring myself to leave the car, but I can't find my voice. I know it's not right, but part of me wanted them to keep going, wanted them to hurt this woman.'

My mother pauses, looks to the peak of the hillside as if expecting someone to appear. When they don't, she sighs, continues.

'Well, I get my wish. Charlotte's snuck out the side of her house, got into her car without us hearing. She reverses out, takes off. We give chase. First, it's just to scare her, then Daniel rams her, and before we know it, she's left the road. Oh, the screeching sound… I don't know if she's alive or dead, Henry, and Daniel won't let us out to check. It's a dark back road nobody uses and we just drive off. We get back to Janice's, stay the night. I have to look at you and Graham and pretend nothing happened. We don't even call the police or an ambulance. I picked the phone up so many times, Henry, I just couldn't… And I'm up all night thinking about what had happened and the next day the news reports a local lady dying in hospital following a hit and run.

'And yes, I felt awful. We'd gone too far, we'd let rage push us, and it resulted in what rage is best at: destruction. But I also felt relieved, and I latched onto that relief, and it told me that what happened was an accident, that I couldn't have done anything to change it. I told myself that lie every single day for years and years.'

My mother stops, forgoes the handkerchief and uses the back of her hand to wipe more tears from her eye. We wait, but she doesn't continue. This is the most I have heard her speak in one sitting for decades. Maybe she's run out of words?

I need her to finish the story, though. 'What about the baby? When did you find out it survived?'

My mother shakes her head. 'Not until Graham called me.'

'When was that?'

'About a year ago.'

'So, this whole time…'

'I didn't know. Honestly, I didn't. They never reported it in the news, and—'

'What did Uncle Graham say?'

'He was so angry at the way that woman had left him, and with your father's death… We thought he'd cast her from his mind. I don't know when he'd started digging into her death, when he'd found out about the baby. But when he called, he believed the child had found her family roots, something leading to Janice. The trail ran cold there; Graham was sorting through rumours of her fate. Ending up in a cave was one of them.' My mother shudders. 'I don't want to know what's in there.'

'You already thought you killed her as a baby,' I snap, 'what's the difference now?'

My mother holds her hands up in mock surrender. 'I can't change what happened, can't erase mistakes. But if ever there were a chance to make amends…'

'It's too late for that.'

'It's never too—'

'Did you help Uncle Graham?'

My mother lowers her hands, puzzled.

'When he called and told you about Lillian, did you help him find her?'

She shakes her head.

'Did Aunty Janice know he was looking for her?'

She shrugs.

I stand. 'Then I'm going to do what Uncle Graham should have done.'

'Where are you going?'

I ignore her.

'Henry? Where are you going?'

I head up the hillside, my body heaving, fighting a waterfall of tears desperate to escape.

'Don't call the police. Please!'

I have to stay composed, have to push everything down just a little longer.

'It's your family, Henry! I'm your mother!'

I reach higher ground, turn to look back at her.

'Let our mistakes stay buried,' she sobs before burying her face in her hands.

I think of Leonie Haynes, of Lillian's extended foster family. Never knowing Lillian's fate. Clinging to the hope that a plaque in Karrakatta Cemetery will one day be unnecessary. I think of how this secret has made my mother withdrawn from the world. From me. Fighting guilt every time the memory is triggered. Convincing herself that Charlotte's death was for the best, as if the woman's life meant nothing. As if her baby's life was an inconvenience to eradicate.

'Henry! Please!'

I take out my phone. Bring up Gary's number. Begin the hardest call I've ever had to make.

CHAPTER FORTY
HERBERT WEEK

'Another beer, Henry, mate?'

A glass is thrust into my hand. I look up from my seat to see Kevin doing his best to appear cheerful. We've been back at the brewery for twenty minutes, and I'm already into my second pint.

After making the call to Gary, several officers had turned up, then put out a request for a specialist to identify a burial site. The officers took our details, detained my mother to retell her version of events at the station, then allowed us to leave. Gary's call, which suited me fine. He knew we'd be sticking around town, but I no longer wanted to be the first to see what they exhumed, reality sinking in.

I just wanted to hide in the studio, but the wake presented a brief return to normalcy. Keeping up appearances for Uncle Graham. And a good distraction.

'All good, Henry? You don't like the stout?' Jock's standing beside Kevin, a worried look on his face. Is he concerned we're not having a good time, at a wake? No, that's a stupid thought. He just wants to make sure we're taken care of.

'All good, Jock. Thanks for this.' I wave my hand around, encompassing the small crowd of chatting, drinking mourners.

Leonie Haynes isn't amongst the crowd. I've missed another opportunity to talk about Lillian, to get her photograph. My body's response is to down the beer in my hand in three quick gulps. Jock disappears for a moment, then reappears with another pint.

'Remember, your aunt paid for it.'

'Then keep them coming. And make sure you take care of everyone else, too. Especially Trent. Get him some top shelf whiskey.'

'If ever there's a time to drink irresponsibly,' Kevin adds, 'it's at a time like this.'

'I didn't hear you utter the term "drink *irresponsibly*",' Jock jokes.

I raise my fresh glass. Five days ago, I drove down to Margaret River to prepare for Uncle Graham's funeral. That was already depressing enough. Now, I've exposed my family as a bunch of murderers, keepers of long-held secrets and hosts of a hidden computer network. I will return to Perth knowing up to five family members may face trial, not to mention Uncle Daniel's mates. Because of me. Five family members, including my mother, whose confession I couldn't ignore.

Now I've lost everyone who raised me. On top of that, I failed to help prepare my uncle's funeral, failed to even see the end of it.

I down my new beer, smack my lips together.

Kevin and Jock pat me on the back, then disappear to another part of the room. Kevin's happy to take over as host, keeping everyone plastered. Responsibly.

Lucy returns from the toilet. She takes the empty glass from my hand, runs a finger under my chin and tilts my head to meet her beautiful green eyes. 'I know that look. Whatever happens, you'll always have me.'

I try to smile. It's a thought that thrills me, but one I'll be more appreciative of later.

'Maybe they'll all get let off,' I mumble.

'What's that?'

'Everyone's confessing to stuff, but there are no other witnesses, not much evidence.'

'The police will gather enough evidence, especially if something's in the cave.' Lucy leans in, kisses me on the cheek. 'You're a good man, Henry. Not like them. And you did the right thing.'

I'm about to ask her why doing the right thing feels so fucking awful when my mobile rings. It's Gary.

'What's happening?' I almost shout as I start the call.

'Easy, we're just gathering evidence.'

I look at my phone, at my wife, our surroundings. Has Gary bugged something, or is he the master of coincidence?

'Henry, you there?'

'I'm here.'

'You know, we're officially going to call this Herbert Week, to explain the extraordinary jump in overtime hours.'

'Better than arresting wine-soaked tourists, I guess,'

'That's not all that happens on our slice of earth, and you know that.'

I motion to Lucy. We head to the grassed area, away from the noise. 'You mentioned evidence?'

'A local brought in an old service dog. German Shepherd. We've used it before. Took about ten minutes to detect a body.'

I shudder, turn my phone's loudspeaker on. I need Lucy to hear this, regardless of who else can. 'Is it… Was it…'

'We haven't dug it up. The dog just got the scent, confirming there's something there.'

'Near the holes?'

'Close. A couple of metres deeper in.'

'When…' I swallow a rising lump in my throat '…When will you know? For sure.'

'It'll be a while.'

'Like, a day?'

'You remember procedure… We need to get a team in to dig. Then if we find something, there'll be testing, investigations, paperwork, paperwork, paperwork. This isn't a *days* thing, it could be weeks till we know who it is.'

'What do I do in the meantime?'

'Today, you finish your uncle's wake, do what you need to do. That's why my team let you leave. But before you head back to Perth, you all need to see me at the station. Help me with my paperwork. Help make sense of what the hell has been happening.'

I know Gary has asked for patience. I know I should be talking and drinking with everyone at the brewery, honouring Uncle Graham. Keeping myself distracted. But all the pints in the world can't stop me thinking about what's lurking in the cave, what my relatives are saying at the police station. I last an hour before asking Lucy to come for a walk with me.

We make our way into town. Lucy points out some shops and I remind myself she's hardly seen anything. Nor have I, really, the town's epicentre a blur. Will we be able to return to Margaret River for a real holiday, or will be it be forever tainted by everything we've discovered?

'Can we go into the bookstore?' Lucy asks.

'Maybe later.' My voice is a little slurred. Regardless of the alcohol swimming in my system, there's only one destination in my mind.

I stop.

'You know what?' I try to take Lucy's hand, miss the first time. 'Bookstore sounds great. I've just got to… I mean, I need…'

'To sort things out at the station?' Lucy leans in, kisses my cheek. 'You want a mint for your breath?'

'A mint would be great. Hey, how come we don't say mint and pint the same way? It's just the first letter that's different.'

'Great question. Maybe don't ask Gary, though. He's got enough to deal with. And take as long as you need. I'm going to see what else this Robotham guy's written.'

I wheeze my way into the station, where the same woman greets me at the desk with a suspicious smile.

'Hi, Carol,' I manage. 'Carla?'

'Carla.'

'Gary in? Sergeant Winters?'

'Wait here. Harry, right?'

'Henry.'

Carla's smile widens. Now we're even.

I collapse on a chair. Wait as the minutes tick by. I should have turned myself in long ago. Made myself available for deeper questioning, explaining my behaviour throughout the week. Following procedure, cooperating with local law enforcement. Gary's going to lose his job if a colleague complains about his leniency towards me. I need to be innocent in everyone's eyes, not just his.

I lose track of time. Almost fall asleep. Three pints will do that.

Someone rocks my shoulder. I open my eyes, shrink back against my chair. It's just an officer, though, a young man I've never seen before. He asks me to follow him through the station. Leads me to a small, enclosed room. It's got a tiny desk and three chairs, no decorations. I'm offered a coffee, which I accept with a little too much enthusiasm. The officer tells me he'll go and make it. I sit as he leaves the room. The door shuts with a click.

Fuck. I've made a gigantic mistake. Gary must still be out at Aunty Janice's property. He won't be here to corroborate my story. Someone with a chip on their shoulder, like bear officer, is going to interrogate me, lump me in with the rest of my sick family. A six-for-one deal.

No. I wanted this. I expected this. The alcohol's messing with my brain. Or is it the trauma of everything that's happened? Is this the onset of a breakdown? I did just call the police on my mother, after discovering the burial site of my half-sister. Not to mention the funeral I ruined, the multiple lives I put in danger, the constant threats to my own life. At some point, my mind is primed to snap, right? Maybe I've reached that point.

Where's Lucy? I'm so much stronger with her by my side and I didn't ask her to join me. She just wants the best for me, is clearly still in love with me. What's going to happen if I'm imprisoned on some technicality? Lynden could get a lawyer that twists everything around, makes it my fault I got abducted and bashed my way to safety.

I start sobbing. Real make-every-limb-shudder-as-if-something's-trying-to-escape-your-body sobbing. I can't stop, every beer-infused thought working its way through me.

At some point, the door opens. Gary steps inside, still in his suit, accompanied by the young officer.

'Oh, thank God!' I take a deep breath, wipe the mess from my face, sit upright. Pretend everything is completely normal.

'Henry, I said to finish your uncle's wake, pop in before going back to Perth.' They round me, take a seat on the opposite side of the desk. Gary doesn't introduce the young officer.

'We'll be leaving tomorrow morning,' I offer, which might be the truth, 'so I wanted to get this done now.'

Gary swipes an invisible fly. 'You've been drinking, you sure you want to do this now?'

I nod. 'I feel a little better.'

Gary produces a notepad, flips it open, reads a few notes.

'Wait,' I say, panic returning. 'Am I here to help make sense of things, or are you looking for a reason to take me to a holding cell?'

'Information, mate. If I doubted you, I'd have arrested you days ago. Or several times after that.'

I try to smile.

'As I said at the funeral, the tech team loved what you found at the cottage. Apparently, you helped uncover a smorgasbord of online schemes. Pretty unique for our little patch of Australia.'

'What type of schemes?'

'Besides the VPN hosting, a server linked to websites hidden in the deep web. Or the dark web. I don't know the difference, and I've written both down. They're hosting a range of things, though. Australia's own PirateBay. I can't go into more than that, except to say they also seem to store a lot of photos and video footage of people around town. Both tourists and locals. A lot of hidden cameras we weren't aware of. They've called more tech guys to come and investigate, so it's out of my hands now. I'll let the big boys deal with all that paperwork. At least it means we have justification for Herbert Week's overtime budget. We might even make front page of the papers.'

'So, my uncles are criminals in every sense of the word?'

'The internet's the new land of gold, for all the wrong reasons. But I'm with your earlier thoughts, I think they had outside help with the setup. I'll note it in my report.' He taps the pad.

'Everything you said in church, you got that from your uncle, Graham?'

I tell Gary about the clues within the funeral list. What it led me to understand. How my father's family reacted. The aftermath, with my suspicion of Aunty Janice as balaclava-face, trying to clean up everyone's mistakes. Gary's heard a lot of this already, but he doesn't stop me, takes more notes, points a few things out to the young officer.

'I can designate time to build a file on Lillian, now,' he says. 'But nobody's willing to shift any blame to your aunt, even with a body on her property. Early days, though. I'm sure we'll break the hold she has on your family.'

'She doesn't have a hold on me,' I say. 'Guess that's why Uncle Graham knew I'd follow his clues.'

'Do you want to talk to anyone from your family now, while they're being held?'

I thought I did, but find myself shaking my head.

'Well, you'll be called to witness for several charges. And if they come up, we'll be able to explain away some of your actions. I've already taken a call from the priest, and he's offered his understanding and forgiveness.'

'I hope Uncle Graham can forgive me.'

'After all you've done?' Gary shakes his head. 'I know it's not the result you were hoping for but look what you achieved.'

'I just made sense of a crime my uncle should have reported to you.'

'We won't know why he hid it from us.'

Hid it? I close my eyes, a theory boiling to the surface; something that's nagged at me ever since Uncle Graham's phone call.

'He knew he was going to die,' I whisper.

'Come again?'

'I got to Uncle Graham's house three days after he died, and Aunty Janice had already boxed everything up. Tubs were missing. The phone line was down. Most furnishings were gone. Clothes and sheets and everything, the place stripped bare.'

'People cope with grief in unusual ways.'

'Grief? No.' I open my eyes. 'She was looking for something. Removing evidence. She suspected Uncle Graham was searching for Lillian. Mum said he called her a year ago, gave her some theories. He's been working on it this whole time. And then, with his diagnosis, it becomes a race to the finish line. He finds the cave, starts digging. He asked me to keep digging, on the phone. I thought he meant dig for information. What if it had a double-meaning, though, like all his clues? What if he had to resort to all the secrecy to fool Aunty Janice, to make her think he'd given up?'

'We won't be able to prove it. And if he thought he was going to die, wouldn't he have just come to us, anyway?'

'Janice could have held something over him. Or maybe he thought she held something over the police? I know, it's a thin theory. But when Uncle Daniel took the roo video of me, he said he owned me. Mum told me she was forced into silence after Charlotte's crash. They had a photo of Uncle Roland's car—maybe his own wife held that over him? Everyone blackmailed. And then… maybe it fell apart cause Aunty Janice caught Uncle Graham digging in her cave.' I reach out, grip the table. 'She hadn't wanted me to see his body. Someone had written it off as a fall, hitting his head on the toilet. But what if…'

I can't finish the question, fighting more rising tears.

'The truth will come out,' Gary offers.

'If you can prove it?'

They can't even examine my uncle's body. It's ash by now.

I pull back from the table, stand. 'I need to be with Lucy.' I reach out to shake Gary's hand. 'Thanks for everything you've done to help me. You went far beyond your duty.'

Gary rises, returns the handshake. 'We'll keep you posted. I know this is the furthest thing from your mind, but the offer of employment still stands. The way you've pieced everything together, you've got the instinct of a detective in you.'

'With my family background?'

'You still don't remember me well, do you? Senior year, police arrested my father. Failed bank robbery. Everyone called me Getaway Gary, like I was the driver in the entire scheme; even though I was in class at the time.'

I don't remember that at all. A moment that impacted Gary's future, and I was too busy feeling sorry for myself to register it.

'Point is, we're not our parents. Or family. Not always, anyway. We're the occasional exception, and that's something to unite us.'

'I'll think about it,' I offer.

After all I've lost today, it's a tempting ray of hope. But I can't do anything until I know what's buried in that cave. Until I know how many secrets a patch of earth can uncover.

CHAPTER FORTY-ONE
WHERE DO I START

My mobile phone is ringing. I reach into my pocket, but it's not there. I roll out of bed—drowsy but sleepless—and follow the sound across the studio, retrieve it from the now-empty coffee table.

It's nine-fifteen in the morning. The closed blinds suggested otherwise.

'It's my day off,' Gary says, 'but they've given me an update.'

'Let's hear it.' I walk back to the bed, nudge Lucy. She stirs, doesn't wake.

'It's not much.'

I walk out onto the decking, blink away the sunlight, find myself taken back to the moment outside the cave. 'Anything will help me at this point.'

'First off, doctors say they'll bring your uncle, Daniel, out of his coma tomorrow or the day after. Once he's alert, he might give us a lot of answers.'

I don't know how to respond to that, so I stay silent.

'Second,' Gary continues, 'the team at the cave had some overtime approved. They've already uncovered the body.'

'Was it… could they tell who…'

'Several indicators confirm it's female. That's all I know. They've got to work around the area, then take everything in for processing. No identity, yet. Paperwork, paperwork, remember? I just didn't want to leave you hanging. There's definitely a body, and it's definitely female.'

I thank Gary for the update and end the call, then creep back into the studio. Lock myself in its bathroom, slide into the empty spa. Curl into a foetal position. Think about the woman buried in the cave. My sister. Who I never got to meet. I bring my arms up to smother my mouth, and scream.

Lucy and I check out of the studio, drive her car to Busselton, to the funeral director.

'I'll see you back home,' Lucy says, parting ways with a kiss, her lips lingering on mine.

'Wish we could go together.'

'I know.'

'Tell your parents I'll see them soon.'

June appears as Lucy drives away. She's carrying two boxes. One holds the display items from the funeral. The other holds my uncle, his ashes in an urn. June explains all this while I'm wondering where I'm supposed to take the ashes. Apparently, the director has mailed further instructions from my uncle. They'll arrive in the next week. Or two.

'Thanks for the interesting funeral,' June says, carrying a box to my car. 'I thought this job was just the same old thing every day. Then you came along and added some sparkle to it.'

'Glad I could help.'

'I might even write a book about it one day. Lonely funeral worker gets entangled in a dramatic cold case.'

'Entangled?'

'Well, it'll be fiction. I'll have to exaggerate the drama.'

I shut the car boot, the boxes wedged against a cracked cricket bat. 'Not too much to exaggerate. And lonely? What about Trent?'

She chuckles. 'Well, he gave me his number, but I don't think he's my type.'

I nod. 'Probably for the best.' Despite Gary saying we're not all bad, I'm hardly going to encourage someone to be with my family. 'Take care of yourself. And thank *you* for all you did yesterday.'

'All part of the service.'

'It was more than that, and you know it.'

My car starts without any shakes or rattles, unopposed to the overnight stay. I adjust the rear-view mirror, glance at the dashboard. See the indent left behind by Uncle Daniel's knife. If he recovers, will he blame everyone else, or will he continue to be the scapegoat?

I ease the car onto the coastal road, but I don't travel far.

There's one last stop I need to make.

I find her standing outside Busselton Jetty's ticket booth, chatting to the lady manning the till. She's in her volunteer's uniform, with a black bum bag wrapped around her waist.

'Hi, Mrs Haynes. Back already?'

She halts her conversation, turns, takes me in.

'Thanks for coming to the funeral yesterday,' I add.

'My pleasure,' she says.

'My uncle talked to you about Lillian, didn't he? Established a bond with you. That's why you came.'

Leonie leaves the booth, steps out into the strengthening sunshine. 'I needed to be sure your intentions were the same as his.'

'Which were?'

'To find one of my girls. To help her.'

I hesitate to tell her about the discovery in the cave. It's only a matter of time before she'll get a call. 'I'm sorry we failed.'

Leonie leads me along the jetty, back towards land. 'I may have bent the truth on one of our previous meetings.'

'What do you mean?'

'The last time I heard from Lillian, she said she needed to disappear for a while. She had things to sort out, said it was safer if she was alone. I've helped the illusion that she's no longer around, although every day I long to see her, to talk to her. I didn't make it a priority to continue raising her disappearance with the police, and I should have. Tiffany knew this. It seems to have caused a rift. It's why she writes to me now, doesn't call.' Leonie pauses, clears her throat. 'I always carry a photograph of Lillian's plaque. If people ask me about her, I'll show them, stop them looking. Should she turn up again, it will be a wonderful turn of events. If she doesn't, I'm realistic about the worst outcome.'

I want to tell Leonie that she needs to prepare for the worst outcome, but all that comes out is, 'Do you have any photos of Lillian with you? One of her when she was…'

'Not a plaque?' Leonie thinks about this for a while. 'You know what, would you like an ice-cream?'

I'm thankful for the diversion. 'That would be lovely. I think I owe you a triple scoop by now.'

'No. My treat this time. What flavour would you like?'

'Something with caramel?'

Leonie links her arm around mine as if she's escorting me to a fancy restaurant. 'You know, I think I'll try something different today.'

'Yeah?'

'Strawberry. I love strawberries.'

I smile. 'Sounds delicious.'

We order, collect our ice-cream, head to the beach. After Leonie's licked away half her first scoop, she points to a limestone wall on the edge of the sand. 'Let's sit.' She uses her free hand to remove a piece of photo paper from her bum bag. 'What would you like to know about Lillian?'

What *do* I want to know? There's so much, I can't pick one thing. 'Everything,' I answer. 'As much as you want to tell me.'

'How long have you got?' she chuckles. When she sees I'm serious, she rests her ice-cream cup on the wall. 'Well, where do I start? She's incredibly smart and fiercely independent, which often got her into trouble. But she'd win you back with her amazing smile, which always seemed to come from her eyes. Beautiful, round eyes. Just like yours.'

She hands me the photograph, tells me I can keep it. It's of a woman in her late-teens, early twenties. She's right. Lillian's hair is as wild as her mother's. Her skin is a darker shade than mine. But our eyes are the same.

CHAPTER FORTY-TWO
A HUNDRED PER CENT SURE

Even after quitting teaching, I'm amazed at my ability to amass paperwork. We've been back in Perth for three weeks, and I can no longer see the oak wood of my study desk. I need to leave the mess for a while, get some coffee, reclaim some sanity. I call out for Lucy, ask if she'd like one too, then realise she's at work.

I'm all alone. With my paperwork.

After a decent break, I force myself back to the desk. I have to clean it. Besides, it's an excellent distraction. Better than drinking. Maybe. I shuffle things around for half an hour until I can look at the big three—correspondence drawing my immediate attention.

The first is a collection of letters and forms from Uncle Graham's lawyers, ready for me to sign. I don't know if he intended to leave me his property but given what's happened to the rest of the family, everything's coming my way. Two properties with mortgages, rates, bills? I don't know how I feel about that. I glance behind me, trying to spot the lounge room's fireplace through the doorway.

'Thanks, Uncle Graham,' I say, directing my words to the urn resting atop the mantlepiece.

It's revenge for putting him there. And the funeral. Although his final letter put the onus on me to decide whether to bury his urn—no last clues, or an explanation for his approach—and I haven't decided what I'll do.

'If I keep your house, can I scatter your ashes there? Or should I just give your house to Kevin?'

No response. I haven't resorted to two-way conversations with ghosts. Yet.

The second pile of correspondence ties to the first. Paperwork from Gary, a contract of sorts to join his unit. With medical forms, referrals to a psychologist, and a dozen more things to fill out. Lucy's helped me read over it, highlighting some of the key details. If I take the job, I could take my uncle's house, leave Perth behind. It sounds simple, but it's a leap I don't know if I want to make, back into something I've already tried. Something I didn't think I'd ever wish to do again. I've looked into other avenues of law enforcement, as Lucy suggested, but the window to make a choice is closing.

The third piece of correspondence is from Leonie Haynes. Many senior citizens have mastered the art of technology. Emailing, keeping in touch with relatives via social media and video calls. Not Leonie. She's written me a letter. *Hand*written. With Uncle Graham gone, she may be the last of a dying breed.

After our talk about Lillian, I'd left my Perth details with her. A week ago, her letter had arrived. She'd revealed more about Lillian, details about what drove her as an adult. Even though she loved palaeontology, Lillian had been studying linguistics. She'd wanted to travel the world, learn different cultures, teach English to those learning it as a second language.

I've framed the photograph Leonie gave me. It's on the edge of my study desk, Lillian's face peeking over the paperwork. Beside it, the typewriter named in her honour.

The phone rings deeper inside the house. The landline. I let it go. There used to be three types of people who called my landline, now it's just one: telemarketers. I hear the digital answering service kick in, then the beeps to let me know the caller hung up.

My mobile rings.

I fish it out of my pocket, check to see who's calling. I'm hoping it's Lucy. We've talked about going on a lunch date this weekend, maybe somewhere in the Swan Valley. I've narrowed it down to three places.

It's Gary.

My fingers are shaking so much, it takes a while to answer the call. 'You're not hurrying me up on the paperwork, are you?'

'No, take your time.'

My brain confirms my body's reaction. 'What did they find, then?'

There's a crackle over the line. Gary sorting out his notes. 'We've identified the body in the cave.'

'And?'

'It's not Lillian.'

I almost drop the phone. 'What?'

'They made a cast out of some fingerprints, then ran dental tests. When it didn't match with what they had on Lillian, we went with a different hunch.'

A wave of adrenaline lifts me out of my seat, sends me pacing down my passageway. 'What hunch?'

'Leonie Haynes told us one of her foster kids was very close to Lillian. They moved out together at eighteen. Her name was—'

'Tiffany?'

'Tiffany. She lived with Lillian, came back to stay when they locked up the ex-husband. We think she pretended to be Lillian, tried to get some answers, got killed for it.'

I drop onto my couch. 'That's a hell of a hunch to run with.'

'Well, Daniel's recovered enough and he's quite talkative, given the multiple charges he's facing. And, because his sister's tried to pin everything on him. He divulged a lot of details we'll now have to confirm. Apparently, someone came to Roland's house, claiming they were Lillian, trying to trace their family origins. Janice told her to go away, with far less grace. But the girl kept coming back, then started threatening private investigators, lawyers. Said she knew what had happened to her mother.

'Daniel said she'd made the mistake of admitting they were her only family, that she had no one else. Maybe she'd said that to force some compassion, but it worked against her. Janice allegedly had them end things, thinking nobody would care. One death to cover up another. They used the cave on the property. I checked, and nobody reported someone missing. Nobody came looking for the body. Then, years later, you and Graham started asking Daniel about Lillian, as if she was still alive, as if she was someone you were trying to meet. His drug-riddled brain couldn't cope with that. Hence the abduction and bizarre behaviour.'

'If you believe that story.'

'If we believe it.'

'So, Lillian's alive?'

'We can't confirm that. She's just not the body in the cave. Identification goes to Tiffany Haynes.'

'Are you a hundred per cent sure?'

'We're certain.'

'And the real Lillian's never come forward about this? Never reported Tiffany missing?'

'We can't find any record.'

And Leonie wouldn't have, because she thought Lillian had gone into hiding.

'Leonie Haynes has received recent letters from someone she thought was Tiffany,' I think out loud. 'We need to see them.'

'I'll get someone on it, right away.'

I end with a stream of thanks and hurry back to my desk. My hands are shaking even more. I push down the pang of guilt for undervaluing the life of Tiffany Haynes, focusing on the fact that her death opens a whole new world of possibilities for Lillian. The happiest one being, she's still alive.

I wish I knew why she's hidden this whole time; why she kept Tiffany's death a secret. Whether it was something to do with the ex-husband or my psychotic family.

I grab the picture frame off my desk, stare at Lillian's face as I dial my wife. Gaze at the wide eyes that are indeed a match with mine—my sister, I'm a hundred per cent sure.

Lucy doesn't answer. I leave a message. Sputter the details, redial, leave a more coherent recording. While I'm relaying the news, I can't help but think of all the possibilities before me.

Uncle Graham would be proud of what I'd accomplished, excited by Gary's phone call; but he'd say there's still work to do.

Still one item on the list.

Find Lillian.

TO BE CONTINUED IN

PAY FOR
YOUR MISTAKES

ACKNOWLEDGEMENTS

This book is the first in a series, the origin-like *Lillian* story arc that will see Henry Herbert (and those in his life) evolve over the next four novels. I can say that with confidence—I've drafted books two and three, and I'm writing number four! But let's focus on this book for now, because it's the one you're holding in your hands (or on your device). Which means everything to me—you've read something I've created, a story that's travelled beyond my imagination, and I cannot thank you enough. I hope you have seen what I'm developing with Henry and the supporting cast and join me for the next books as he becomes a... (Well, that's a secret for now.)

After reading this novel, you must think I've somehow emerged unscathed (or scarred) from a traumatising family. There are shadows of my life in here, but nobody in my family has run an illegal network or covered up a murder. That I know of. My family is always supportive, although the extended family is much like Henry's—we don't see each other often enough, missing lives lived between visits. This played a part in Henry's disconnection from everyone. A few other family events shaped this novel's direction. Too many members passed away before and whilst writing this novel. Aunty Leonie, Uncle Allan, Aunty Jeanette, and the one that hurt the most, my grandmother, Shirley Leece. I tried to channel this into the grief of Graham's funeral, but Henry hasn't let everything out yet, hasn't processed it all (just like real life).

Both sides of my family are connected to the Margaret River region and its surrounds. My parents grew up in Busselton and Bunbury. One grandfather owned a bakery in Busselton, one owned a butcher's shop in Boyanup. Graham's property is based on one that my grandmother often took me to, a family friend in Margaret River. But me, I'm a Perth city boy. I visit Margaret River when I can, trips used to take photos, make notes and decide on that body location. I wanted Henry to be like me—going to this different world only hours away, approaching it like a tourist until he realises what he's there to do. So, my apologies go out to the local citizens of the Margaret River region—if I've got things wrong, blame Henry's tourist lens. If I've offended a business or location (even with their changed names) through my depiction, that's because things needed to be a certain way for the plot to work (especially liberties I took with the operations of the police force). It's not because I despise the town or its people. Margaret River is a magical place to me, a perfect escape from this city boy's life. I hope you felt that, too. I wanted to keep actual locations in this novel so people can take a trip and spot everything I mentioned—something missing from a lot of Aussie noir. Anyone hiring a tourism ambassador?

My grandfather has read every manuscript I've ever drafted. He always gave honest feedback on my work, which shaped the final product. Sadly, his eyesight was too poor to read this one, but I could explain what it was about and he wanted nothing more than to see it out in the real world. I hope I've made him proud.

My wife, Avril, is another brutally honest reviewer that I'm always happy to share my work with. Unfortunately, she's read so many iterations of this novel (started pre-COVID), I think she's confused as to the final edit I've ended up with. I cannot thank her enough for her patience in that regard, and for giving me time to stay in my head and write, knowing I'm a million miles away when I'm in the zone, even if I'm sitting right next to her. Same goes to my children—I'll always try to spend time with you, but thanks for giving me the occasional space to write.

A huge thanks to other early readers of this novel, especially Larissa Ariyaratne and Chris Simms, and to my future readers. Until the next one, take care and enjoy your time with family—the one you were born with or the one you've made.

ABOUT THE AUTHOR

Craig Bezant hails from Perth, Western Australia. His short fiction has appeared in numerous magazines and online publications. Craig created and edited the award-nominated *Eclecticism E-zine* before co-founding Dark Prints Press (2010-14). Since then, Craig has edited and published the work of over 100 of the world's best crime and horror authors, including Lawrence Block, Chris Simms, Jonathan Maberry, Joseph D'Lacey, Angela Slatter, Gary A. Braunbeck, Alan Baxter, and Stephen M. Irwin.

Craig won the 2012 Australian Shadows Award for Best Edited Publication (*Surviving the End*). He was guest editor for *Midnight Echo #10* (AHWA), an Associate Editor for *HorrorScope*, and a judge for the 2009, 2010 and 2022 Australian Shadows Awards. He is also the author of the children's adventure novel, *The Flats*.

Craig loves reading (when he's not writing). He also loves Lego, basketball, video games, typewriters and tattoos. Of course, his family is everything. (They didn't make him say that. Honest.)

Visit Craig's website: www.craigbezant.com